DISCARDED

MAY YOU ENJOY THIS BOOK

The Public Library is free to all cardholders.
You can increase its usefulness to all by returning
books promptly, on or before the "Date Due".

If you derive pleasure and profit from the use of
your public library, please tell others about its
many services.

THE NASHUA PUBLIC LIBRARY
2 COURT STREET
NASHUA, NH 03060

Pure
Fiction

Also by Julie Highmore

Country Loving

Pure
Fiction

JULIE HIGHMORE

review

First published in 2003
by REVIEW

An imprint of Headline Book Publishing

10 9 8 7 6 5 4 3 2 1

Cataloguing in Publication Data is available from the British Library

ISBN 0 7553 0606 6

Typeset in Garamond by Palimpsest Book Production Limited,
Polmont, Stirlingshire
Printed and bound in Great Britain by
Clays Ltd, St Ives plc

HEADLINE BOOK PUBLISHING
A division of Hodder Headline
338 Euston Road
London NW1 3BH

www.reviewbooks.co.uk
www.hodderheadline.com

For Sophie, James and Tom

AUTUMN

ONE

'So you're stuck again?' I said, phone in one hand, Georgia in the other.

'Looks like it. I've got a meeting arranged for ten o'clock. Silly to drive all the way back in the morning.'

'I suppose so.' Where had she said she was?

'So, see you tomorrow then.'

'OK.'

'Oh, and, Ed . . .'

'Mm?'

'I'll need my cream silk shirt for Thursday.'

This was so Bernice. No, 'How's Georgia been?' or, 'Sorry I can't make it back the one night a week you go out, Ed.' Did I believe her anyway? She was on the mobile, so could have been anywhere. Just outside Oxford in a Travel Inn. Clive running a finger down her back while she talked to me.

I hung up, put Georgia down and loaded more paper into the printer, wondering if I'd finally finished the thesis. Probably not.

There were always little things to fuss over: should I double-check that quote; would 'moreover' be better than 'furthermore' . . . God, I was tired of it. Although pleased with my gargantuan achievement I'd have been happy never to hear, see, speak or type the words 'Exchange Rate Mechanism' again.

I glanced at the clock. An hour till the reading group, or 'reading circle', as Bronwen liked to call it. She'd been the initiator; putting up a notice in the branch library where she worked, as well as in others around town. Organising a hosting roster. I'd excused myself from that, what with our house being the size of a fridge and Bernice banging away on the computer in the living room all evening. Anyway, a reading circle kind of appealed. It sounded welcoming and cosy. Like we'd all hold hands while we discussed the book; try to make contact with the deceased author, maybe. 'Virginia Woolf, can you hear us? . . . No sorry, not you, Thomas. Virginia.'

There'd been a phone number on the notice – 'Or see Bronwen in this library', it said. I went and found her. She was somewhere in her forties, with wild dark hair, opaque tights and flat velvet shoes. She had something of the Eleanor Bron about her, but without the sex appeal. Her chest was on the large side. 'The first meeting will be here next Tuesday,' she whispered. 'Seven thirty. Do come. We're hoping it won't be all women.' I was hoping it would be, but quite a cross section came along the first evening. Eleven in all. We sat and chatted. 'Fiction only, I think,' said Bronwen, and we all agreed. Then for some reason she asked me to choose the first book. '*Ulysses*,' I said immediately. 'Always meant to read that.' There was a communal groan and only six people turned up at

Zoe's house the following Tuesday, one of whom – Bronwen – had got to page eighty-three and was given a round of applause. As there then wasn't much to talk about, Zoe suggested a game of Taboo, which was fun. Actually, I think most of us wouldn't mind playing Taboo every week.

I closed the computer down and checked the time again. Twenty to seven. Too late to ask Natalie over the road to baby-sit, and besides, did I really want to give eight pounds to a fifteen-year-old who does her homework on a laptop I'd swap a finger for, all to discuss a book I was indifferent about with people I barely knew?

'Right,' I said, lifting my daughter from her little seat and kissing her downy head. 'I hope you've been reading your Brontë, young lady.'

Kate – forty-two, furniture restorer with her own shop and currently unattached – couldn't take her eyes off Ed's chest. Firm, lightly tanned, just hairy enough. He'd unbuttoned his shirt with one hand before popping the bottle in his daughter's mouth and looking up at the startled group.

'You're supposed to do this now,' he told them and laughed. 'You know, skin on skin. Makes her feel she's being breast-fed.'

Bob – late-fifties and a flooring specialist – said he'd got through fatherhood without once changing a nappy.

Bronwen, frowning, asked Bob if that was really something to be proud of.

Donna – pretty, blonde ponytail, twenty-one and mother of two – sighed and continued picking at her nail varnish.

They were in Bronwen's house waiting for Zoe: early thirties, daily commuter to London, attractive and clever but highly strung. After they'd completely run out of things to say about Ed's baby and Bronwen's carrot cake, Zoe arrived in an oatmeal suit and perfect make-up, blonde highlights streaming behind her.

'Sorry, gang, sorry,' she panted. 'Train problems again. It is still *Jane Eyre*, isn't it?'

'Yes,' they chorused, books on laps.

A mildly overweight middle-aged man with a pleasant face, thick but receding hair, a corduroy jacket and a tattered book in his hand, hovered in the doorway.

'Oh, and this is Gideon,' said Zoe. 'He's staying with me at the moment. Hope you don't mind him sitting in?'

Gideon said, 'Hello,' and attempted a smile, but looked as though he now regretted tagging along. Seven people in Bronwen's cluttered front room was probably six too many. Bronwen moved the cat, brushed at the hairs it left behind and offered Gideon the end of the sofa and some carrot cake.

'She's a right bitch, that Blanche Ingram,' Donna announced after Ed had put his daughter down and read a passage. Beautifully, Kate thought.

Jane Eyre had been Donna's choice. She said she'd been doing it at school when she 'fell' with her eldest and didn't finish reading it.

'So I never found out if Jane got to shag Rochester,' she'd explained to the group. 'No, no, don't tell me.'

'Why are attractive, confident women always considered bitches?' asked Bronwen.

Donna rolled her eyes and said, 'Pardon me for breathing.'

'Actually,' ventured an unfamiliar voice. Everyone jumped and turned in Gideon's direction, 'Blanche does play rather an important role *vis à vis* the fire, stroke, ice symbolism that runs through the novel.'

Nobody said anything and so he continued, hoisting himself with some difficulty to the edge of the sofa, then clasping his hands. 'You see . . . Brontë, whether consciously or not, brought into her novel an unusual amount of *red* . . . symbolising Jane's inner fire, fervour, courage . . . and also *white* . . . representing the coldness of the world and those she encounters during her wretched childhood and early adulthood.'

Kate scanned the rest of the group. Had she been the only one not to spot this? Donna was frantically note-taking, so she guessed not.

'Go on,' urged Bronwen, looking slightly aroused.

'Remember young Jane at the Reeds' house, reading solitarily in the window seat behind "folds of scarlet drapery"? Looking out at a "pale blank" world?'

The women nodded, the men pretended not to be listening.

'And the room Jane's locked in as a punishment is the Red Room, reflecting her fury at her unjust treatment. Her best friend at school – a warm but strong, stoical person – is called Burns, with all that connotes. As for Blanche Ingram . . . well, to blanch means to whiten. *Blanche, bianca* – cold, sterile, shallow. The very opposite of the loving and passionate Jane Eyre, with her strong and rich inner life. Something that carries her through all the rejection and turmoil.'

Georgia suddenly let out a long wail – almost as though Jane's story was too much to bear – and Ed picked her up and held her contorted little face against his shoulder.

'That was *terribly* interesting,' sighed Bronwen.

Gideon gave a brief nod and sank back into the sofa, while Ed said, 'Hey, hey . . .' to his fractious baby, and stroked her head and rocked her. 'What's the matter?'

'Maybe she'd like some more milk?' suggested Kate, fingers crossed under her book.

Kate glanced at the clock and saw they'd overrun. Ten past nine and Gideon was still on a roll. 'A happy outcome for Jane, of course, but how disappointing that Brontë chooses to collude with the dominant ideology and has Rochester maimed and blinded before the socially inferior "plain Jane" is good enough for him.'

Bronwen cried, 'Quite!', Bob grunted, and Donna said, 'I'm just pleased she didn't go off with that religious geezer. Saint John? He was gay, I reckon.'

'Sinjun,' corrected Gideon.

'Wha'ever.'

'Well, thank you, Gideon,' said Bronwen. She got up and went over to her messy, packed-to-the-gills bookshelves and held up *The*

Shipping News. 'So, have we all started reading E. Annie Proulx for next week?'

Kate nodded. She loved the book so much she'd almost finished it, and couldn't wait to hear what the others thought.

'I honestly don't think I'll have the time,' said Zoe, checking for text messages. 'I've got a nightmare of a report to do and a meeting in Dublin. Ready, Gideon?'

'So soon?' he asked. He looked at his watch and frowned. 'What about Bertha Mason?'

'The mad cow in the attic?' asked Donna. 'We did her last week.'

'Ah, shame. I hope you all caught Brontë's "domestic slavery" message?'

Bronwen said, 'Oh yes, Gideon, very good,' and began passing out jackets from a pile in the corner.

Ed, the househusband, said people really should stop thinking of domestic work in terms of slavery. He popped a woolly hat on his sleeping daughter's head and gently tucked blankets around her. When he'd finished he touched her cheek with the back of a finger and smiled. Kate was mesmerised and wondered for the first time what Ed's partner was like. Stunning, no doubt, with a heart of gold, dazzling wit and legs as long as Zoe's. Ah well. She took her little leather jacket from Bronwen and listened to Bob heave himself off the sofa with a lengthy groan.

'Talking of mad cows,' he said when fully upright and zipping himself into fawn polyester, 'the missus'll be wondering where I've got to.'

Kate laughed despite herself. Next to her stood Gideon with cat hairs on his bottom. 'I've just started lecturing here in Oxford,' he was telling Bronwen.

'Really?' she said.

'Well . . . just outside. Molefield College. Do you know it?'

'Oh . . . yes.' Bronwen sounded disappointed.

'It's very much on the up, you know. Hoping to gain university status in the near future.'

'Right.'

'Anyway,' he told the group, 'I'm staying with Zoe while I look for somewhere to live. So I expect I'll see you all again.'

'Oh, good,' murmured Ed.

'Do come along next week, Gideon,' said Bronwen, breathily. 'Is English literature your subject by any chance?'

He smiled and ran a hand through his brown wavy hair. 'Yes, it is. Funnily enough I'm running the Nineteenth-Century English Novel module this semester.'

'Really?' Bronwen inched closer. 'I always think it was such a fertile period for women writers. Do you have a favourite Victorian novel?'

'Mm, let me see.' He tapped his chin with a forefinger, pursed his lips and eyed the ceiling for a while. 'Well . . . I think it would have to be *Middlemarch*. George Eliot weaves a wonderful tapestry of provincial life, throws in an admirable, and again *passionate* heroine, and to top it all gives us the perfect omniscient narrator.'

'I totally agree!' cried Bronwen. 'It's always been my favourite too.'

'Hang on a minute, Bron,' said Donna, slipping her arms into pale denim. 'I thought you didn't like books written by blokes?'

Gideon laughed heartily. 'Ah yes, the old ones are the best.'

Kate thought she'd walk home from Summertown. It was a warm evening and although it was dark there were plenty of people on the streets. As she wandered towards her house through the back streets of Jericho, lights were on but curtains were open, so she checked out front rooms: a total Ikea job here, an academic shambles there. Mm, love that sofa throw. God, hate that rococo through lounge. Occasionally she'd get ideas this way; other times she wanted to knock on a front door, hand over a card and say, 'No offence, but your décor's hideous. Why not come to my shop with a thousand pounds or so?'

She turned into Alice Street, a slight detour but worth it for its interiors. It was made up of two rows of tiny straight-on-to-the-pavement terraced houses, all done up and neat as pins, and the most expensive, per square metre, in the city. Some said in Europe. Each house had been painted a different colour in an attempt at an overall funky/chic effect. Only one, in the middle of the north-facing row, was letting the side down: stone cladding, carriage lamp, surround-sound TV they were sharing with the street. Kate crossed over to avoid it, and was nonchalantly peering into front rooms again, when all of a sudden a man loomed to within inches of her. He was up against the inside of his window, arms held high and spread out. She stopped in her tracks and let out a small scream from the shock of it.

*   *   *

I'd just settled Georgia and was closing the living-room curtains when I saw Kate from the reading group outside making odd noises. If she woke the baby I'd kill her. I hurried to the front door, which didn't take long as it's right beside the window, and asked if she was all right.

'Oh, crikey, it's you,' she said, obviously shaken. 'Um, yes. I'm fine now.'

'It's not the colour of the house, is it? Only we weren't sure about the purple.'

'No, no. You can hardly see it in this light. I mean . . . I'm sure it's lovely. You gave me a fright, that's all. At the window.'

'Really?' I said, unable to remember the last time I frightened a person. When I was ten I hid under my brother's bed one evening and grabbed his bare ankles with a loud roar. I've heard he still can't sleep in a bed on legs. 'It's just that the curtain hooks get stuck,' I explained to Kate, 'and you have to give them a yank.'

'Right.'

'Um, would you like to come in? We've got some flower remedies somewhere, left over from Bernice's labour. Good for trauma.'

She laughed. 'No, it's OK, thanks. I'm all right now.' She wrapped her jacket tightly across her chest and folded her arms. 'Did they help her? The flower remedies?'

'Actually, they were for me. Helped a lot, yeah. Well . . . how about a cup of tea then?'

She twisted a slender wrist and looked at her watch. She was quite fanciable, Kate. Hard to put an age to. Thirty-four, thirty-five?

About five two or three and attractively waif-like. Nice hair, dark and curly and shoulder-length. Brown eyes, sweet voice. Not the most talkative member of the group so still something of a mystery.

'OK, then.'

She came in and I gathered Georgia's bits so Kate could sit down. 'Lovely house,' she said. 'I didn't realise you lived so near to me. Where's, er, Bernice did you say her name was?'

'Yeah. She's away on business. Back tomorrow.'

'What does she do?'

'She's . . .'

I wanted to tell her Bernice was an expert on the mathematics of knots. One of the best in her field. Which she'd have been on her way to becoming had she not given up on her D.Phil. when she found she was pregnant, saying one of us had to be a grown up and it obviously wasn't going to be me. *And*, while she was at it, never mind that her doctoral thesis might be of enormous benefit to humankind whilst mine would only be read by the examiners, and possibly my parents. After a promisingly romantic beginning, our relationship had, by this point, soured somewhat, and Bernice was regularly this direct with me; rude some might say. But I decided to put it down to pregnancy, and made her bowls and bowls of the French onion soup she was craving while she filled in application forms. One company called her for interview, and, after hiding her bump, she landed a job as a sales rep, flogging study guides; a job she proved surprisingly good at. She took a few weeks off to have Georgia but couldn't wait to get back to work. Motherhood comes to Bernice like knitting comes to dogs.

'. . . in publishing,' I told Kate. 'Academic.'

From the long thin kitchen – an extension that ate up ninety per cent of the garden – I could see Kate looking around thinking, Ah, so that's how they can afford Alice Street. Should I tell her we're renting dirt cheap from a friend who's abroad, in exchange for decoration and maintenance? I thought not.

I took two mugs through, handed her one and sat in the rocking chair. 'So what did you think of our guest speaker this evening?' I asked. I couldn't help noticing the women had been hanging on Gideon's every word. Donna even took notes.

Kate blew on her tea and took a dainty sip from the mug, slim fingers coiled around the handle. 'Bit of a tosser,' she said in her delightful soft tones. She looked around her. 'I can see why you can't hold meetings here. You'd have to seat us in a long line, wouldn't you? We'd all be talking to a wall.'

I thought: If she wasn't so cute I'd be insulted.

'On the other hand,' she added with a big grin, 'we could stick Gideon right on the end in the kitchen. Let him tell the cooker all about the overuse of the pathetic fallacy in Victorian literature.'

I laughed and we talked about Georgia for a while. I got the impression Kate was quite smitten with her; she'd hardly taken her eyes off her when I fed her at the meeting. I topped up our mugs and we chatted a bit about my thesis and her shop. She didn't mention

14

a bloke, but then again I didn't ask. We seemed to be hitting it off pretty well. Then Bernice rang.

Kate thought Ed was charming and funny until he picked up the ringing phone.

'Oh, hello again,' he said flatly. 'Yes . . . No . . . No. I did that today . . . *No*, but I'll do it tomorrow . . . *No*, it won't be too late . . . Yes, I did . . . Sixty-three pounds . . . Well, it was the cheapest I could find . . . No, *you* fucking take it back . . . OK, OK . . . Chill, will you? . . . I said OK, didn't I? . . . Bye.'

He returned to the rocking chair, eyes blazing, and picked up his mug. 'Bernice.'

Kate nodded.

'Where were we?' he asked, breaking into a big broad smile.

Kate was slightly taken aback. *Split personality* she added to her mental minus list, underneath *Quite young – 35ish?*, *Already partnered* and *Patch of baby sick on shoulder*. She said, 'I was boring you with my furniture business.'

'No, not boring at all. What's boring is John Major, Norman Lamont and Black Wednesday.'

'Well, yes, I can see that might be,' she said, and laughed, but he suddenly looked hurt. 'When you've spent three years researching it, I mean.'

'Yes.'

It felt like time to go. At the door she thanked him for the tea.

'My pleasure. Are you going to be all right walking home? You won't be screaming at windows or anything?'

'That would depend, really.'

'Well . . . bye then.'

'Bye.'

'See you next week at Bob's?'

Kate nodded. 'Or pop in the shop if you're passing.'

'OK, yeah, I might.'

On the winding route to her house she came up with some plusses: *Handsome, but not perfectly so – like a slightly irregular Hugh Grant. Glorious chest. Witty. Warm. Intelligent. Hates Bernice.* Before reaching home, she'd moved *Quite young* from the minus to the plus list.

After they'd left and she'd cleared away plates and cups and hoovered up bits of cake, Bronwen emailed the other members, with the exception of Donna, whom she'd have to phone.

Dear Reading Circle – change of plan. Read Middlemarch, not Proulx! I've a spare copy if anyone wants it. Bronwen

Three of them picked up the message before going to bed. Kate was hugely disappointed. Ed thought, Why doesn't Bronwen just drop her knickers for Gideon and be done with it? Zoe guessed she'd have to skip the next meeting, but knocked on her spare bedroom door and told Gideon of the change of book, just in case he was thinking of going along again. Gideon thanked her, said good night and turned to beam at himself in the mirror. He'd obviously been a big hit with the group.

In a semi in Marston, Bob, who tended to pick up emails first thing, was sitting in bed with *The Shipping News*. 'Bloomin eck,' he said, frowning and scratching at his cheek. 'I thought Charlotte Brontë was hard going.' He flicked back a page to reread it. 'Bronwen said we might find E. Annie's sentence structure challenging.'

'Oh dear, poor you,' said Christine, beside him. She couldn't recall, in all their years together, having seen Bob read a book written by a woman. Now he'd been forced to read two in a row. 'Why don't you try the Follett I got you from the library?'

'Good idea,' he said, closing the book and shaking his head at it. 'I reckon she was two sheets to the wind when she wrote this.'

Christine smiled sympathetically, ruffled the one or two hairs Bob had left, then went back to the article on how a paste of sodium bicarbonate and water would remove all those stubborn marks on your cooker and leave it sparkling. She thought she'd definitely try it tomorrow. Mind you, Bob had used that sodium bicarbonate toothpaste for a while and it did nothing to lift his tea stains. She flicked the page over to an interview with Michael Aspel. Now there was a man with a good head of hair and sparkling teeth.

TWO

Donna was in her neighbour's living room, yawning. Not because she was tired but because she was bored with the lot of them. All smoking and swearing at their kids, moaning about blokes or pulling to bits some poor girl who happened to have finished school and was doing something with her life. Shelley was going on and on about Lee.

'So I says to him, I says, ere, if you wanna see Lara every other Sundee, then I wanna see some dosh. Kids' clothes don't grow on trees, I says. He says, yeah, and neever do jobs. Annoying git.' She stopped to draw on her cigarette. 'Anyway . . .'

Donna leaned back and closed her eyes. She could understand why those guys sometimes flipped and gunned down a roomful of people. OK, Shelley's ex wasn't exactly Father of the Year, but then neither were the dads of her own two boys. Of course, being inside made it a bit hard for Carl to shine as a father. And did poor Mark even know he had a kiddie? Ryan crawled on to her lap, crying, and said, 'Lara bited me.'

She kissed him better and they sat for a while watching the other kids battling with one another. All of them were named after some pop star or Lara Croft or something: Kylie, Robbie, Britney, two Brooklyns.

Got to get away, thought Donna. What she really wanted was to study English – which she'd loved at school – and maybe get a degree. But no way would she tell this lot. They felt they'd read a book if they flicked through the Argos catalogue.

'What's the matter with Ryan?' asked Shelley. 'Ere, Ryan, what's up?'

'Lara bited me.'

Shelley ground her cigarette in a saucer, blew smoke out her nostrils and grabbed her daughter by the upper arm. 'What,' she shouted, placing a firm smack on Lara's leg, 'have I,' smack, 'told you,' smack, 'about hurting,' smack, 'other kiddies?' Smack.

Lara cried a bit and rubbed her sore leg, then hurried across the room and bit one of the Brooklyns; to which her mum gave a long throaty laugh, pulled another Marlboro Light from the packet and said, 'She's a right headcase, she is!'

Back at home after she'd collected Jake from school, Donna looked up the number of the college of further education and a nice woman told her everything she needed to know about doing an Access course. Well, everything except how to finance herself and the kids while she did it. Would she still be able to sign on? She phoned the DSS but they'd gone home for the day.

'Oh well,' she said, and turned her mind to how she and Ryan could get out of Lara's second birthday party tomorrow. No way could she afford a present, plus she'd have to get someone to look after Jake, who wouldn't be seen dead at such an event now he was five. What's more, Lara was having her tiny two-year-old ears pierced as a birthday present from her mum, which Donna definitely felt inclined to phone the Social Services about.

Bob was sitting at the dining table with a pen and a large Basildon Bond pad. Bronwen had suggested they all write a bit of an autobiography about themselves to present to the group at some point. 'Whenever you're ready to share,' she'd said.

Bob Proctor, he wrote, in his curly forward-sloping lettering, and underlined it. *I was born in 19— Well never mind that, in what they now call Humberside, but we called North Lincs. Five of us lived in a three up two down terrace in a street where someone was always shaking a cloth out of her front door.*

Who the eck's going to want to know all this? thought Bob, but he ploughed on.

I left school at fifteen and was an apprentice electrician until Mr Trinder the boss disconnected the wrong circuit one day and electrocuted himself to death with Mrs Spencer's bathroom light. I then turned to carpet fitting as a career. It was at a time when wall-to-wall was taking off so no shortage of work there. I met Christine on holiday at Skegness Butlins in the summer of 1964. Christine was from Preston and everyone in her family was Our Something. Still are. By Christmas we were wed and a month later Heather was on the way. After her came Keith and I'm now the proud grandfather of two. Our Heather hasn't married but manages to keep herself busy with a prize winning brass band.

I'm still in the flooring business. Got transferred to Oxford in 1987 to manage Plus Floors newest branch, but have been semi-retired since last March. Not my choice. What they call rationalisation. They've got a pipsqueak called Bradley in charge now who ticks me off when I talk in feet and inches. Never mind that that's what the customers want to hear. My main hobby is coarse fishing but I also have a keen interest in trains. I don't go in for spotting like our Keith, though. Too nippy at the end of them platforms.

I joined Bronwen's reading circle with my wife's encouragement because although I like a good book I have the annoying habit of not finishing them. I have suspected, mind, that Christine just sees too much of me these days and wants me out the house.

Right, that'll do, he thought, then typed it up on the computer with two fingers.

Kate had a work experience boy in called Duggie. Sixteen, baseball cap with a hood over the top, trousers you could fit three men in. He wasn't interested in furniture restoration and decoration, he just lived opposite and didn't want to travel too far. 'It was you or Lorna's Lingerie,' he told her. 'Only Lorna said no.'

Duggie couldn't be bothered to get the hang of the till, or sweep up or make coffee properly, and twice came back from town with Coke and Mars bars, rather than the sandwiches Kate had ordered, so on day four of ten, she gave him a fatally cracked, woodwormy old chest to clean up and decorate in any way he wanted. It kept him out the back, which was good, as he was scaring the customers.

It had been quite a slow day. Part-time Miles was manning the shop and Kate was in the 'studio', painting. This was a special order for a haughty, well-dressed man who wanted something similar to the wardrobe Edward Burne-Jones gave the William Morrises as a wedding present – all stunningly decorated with scenes from *The Canterbury Tales*. He'd handed over his beautiful old wardrobe and said no longer than three weeks, if she wouldn't mind, as it too was a wedding gift. At first she was nervous and lost sleep over it, but after an entire day in the Ashmolean Museum, staring at the original and making lots of sketches, she eventually summoned the courage to start. For two weeks now, she'd worked on nothing else and, to her eyes anyway, it looked better than Burne-Jones's.

Beside her, Duggie was halfway through painting a nude on his blanket box, copying from *Razzle* and giving his woman even more improbable breasts than those of the model. Kate had put some music on to avoid having to make conversation; never easy at the best of times, but even trickier with dusky 'Suki' lying on the floor between them, sucking a finger and showing off her extensive bikini-line wax.

After half an hour or so, Miles stuck his head round the door. 'Kate, there's a Mr Phelps here from Thomas Cranmer School. Come to check on Duggie.'

Duggie froze and said, 'Shit!'

'He's through here, is he?' boomed a loud schoolteacherish voice.

22

'Quick,' hissed Kate, thrusting her brush into Duggie's hand. 'Swap places.'

He gave her his flesh-coloured brush and they hurriedly jumped into each other's positions. As she turned to greet Mr Phelps, Kate slid Suki under the ground sheet.

'How's it going then, Duggie?' he asked, and without waiting for an answer said to Kate, 'Been a big help, has he?'

'Oh yes.'

'I say, Duggie!' exclaimed Mr Phelps as he skirted the wardrobe. 'You're doing a superb job here. Been hiding your artistic talents from us at Thomas Cranmer, eh? Extraordinary!'

Duggie stepped back and chewed on the end of the brush. 'Mm, yeah, I'm quite pleased with it.'

Mr Phelps looked over to where Kate was dabbing at a hand on the blanket box. Not so much a hand, Kate noticed on taking a better look, more five chipolatas sprouting directly from the woman's wrist. 'Yes, well,' said Mr Phelps, screwing up his eyes behind his glasses. 'I've never pretended to understand modern art.'

He thumped Duggie on the back. 'Well done, lad. We know who to get to do the school production scenery in future, don't we?'

He jotted down some things in a folder, bade Kate farewell and went off to surprise another small business.

I was standing mesmerised by this pink-and-white polka-dot coffee table in Kate's window, when a man flew out of the shop in a terrible suit. 'I really think you should consider doing A level Art, Duggie,' he shouted. He tucked a folder under his arm and almost walked into a cyclist.

'OK, I'll do that, Mr Phelps,' said a lad standing at the door with paint on his face. 'Dickhead,' he whispered under his breath.

'Is Kate in?' I asked him.

'Yeah, she's out the back.' He turned round and held the door open for Georgia's buggy. 'I'll show you.' We passed a guy of around thirty at the counter, flicking through a magazine and looking as though he'd really rather be somewhere else. 'Through here,' said the boy.

Kate was wearing a paint-splattered shirt down to her knees, which she whipped off the moment she saw me. 'Ed! Hi!' she said, and laughed manically. 'It's just one surprise after another today.' She looked over at the boy. 'Make us a couple of coffees, would you, Duggie?'

'Yeah, alright. I think I owe you one.'

'I seem to keep scaring the life out of you,' I said when he'd gone.

'No, no, it's not you.' She explained that the boy's teacher had almost caught him indulging in pornography during his work experience, and nodded towards an appalling nude painted on the lid of a big box.

I took a closer look. 'Um . . . why's she balancing two jam tarts on her breasts?'

'I don't think she is.'

'Ah. And this would be . . . ?' I asked, pointing.

'A hand.'

'Of course.'

Kate's current project was in an altogether different league: a beautifully painted wardrobe. Obviously, I heaped praise upon it.

Duggie was suddenly back with us. 'Blimey, that was quick,' I said when he handed me a mug of something I could do nothing but stare at for a while. Who'd have thought you could go that wrong with instant granules.

'Sorry,' whispered Kate.

Duggie went back to work, and Kate and I took Georgia out into a small courtyard filled with pot plants and cast-iron furniture. It was a bit nippy in the weak, late-September sun, but better for Georgia's tender little lungs than all those paint and turps fumes.

Kate fed her coffee to a bay tree and I handed her mine to do the same with, then, for want of something more original, said, 'How are you getting on with *Middlemarch*?'

'Fine. I've read it before, of course.'

'Me too.' Well, I saw it on TV. Same thing.

'So, you'll be at Bob's on Tuesday?'

'Yeah.'

'And Georgia?'

'Bernice promised she'd baby-sit.'

'Baby-sit! Strange word to use.'

'Mm, well, it's just not Bernice's thing,' I explained, 'mother-hood.'

Kate shook her head and I could see she was thinking, Bitch. Which was good.

'I used to get terrible separation anxiety,' she said, 'when I had to leave Charlie.'

'Charlie?'

'My daughter.'

Now she definitely hadn't mentioned a daughter before. I was slightly thrown for a while, but then suddenly saw Kate in a new light: hand-in-hand with a miniature version of herself, matching cotton dresses and sunhats.

'She's fourteen,' she said, almost sadly. 'I don't see much of her now.'

'No?' Perhaps she was in care, or living with her father. It seemed best not to enquire.

'I never go in her room, and she hardly ever comes out of it.'

'Oh, I see. Well, it's probably for the best. I was horrible at fourteen.'

'Surely not,' she said, suddenly smiling. 'I bet you were quite sweet.'

Was she coming on to me? I thought I'd reciprocate. 'You must have been really young when you had Charlie.'

'No, I was twenty-eight.'

'Christ, you don't look your age!' I cried, aware that it wasn't quite coming out as a compliment. More like, 'You mean you're *that* old?'

'Thanks,' she said. 'How old are you?'

'Thirty-five,' I told her, adding on three years.

Well, why not.

*   *   *

26

Gideon was hungry. He opened Zoe's fridge and found two celery stalks – so limp that they dangled between the shelf gaps. No milk, he noticed with a sigh. There was only half a jar of some carrot drink in the door, along with that ghastly 'virtually fat-free' sunflower stuff of hers. Whatever happened to butter, he wondered, taking all three items out.

He spread see-through margarine on the solid chunk of wholemeal he'd discovered in the bread bin, then, yanking off the leaves, laid the celery on top. A bit of Branston wouldn't go amiss, he decided. After a quick search, he sat down at the table with a bottle of Tabasco, wondering how safe his crown would be when he bit into that bread.

While he ate, Gideon listened to *The Archers*, reluctantly and with a heavy heart – he and Penelope had never missed an episode. Did she now tune in with Graham, he wondered. One of her innovative casseroles steaming before them?

No, it didn't do to dwell, Gideon decided, as *Front Row* began babbling away in the background. The British pop scene, an installation at some gallery in Manchester – not hugely interesting to Gideon, who was waiting for *Any Questions, Letter from America* and *The Friday Play*. Should he perhaps do a little work on *Wuthering Lows: The True Story of Haworth*? He fetched his files from upstairs and started reading the eighty-one pages he'd written so far. Fascinating, he kept telling himself, but halfway through his eyes grew heavy and his chin made its way to his chest and he gave up. A little motivational research trip to Yorkshire was called for, he decided. Next summer, perhaps?

He bundled his papers back in their box files and drummed his fingers on Zoe's tiny kitchen table. A good book, that's what he needed, what with no marking to do and an entire weekend stretching ahead. That rather nice woman at the reading group – Barbara? Bridget? – had recommended her library as one of the best branches. Ah, yes . . . now that would be something to do tomorrow.

Halfway through *The World Tonight* – the Middle East, tedious speculation about interest rates – Gideon felt he'd had enough and took himself off to bed via the kitchen, where he filled a bowl with Zoe's muesli, trying at first to eat the dry mixture with a spoon but then opting for a palm-to-mouth method. At 11.20 he eventually turned in with Tobias Smollett's *Humphry Clinker*: a dog-eared old favourite Penelope had given him on their first wedding anniversary. 'For my darling, Giddy,' he read for the thousandth time. 'With all my love, Penelope.' She'd never liked her name to be shortened, so they were Giddy and Penelope. He'd rather liked his pet name, thinking it suited the way he felt: giddy with love and happiness. Until Graham came along, that was.

Bronwen was trying to keep her heavy eyes open as she lay in her Victorian brass bed, listening to *Book at Bedtime*. It was a rather gripping tale by a young Indian writer, but even this couldn't stop her mind drifting off to having to go to work in the morning, and whom she might take to the Holywell Music Room tomorrow evening. She'd bought two tickets, thinking her father might be up for it, but had called in on her way home to find him still in his pyjamas and talking to the sideboard. The house was ice-cold and his nose dripped. 'Daddy, you'll catch your death,' she'd told him, and bundled him into his dressing gown. He really was becoming quite a trial, poor dear. Luckily for her he had Mrs Cornish going in most days, turning his Stravinsky down and retrieving the kettle from the garden.

She'd go to the concert alone, no doubt. Perhaps they'd take her spare ticket back on the door. One would think that a Tibetan tantric choir, albeit one from Banbury, would consider it bad karma not to.

After spending a full hour agonising over a semicolon, I decided life really was too short – plus it was the weekend – so slotted Georgia into her going-out gear and headed for the shops. It was eleven o'clock and Bernice was dead to the world. With a bit of luck she'd stay that way till Monday morning.

As usual, heads turned when I walked down the street. Nothing to do with me, just women of a certain age giving Georgia the eye. I used to get quite nervous when they came up and said, 'Hello, *beaut*iful,' not realising that all women over fifty were this forward with babies. I saw them as possible menopausal abductors and pretended she only slept an hour a night to put them off her, but then grew to not mind at all; regarding it, in fact, as a kind of service to the community to be displaying my daughter in public.

'She's sleeping right through,' I was now telling an interested party in the Superdrug queue.

'Oh, you're a *very* good girl,' she said. 'Yes, you *are*.'

Georgia attempted a smile and waved a fist haphazardly and the woman went into raptures. 'Oooohh,' she said with a fixed grin and wild eyes. 'I could take you home and eat you, you scrumptious little thing.'

No she bloody couldn't. I reverted to my theory that they're all possibly unhinged, these women, and moved us to the next till.

'Ted?' I heard someone say. My shoulder was tapped and I turned. It was Gideon with Vosene in his hand.

'Oh, hello,' I said. 'Ed, actually.'

'Ah, yes.'

The queue wasn't budging and it occurred to me we'd have to make conversation. I tapped a foot and scratched around for a topic. The weather? Medicated shampoo?

'So, what's the verdict?' he asked.

'Sorry?'

'*Middlemarch*.'

'Oh, right. Mm, yeah, really enjoying it.' We both went forward one place. 'Great characters.'

'Indeed, indeed. That's because Victorian readers liked to – ' he popped his Vosene in a pocket and drew inverted commas in the air – '*see* their fiction. Pre-cinema, of course. Eliot was exceptionally good at doing this without overdoing it. You know she was widely acclaimed to have taken the Fieldingesque

branch of literary pictorialism to a new and far more sophisticated level.'

'Really?'

'See Dowden,' he footnoted, and I wondered if I could slip back
into the abductor's queue.

We moved towards the till again. 'Why don't you go first?' I
suggested. 'As you've only got one item.'

'Jolly nice of you,' he said, squeezing his girth past us, then
looking bewildered at his empty hands.

'Pocket,' I told him.

'Ah.'

It was early Tuesday evening and Christine had changed her mind
twice about which coasters to put out for Bob's reading circle. In
the end she settled on the Composers of Europe. After opening
up the nest of tables and spreading them around her seating
arrangement, she put Verdi and Beethoven on one, Bach and
Mozart on another and Elgar and Handel on the smallest. Maybe
Handel shouldn't go on the smallest, she thought, with that big
head. She swapped him with Verdi, then sat down and went
through a mental checklist: cups and saucers bleached; prawn
mayonnaise/ham/cheese-and-onion sandwiches made, crusts off;
sausage rolls almost done; Victoria sponge on doily on cake stand;
cloakroom scrubbed, polished and vacuumed; Bob's record of train
sounds hidden.

An hour later she was sitting in the corner watching them all.

She'd once read that a good hostess always devises a way of remembering a stranger's name. If they're called Peter, imagine them sitting in a saucepan – Peter Pan. That sort of thing. But she'd decided that was going to be a bit hard with the number of strangers now sitting in a circle in her living room – not all of them, she noticed, making use of their coasters – so this afternoon, Bob had written down descriptions for her. She took a sneaky look at them under the knitting on her lap.

'DONNA – scrubber, silly shoes. ED – namby-pamby, new man, pretty boy. KATE – never says a word, looks the spitting of our Heather. ZOE – posh, bottle-blonde, stick insect thin, always late. GIDEON (if he comes) – scruffy, clever dick, know-all. BRONWEN – breasts you could use as battering rams.'

Christine matched everyone with their descriptions and memorised their names, then looked at her watch. Almost time for the nibbles. She might have done too much, what with Zoe not being here. She looked at her watch again. Goodness knows how they were finding so much to say about one book. Come to think of it, the chap called Gideon was doing all the talking. He was sitting with his back to her on a dining chair. Odd socks, she noticed, and a hole in his jumper that she knew she had just the right colour yarn for.

'. . . good lady wife is going to supply us with refreshments,' Christine suddenly heard Bob saying and she leaped up, sending her knitting flying.

If it hadn't been for Kate's thigh regularly brushing against mine on the sofa, I'd have got up and gagged Gideon with his grubby checked scarf.

'The irony, therefore, is omnipresent,' he'd announced just before the break, folding his arms and smirking.

'So . . .' Donna asked, leaning forward and chewing lightly on a pen, 'what's the difference between omnipresent and . . . hang on – ' she flipped through her spiral notebook 'om-nis-ci-ent?'

Gideon looked around the group. 'Perhaps someone else would like to enlighten Diana?'

'Donna, actually.'

'Yes, of course. How about you, Bill?'

'Bob,' we all snapped.

'Bob. Right.'

Bob's eyes had jumped around in a panicky fashion for a while, before he looked at his watch, said, 'Ah!' and declared it time for refreshments. Christine had then sprung from her armchair in the corner, galloped to the kitchen, banged around a bit and returned, flushed, with a hostess trolley laden with minute sandwiches and a cake on its own glass stand.

'Here you are, Ed,' she said, handing me a plate and patterned serviette. 'Do help yourself, Kate. There are sausage rolls on the bottom shelf, Gideon. They're still a bit hot, Donna, so watch your tongue. Can I top up your drink, Bronwen?'

'This is brilliant,' whispered Kate by the coal-effect fire. She popped an entire sandwich in her mouth and I did the same. 'Do you think Bob would mind if we met here every week?'

'I dunno. I think Christine might have a breakdown. All this food. And have you ever seen such a clean and tidy house?'

'Probably not.' Kate looked around at the polished wood and glistening ornaments. 'Uh oh,' she said. 'I think I spot litter.'

She bent down and picked up a piece of paper, then stared at it for a while, the colour, I couldn't help but notice, draining from her cheeks.

'What is it?'

She folded it twice, said, 'Nothing', tucked it behind a shepherdess on the mantelpiece and went back to the food trolley.

Of course I had to have a look. I eased the piece of paper out, slipped it into a trouser pocket and asked Bob for directions to the toilet.

'Namby-pamby, new man, pretty boy' – huh!

It was true Kate hardly ever said anything, but then who could with a clever dick know-all in the group. The finger of suspicion for this list pointed at Bob, the only one missing from it. Or Christine? No, not Christine I decided as I took a pee. A woman with a crochet runner on her toilet cistern would never be that disrespectful. I stuck the piece of paper behind a bottle of eau-de-Cologne and returned to the living room, quite pleased it wasn't me with breasts like battering rams.

'So . . .' Kate was saying. Was she ever going to shut up? 'Although George Eliot often portrayed social groups at leisure, just as Jane Austen did, such scenes are part of a much broader canvas than

34

was ever attempted by Austen, and also show far greater knowledge of natural social discourse.'

Actually, I was enjoying this. Primarily because Gideon wasn't.

'Do you know,' Kate continued, just as poor Gideon was drawing breath to say something, 'that nowhere in Jane Austen's novels do two men have a conversation together? Eliot, on the other hand, has her male characters discussing politics, medicine, the coming of the railway, farm practices . . .'

The doorbell played 'Frère Jacques'.

'Goodness, who can that be!' exclaimed Christine, and once again leaped from her armchair.

It was Zoe. 'Hi. Hi. Sorry. Sorry. I wasn't going to come, but the drive from the airport was quick and I thought Gideon might like a lift home. Have I missed much?'

'Yes, you have,' I said. 'Kate's been telling us some fascinating things about *Middlemarch*.'

Bronwen said, 'As has Gideon,' and Gideon gave the group a smug-bastard bow of the head.

I turned to Kate beside me and whispered, 'Where did you get all that from?'

'Did it for A level.'

'Cheat.'

When, later, we all stood up to leave, I half expected Christine to produce going-home bags filled with crayons, balloons and cling-filmed slices of her sponge cake. Instead, she appeared with all our coats, and, carefully remembering which belonged to whom, handed them out.

Meanwhile, Bob was piling up the dirty plates and glasses. I sidled up to him. 'Fancy a couple of jars down the pub, mate?' I said, as deeply as I could manage. 'Or have you got to stay and help the boss clear up?' I nudged him and did my best blokish laugh. 'Eh?'

'Another time, maybe,' said a puzzled Bob.

Thank God.

Donna came over to say goodbye to Bob and thank him ever so for all the sandwiches and whatnot. 'Are these your kiddies?' she asked, pointing at an array of family photos.

'Yes they are,' said Bob, obviously delighted at her interest. 'Those are the grandchildren, Nathan and Kimberley. This is our son, Keith. And this – ' he picked up a gold-framed photo of a chubby-faced woman with bushy eyebrows, buck teeth, four chins and a crooked smile – 'is our Heather.'

Well, of course I laughed. Which probably wasn't too polite, but I managed to convince Bob I'd just remembered a joke I'd heard. 'Too filthy to tell in front of the girls,' I said, with another matey nudge.

When he'd wandered off, I called Kate over and pointed at the photo.

'What?' she asked.

I was shaking with suppressed laughter, tears welling up in my eyes. 'Heather,' I managed in a strangled voice.

'Bloody hell,' she shrieked. 'Tell me I don't look like that!'

The room was suddenly quiet. Bob looked a bit sheepish, and Christine began frantically searching the area around her armchair. 'Um . . . I seem to have lost a piece of paper.'

'Is this it?' asked Donna, pointing at the sideboard. 'It was on the floor in the cloakroom.'

Bob dived for it and thrust it into a shirt pocket, then patted the pocket several times. 'Shopping list,' he puffed. 'Christmas shopping list.'

'Oh right,' said Donna. 'So . . . er, what's a scrubber?'

'Scrubbing brush,' answered a quick-witted Christine.

Donna frowned; probably wondering why Bob and his wife were buying her a scrubbing brush and some silly shoes for Christmas.

'How did you get here?' I asked Kate outside.

'Bussed.'

'Can I give you a lift?'

'Great, yeah.'

'The car's just around the corner,' I said, leading the way. When we got to Bernice's ancient, much-cherished, resprayed-lilac Morris Minor, I did, all of a sudden, feel something of a namby-pamby, new-man pretty boy, especially when Kate laughed till she almost wet herself. Which wasn't nice.

After Bronwen had attached her bicycle to the inside of her front railings, she yanked off her helmet, unlocked her door and went straight to the computer. A message from Hamid. Great. She smiled to herself as she read it and emailed back immediately, telling him about the beautiful colours the trees were beginning to turn in Britain, and that she hoped he was 'keeping up his studies!' She deleted the exclamation mark. Hamid had put them after every sentence in his message. 'I have a new baby sister! The rainy season has ended! We are missing you very much!' She pictured him in an Internet café in Calcutta. A handsome young man, no doubt. She really must get back to India soon. But of course there was Daddy to consider now.

By eleven she was in bed, lights out and pictures of books, books and more books filling her head as she drifted off. Stacking them, shelving them, issuing them . . . At one point an image of Gideon's rather nice face slipped in and she inadvertently date-stamped him.

Bob had read the group his autobiography. How sad, Kate had thought while listening, but then again how admirable, almost Buddhist, to be content with so little. At 11.15 – exhausted but not yet sleepy – she sat at the computer and started writing hers. *Kate Anderson (artist/shopkeeper). I grew up in Croydon with an older sister (taller, thinner, blonder), a flamboyant (for Croydon) mother who took up pottery, did amateur dramatics and had a lot of male friends, and a father who caught the 7.24 to Whitehall every day. My parents divorced the minute I left for university and a Fine Arts degree. Dad bought Mum out of the marital home and she and someone called Eric now make pots and offer* chambre d'hôtes *accommodation in Provence. I suppose I should go and visit the witch some time.*

She deleted the last sentence.

At university I did lots of drugs and slept with anyone passable who took an interest in me. I suppose I could use my parents' divorce as an excuse.

No, maybe not, she thought.

I very much enjoyed university life and left with a 2:1 but absolutely no career prospects – the world being full of amazingly talented artists. My father said, 'Why not learn to type?' in that gentle wise way of his. I didn't. I went back to live at home and filled his garage with junk shop furniture that I renovated and/or painted, then lugged off to a friend's market stall. In the evenings I worked in a pub, which was where, aged twenty-three, I met Flash (really Paul, but his surname was Gordon), a musician and signer-on, who lived with us for four and a half years, making my life hell and finally moving out when I announced I was pregnant.

She paused. Bob's life was beginning to look pretty good.

I had Charlotte and continued to live with my lovely tolerant father until Granny died and left my sister and me her house, an arrangement she and my father had agreed upon. 'I have everything I need,' he said. We sold the house and split the money, and I bought an ex-council flat, did it up, made a big profit and, with the assistance of a dodgy no-questions-asked Croydon mortgage broker, bought a largish, in-need-of-some-attention terraced house near the canal in Oxford. I had friends here and thought it would be a nice place for my daughter to grow up. I'm hoping that Charlie has benefited from such a beautiful, stimulating and cultured environment, but, as yet, have seen no signs of it. I get maintenance from Flash, who was celebrated as 'the British Jim Morrison' for a brief spell in the mid-nineties, and who now, with a motley and ever-changing crew, tours the US as a Doors tribute band. My only hobby is my job, unless you count watching low-brow TV in an exhausted stupor. I'm currently between men, but don't half fancy Ed.

She thought she'd edit it some other time.

THREE

Zoe chewed the inside of her mouth as she sped down the M23 towards Brighton. Off the godawful M25 at last. In the cassette player was a Lighthouse Family tape, recommended by a friend who said it had done wonders for his insomnia. It wasn't having a calming effect on Zoe though, so she changed it for some favourite love songs and tried not to worry about Ross, now probably pacing up and down his hotel room wondering where the hell she'd got to.

You'd think he'd be used to her by now. He'd once accused her of being pathologically unpunctual. 'It's controlling, it's attention-seeking,' he'd shouted, 'and it smacks of deep-seated insecurity.' Which was tosh, Zoe decided. She just packed too much into her life, that was all. Look at her now, driving at 80, texting Ross with one hand and working her way through a chicken tikka wrap with the other. The Sinead O'Connor track she usually skipped because it made her cry came on, but rather than use her foot to fast forward, she stuck with it. And cried.

*   *   *

Ross Kershaw, Member of Parliament for an enormous but thinly populated Scottish constituency, married with two teenage children, greying but devastatingly attractive, greeted her in the hotel foyer.

'Only an hour and a quarter late,' he said, pecking her cheek. 'But you look very sexy, so I'll forgive you.'

They took a taxi to a restaurant he knew on the outskirts. 'Best if we're not spotted together in public,' he'd announced three years ago, and as far as Zoe knew they never had been. She hated the secrecy. She hated the fact that he wouldn't leave his wife. But she loved him as she'd never loved anyone, and had decided long ago that she'd do anything to keep him.

They'd met when her firm had been involved in a Labour Party ad campaign, and she'd been given the task of finding a good-looking MP to draw back the women voters who were slowly drifting over to the Lib Dems. She'd gone through a stack of mug shots, and had ruled out the whole of the Cabinet, all of the English and Welsh MPs and half the Scottish ones, when she came across Ross Kershaw and almost fell off her chair. I'll screw this man, she thought to herself, even if I have to pay him. Well, she hadn't had to pay him. Once the job was over, he'd pursued her, and they'd been having furtive dinners in anonymous steak houses ever since. And lots of sex. Often wild. Sometimes way too wild.

They chose from the unexciting menu, and while Ross talked about the speech he was to make at Conference the following day, Zoe got through half a bottle of overpriced Merlot. The food eventually arrived but, as was often the case when in Ross's company, and perhaps because of the chicken tikka wrap, Zoe had little appetite.

Back at the hotel, Ross stripped down to shirt and boxers, formed two lines of powder on the glass-topped dressing table and rolled up a twenty-pound note.

'But what about your speech tomorrow?' asked Zoe, instantly aware of how boring she sounded.

'Have you ever heard me make a bad one? Come on, let's have some fun.'

Zoe was exhausted. She'd worked late the night before, been at the hairdresser's on the stroke of nine and had a bloody awful journey down. She forced a smile. 'OK.'

When she was dabbing at her nostrils and enjoying the rush of adrenalin, there was a knock at the door. 'Ah,' said Ross, winking at her.

Zoe's stomach tightened as he went and opened it, muttered a few words, then returned with a slim and pretty, dark-haired girl of around nineteen. She had long, silky, black-clad legs and high-heeled shoes. Red.

'This is . . . er, sorry, what did you—'

'Chloe,' said the girl, taking off her fun-fur jacket to reveal a skimpy crimson dress, pointy breasts and a twelve-inch waist. She wore a black velvet choker and had a small tattoo on her left upper arm. Ross looked her up and down, gave an approving, 'Lovely,' and led her by the hand to where Zoe was quickly knocking back more wine.

'Zoe meet Chloe. Chloe, Zoe. Neat, eh?' He laughed and slipped one of Chloe's straps off her shoulder while running a hand up Zoe's thigh. 'Now we can really have some fun.'

Zoe stared vacantly at the man she adored, then did what she tended to do to get through these ordeals – dwelled on some other, more mundane and normal aspect of her life. Through the contortions, the groans and the 'Oh, God that's wonderful's of the next half-hour, she concentrated on the reading circle, occasionally smiling to herself at Gideon's completely-lost-on-the-group references – 'Of course, Derrida would challenge that premise' – and at Bob's quaint non-PCness. She remembered Bob suggesting that James Joyce couldn't write a proper sentence because he was a thick Paddy, then telling the joke about how you get an Irishman to burn his ear – 'Phone him while he's ironing!' Bronwen had protested, but there'd been no stopping him. 'And I suppose you've all heard about Mick in his car . . . ? Opened the door to let the clutch out.'

Zoe suddenly found herself laughing out loud, and Ross, currently being treated to a Monica by Chloe, murmured, '*Mmm*, you *are* having a good time, aren't you, darling?'

While Zoe was away, Gideon was scattering pastry crumbs, crisps and dreadful essays over her living-room floor. No proper chairs, that was the problem he thought, as he rolled around on a big red floor cushion and knocked over the remains of his coffee. He scribbled '40%' at the bottom of something a bright four-year-old might hand in, chucked it on a distant pile and sighed as he went on to the next. Not one, but two, had written 'Jane Austin' all the way through, and another – the daughter of a greengrocer, perhaps – had apostrophised everything ending in s: 'After two week's Elizabeth and her sister . . .'

How did they find them, he wondered. Had a frontal lobotomy? Or just forgot to go to school for thirteen years? Then come and do a degree at Molefield!

Still, it was a step up from the Tyneside comprehensive where he'd had the added burden of never understanding a word anyone uttered. For months he felt sorry for the head of Art for being called Martin Bormann, until he'd seen 'Martin Bowman' propped on his desk on parents' evening.

With the last of the essays marked, Gideon turned his attention to a sexy late-night Channel Five film and thought back longingly to Penelope and marriage and never having to think of how the next meal's going to get itself on to the table.

Bernice got cross if I let Georgia sleep all afternoon, because then she'd be up and wide awake and wanting attention all evening, and nothing pissed Bernice off more than that. She'd say, 'I have got work to do, you know, Ed.' Then her favourite line: 'Someone's got to pay the bills.'

I flopped on the sofa and thought, Sod it, I've been up since 5.30, I'm knackered, and what's more I've ironed those horrible blouses Bernice wears now she power dresses. Georgia was dead to the world upstairs, and I intended to have a good, hour-long doze, curtains closed, TV on. I pressed the buttons on the remote, and went through the channels to find the most sleep-inducing programme. Ah yes . . . the Labour Party Conference. I stretched out – as much as one can on a piddling two-seater sofa – punched the cushion a couple of times and sank my head into it. Heaven. Please sleep till 4.30, Georgia, I prayed as my eyes grew heavier. Someone was droning on about the underfunded police force. Or, better still, five o'clock . . .

I jumped at the ding-dong of the doorbell. Shit. Had I been asleep? I couldn't tell. I staggered over to the window and swished the curtain back. It was Kate. Which was fine by me.

She'd obviously woken him. He had lines etched in one side of his face.

'Oh, I'm sorry,' she said. 'Shall I come back another time?'

He opened the door wider. 'No, no, come in. I was just . . . um . . .' He scratched his unkempt hair and yawned. 'Actually, I was kipping. That's what we stay-at-home slackers do, you know.'

Kate stepped inside.

'Tea?' he asked.

'Lovely.'

'That's the other thing we do. Drink tea. Drink tea, take a nap. Drink tea, take a nap. Oh yeah, and get up four times in the night, start the day at six, change countless nappies, find only organic fruit and vegetables to cook and make into sickly purée, then spend hours trying to get said purée into child. Clear up sick. Wash clothes, wash more clothes. Milk, sugar?'

'Just milk, please.'

'Not working then?' he asked when he came back with the tea. He looked all bleary-eyed and crumpled and Kate found herself wanting to cuddle him.

'Just needed to get out for a while,' she said. 'I've left Duggie in charge.'

'Blimey!'

'Actually, he's kind of improving. Better not be too long, though.'

'No.'

They each had one eye on the television, which Kate was hoping he'd switch off, but guessed he wasn't quite awake enough to think of it. 'The Labour Party,' she said shaking her head. 'Who'd have believed it?'

Ed tutted. 'Yeah, I know. The Conservatives are more Labour than Labour these days.'

'No, I mean they're so smartly dressed now. Look at them.'

He rubbed an eye and squinted at the screen. 'Mm, see what you mean.'

'They're far more appealing than they used to be. I mean, this guy who's speaking is really *very* attractive.'

'Ross Kershaw,' said Ed, who might not know his Eliot, but seemed to know politics.

'. . . and to put a stop to the moral decline so evident in our towns and cities—'

'Hey, there's Zoe!' cried Kate, when the camera showed a

woman clapping enthusiastically and giving the speaker a thumbs-up. 'Quick, Ed. Look.'

'So it is,' he said, slapping a thigh and almost slopping tea on the floor. 'Huh. Fancy that.'

'How odd. She works in advertising, doesn't she? I wonder what she's doing there?'

The camera was back on the speaker. '. . . instil a sense of right and wrong—'

'Doesn't Zoe sometimes talk to a Ross on her mobile?' There was another shot of her. Kate guessed the cameraman fancied her. 'I wonder if she's going out with him.'

'. . . prevent young people being drawn into the sordid world of drugs and prostitution—'

Ed said, 'I think he's married.'

'Well, perhaps they work together or something.' Kate stared at the TV again for a while. 'He is gorgeous, isn't he? What did you say his surname was?'

'Kershaw,' said Ed, almost rattily. He turned the volume right down with the remote and moved the rocking chair so it half blocked the TV screen. 'He's not *that* good-looking.'

She smiled at him. 'No, of course not.'

She'd been an hour, so she rushed back to the shop and fell through the door, panting wildly.

'Are you all right?' she asked Duggie. 'Oh God! What's your blanket box doing in the shop? Quick, cover it.'

'It's sold.'

'Pardon?'

'I thought, Well, I'll just try it in the shop, and this geezer comes in and says it reminds him of Go— er, Gogo—'

'Gauguin?'

'That's the one. Anyway, he wanted to know how much.'

'What did you say?'

'Fifty-four pounds ninety-nine.'

She laughed. 'Why ninety-nine p?'

'Things in shops are always summink and ninety-nine p, aren't they?'

'Some shops, yes.'

'He's gone to get his mate's van.'

Duggie leaned back in the chair behind the tiny counter, hands folded on his chest, like someone who'd just concluded a successful takeover of her business. 'How much of the money do I get to keep then?'

'I don't know, Duggie. I mean, you're supposed to be working for nothing. You know, *work experience*.'

'Forty quid?'

'OK.'

When she got home Kate called, 'Charlie?' up the stairs, just to check she was in.

'WHAT!' came the reply.

Right. Charlie was going through an I-*loathe*-my-mother phase. Kate guessed she'd just have to sit it out.

By the time she got to the kitchen and dumped the shopping,

Charlie's unbearable music was thudding through the floor. She was into mixing on her decks, which she did relentlessly with her friend Jack. Said she wanted to leave school at sixteen and be a DJ. The decks, the blood-curdling computer games, the semishaved head and the raunchy Jennifer Lopez posters made Kate wonder if Charlie was your typical fourteen-year-old girl, but, on the whole, she tried not to think about it.

She was tired and had decided in the supermarket just to zap three frozen meals in the microwave; the extra one being for Jack, whose mother now regularly turned up with money for her. 'It must cost you a fortune,' she'd said the first time. 'I know how much he eats.' (How did she know, Kate had wondered.)

She flopped on the sofa while Indian meal number one rotated in the microwave, and found *Channel 4 News*. Crikey, there he was again – Ross Kershaw, speaking to a hall full of delegates. He had warm dark eyes, greying temples and a lovely Scottish lilt, and she was just trying to picture him without his suit when the microwave let out its four shrill beeps.

She fished the packet out of the bin and reread the instructions: 'Pierce lid in several places . . . 4 minutes on Full Power . . . uncover, stir, cover again . . . 3 minutes 45 seconds on Power Level 70 . . . leave to stand 1 minute.' She checked the other two meals and they had completely different instructions. 'Oh, for Christ's sake,' she said, tapping out numbers on the microwave. Perhaps tomorrow she'd just shoot, hang and pluck a couple of pheasants.

'CHARLIE!' Kate eventually called. 'DINNER!' The music thumped on and there was no response, so she took the broom from the cupboard under the stairs and bashed the living-room ceiling. Four feet then rumbled down the stairs.

'Hey, Indian,' said Jack as he lolloped into the kitchen. Jack was one of those boys who suddenly shoot up over a period of about a fortnight, but are left for a long time with their previous width. He had tiny shoulders and a concave chest, but was around six foot two. He said, 'Nice one,' grabbed the ketchup from a cupboard and shook some on to his pilau rice.

Charlie did the same, then looked over at the empty food packets and plastic trays. 'I dunno, Mum. You get lazier and lazier.'

'They just want a reaction,' Kate's *Coping with Adolescents* had told her. 'Resist!'

'I know,' she said with a jaunty shrug. 'I'm terrible, aren't I?'

They disappeared upstairs again, plate in one hand, Coke in the other. Kate ate in front of the television, occasionally looking around at the chaos that was her living room – the easel and scattered canvases didn't help – trying to picture the reading group gathered comfortably here next week. She thought of what she'd have to do to make it go swimmingly, which was basically to get Christine in.

Ed also ate alone – Bernice being caught up in Dunstable – as did Gideon (a day-old sandwich from the corner shop), Bronwen (bean and pulse hotpot), and Zoe (cappuccino in a motorway service station). Donna had chicken nuggets with the boys at six, reading *Middlemarch* beside her plate while they watched the Simpsons on the kitchen portable and missed their mouths.

In well-practised manner, Bob and Christine got all their crockery washed, dried and stacked in the cupboard by seven, so they could settle down for *Emmerdale* with a cup of tea and a custard slice.

'That Gideon,' said Christine during the ads. 'Is he married?'

'Not so far as I know. Says he's staying at Zoe's till he finds somewhere to live.'

'Oh dear. She's such a skinny thing, isn't she? I don't suppose Gideon ever gets a decent meal inside him. No wonder he ate a whole half of my sponge the other evening, not to mention most of the sausage rolls.'

'Ha! So he's a glutton as well as a pain in the proverbial.'

Christine frowned and twiddled her fingers in her lap. Odd socks, hungry, homeless, holes in his jumpers . . . poor lamb. *Emmerdale* was back on and she tried to concentrate, but found herself thinking of that MFI desk of Heather's out in the garage. It'd fit nicely into Keith's old room – sunnier than Heather's ever was – and perhaps they could give him the bookcase from the landing. Gideon was bound to have lots of books. He might like a television in his room for the highbrow stuff: *Newsnight* and what have you. They could view it as a business; a little bit of extra income now that Bob was semi-retired. Like a boarding house – only in a chalet bungalow, and with just the one guest. She imagined Gideon becoming as fond of her Baked Alaska as Bob was.

We were taking a little Sunday-afternoon family stroll around University Parks. Kind of. Any interested observer would have noticed giveaway signs of a dysfunctional unit, the main one being that Bernice could absolutely not walk beside us. She'd lag behind or stride ahead, but was rarely within earshot. We'd done almost a circuit when I turned to comment on the colours of the trees, but found her fifty yards back, chatting into her mobile, hand cupped over her mouth.

'Have you noticed the change in the leaves over the past week?' I asked Georgia instead. She was hung on my back, and as far as I could tell, fairly comatose. 'I think autumn's definitely with us now, don't you? Eh?'

Bernice ran towards me and arrived breathless. 'That was Clive. Got to go into the office, I'm afraid. Bit of an emergency.'

'Again?' I was amazed at how many evening and weekend crises you could have in the study-aid business.

'Don't wait up,' she yelled, now as far ahead as she'd been behind. 'Might have to work all night on this one!'

Jolly good, I thought, and headed for the pond.

Kate was sitting on a bench in the park, chatting with a friend, when she saw Ed and his baby walking down a distant path. 'What do you think of him?' she asked, pointing Ed's way.

'Definitely a ten,' said Maggie. 'Young though. And he's got a baby. So probably married.'

'He is, kind of.'

'Oh, you know him?'

'He's in the reading group.'

'Wow. In that case I'm joining one.'

'Well, plenty to choose from in Oxford.'

'He's got nice hair, hasn't he?'

'Very.'

'Long legs.'

'Mm, and a terrific chest.'

'Kate! Have you . . . ?'

'Uh-uh.' She explained about Ed's breast-feeding.

Maggie nudged her. 'Look out, he's coming this way.'

'Hi,' he said when he reached them. 'Thought it was you.'

Kate introduced her friends to each other and Ed took his baby-carrier off and joined them on the bench. 'Not interrupting anything, am I?'

'We were just clocking the men,' said Maggie. 'You know, giving them marks out of ten.'

'Really? What did I get?'

'Er . . . oh, we don't do dads,' said Kate. 'On principle. Women become invisible to men when they've got kids in tow.'

Ed seemed to think about it, then shrugged. 'Fair enough.'

They were quiet for a while as three twenty-something men walked past, talking loudly.

'OK. Left to right: six, one, five,' said Maggie.

'Uh-uh. Six, one, seven.'

Kate felt Ed's eyes on her. 'God, you're quick,' he said. 'And so cruel! Why give the poor guy in the middle only one point? He looks perfectly OK to me.'

'Cricket jumper,' she told him, and Maggie nodded.

*　　*　　*

We took the back route out of the park and walked, via St Clements, to a café on the Cowley Road, where Georgia decided it was time to wake up and be grumpy. I fed her and did a quick nappy change out the back, then she was her amiable self again. Kate held her while I ate.

We were at a window table and Maggie started up the game again. 'Quick quick, here comes a nine.'

'No. Nice face but a rotten figure,' said Kate.

I was beginning to find this demeaning, but guessed they'd jump down my throat if I said so, and was pleased when Maggie said she had to go and pick up her son from his father's house. She ran a hand down my sleeve and said how nice it was to have met me. Maggie was probably Kate's age but really hadn't weathered well. I wasn't sure I wanted her stroking me.

'Likewise,' I told her.

Kate and I ordered more coffee and sat in my favourite part of town watching multicultural east Oxford pass by. Sari-clad women, Kosovans in pairs or groups – people you never saw in the city centre for some reason. This strange division worked both ways. I knew people who felt, not all that unreasonably, that they'd be taking their life in their hands if they ventured over Magdalen Bridge and into the Cowley Road. Considering its reputation for petty crime, drug-dealing and gang warfare, you'd have thought Inspector Morse might have visited the area, just once. No pristine quads to amble around with Lewis, though; just ninety Indian restaurants, two sex shops and a thousand old-hippie lecturers, still spouting Marx whilst sitting quietly on their three-bedroomed mid-terrace gold mines.

'Ed?'

'Mm? Sorry, miles away.'

'I said they should try to bottle this baby smell.' Kate sniffed at Georgia's head while she rocked her from side to side. 'It's lovely.'

I said, 'Yes, it is,' and thought, What a nice woman, then pictured Bernice frolicking around the empty office with Clive, photocopying her bottom and doing unimaginable things with the stapler. 'Uh, horrible,' I said with a shudder.

'Sorry?'

'Um . . . this . . . er, music. Terrible.'

'Oh, I love Nina Simone!'

Bugger.

FOUR

When Zoe arrived at work on Tuesday she picked up an email from Kate telling her the reading group would be meeting at 7 p.m. that evening, and not the usual 7.30. Now that would be a challenge, she thought, but was determined to make it, having realised that those Tuesday evening meetings were probably the only time she ever relaxed these days.

Ross then called her from his mobile to cancel lunch. She was pleasant about it but put the phone down and quietly cursed him. Never mind, she'd see him Friday lunchtime at his London flat. It had become a regular and definite thing, Fridays. They'd then meet up at the other odd times he could fit her in. He didn't always fly up to Scotland at weekends, which was nice, although she was aware they'd never managed to spend an entire one together. He tended to see her off on the train on Saturday afternoon or Sunday morning with a, 'Simply masses of paperwork to do, sweetheart. Love you.' Which she was sure he did.

Today, she whizzed through her own paperwork, had a meeting

with her boss, two meetings with clients and a very late lunch at her desk, before deciding that was enough and heading for Paddington. On the train she finished *Middlemarch*, closing it with a smile and a wistful sigh that caused the man opposite to ask, 'Good book, then?'

'Very.'

'I've always meant to read it,' he went on.

Oh dear, she thought, a weirdo. Nobody strikes up conversations on trains. Not unless they're on their mobile. He didn't look weird. Thirties. Suit. Briefcase. Rather nice, in fact.

'Take it,' said Zoe, handing it to him. She knew Gideon had a spare one.

The man looked as though she'd just offered him sex in the loo. 'Well, that's very kind. Thank you.' He took a pen from inside his jacket. 'Why don't you write your name and address in it, then I can send it back to you.'

'OK.'

She avoided her usual scrawl and, after taking another quick look at the fair-haired, blue-eyed, lightly tanned stranger, added her phone number and both email addresses.

'Oxford?' he said when she handed it back. 'I'm in Cheltenham. Well, just this side of it.'

'In the Cotswolds?'

'Mm.'

'Nice.'

'Yes, it is.' He offered her a hand and said, 'I'm Matthew, by the way.'

She shook it. 'Zoe.'

'Yes, I know.' He smiled and withdrew his hand and turned to the first page of the book. 'Do you mind if I read?'

'Of course not.'

As the train pulled into Oxford, Matthew looked up at the departing Zoe. 'Thanks,' he said, waving the book at her. 'I will return it.'

'No hurry.'

When she got home there was no Gideon, just his debris. God, he was untidy. She'd only taken him in because he was an old college friend of Ross's sister. As far as Gideon knew, Zoe and Ross had some vague business connection. He'd phoned her early September, introduced himself, and asked if she could recommend any good B & Bs. He sounded very pleasant, so she offered him her spare room for a while, adding, 'The rent would be handy,' before he got any ideas about freeloading.

Five past six. Enough time for a shower.

In the bathroom she was greeted by two pairs of ancient and frayed underpants soaking in slimy grey water in the wash basin.

He'd have to go.

Kate couldn't believe it when Zoe turned up at ten past seven. She'd only told her the earlier time because she was always late. The others were due at half-past. She came clean immediately and Zoe found it hilarious.

'People should have done this with me years ago,' she said,

handing over her coat. 'Jesus, what's that noise? Have you got builders in?'

Kate explained it was her daughter's music, but wasn't sure Zoe believed her. They cocked their heads and listened for a while and Kate could see what she meant. Had Charlie and Jack just been fitting cupboards all these months?

Zoe popped up to the bathroom and looked twice as glamorous when she arrived in the kitchen. Long blonde hair, big blue eyes, perfectly applied makeup. At five eight or so, she towered over Kate. But then so did most thirteen-year-olds.

'I've got samosas for everyone,' Kate said, pointing at her mini food display. 'Or pork pie for the less adventurous. Do you fancy a sneaky gin and tonic?'

'Mm, yes please.'

After tipping far too much gin in a glass, Kate then poured herself a smaller one and took the tonic from the fridge. 'Hey, I saw you on TV the other day,' she said, handing over the glass. 'At the Labour Party Conference.'

'What!'

'Er . . . yeah. The other afternoon. You were in the audience. It was you, wasn't it?'

'God, lucky my boss didn't see it. I was supposed to be in Leeds.'

'That . . . um, what's his name, Ross Kersh—'

Zoe coughed mid-swig and spluttered. 'What about him?' she wheezed.

Kate handed her some kitchen roll. 'He was speaking at the

time. He's quite dishy, isn't he?' Was she just being provocative? Probably.

Zoe dabbed at her mouth, made an effort to compose herself and emptied her glass. 'Yes, I suppose so.'

'And very, you know, upright. Talking about the country's moral decline, et cetera.'

Zoe suddenly started crying, which was a bit of a shock and not at all on Kate's agenda. At twenty past seven it was getting a bit late for a girlie, all-men-are-complete-bastards session at the kitchen table.

'He's a complete bastard,' sobbed Zoe.

Seven twenty-one.

'But he seemed so nice on the television.'

'Ha!'

'Are you and he . . . um . . . ?'

She nodded. 'For three years. Nobody knows. Not a soul.'

Kate thought, Why's she choosing to tell me? Almost a stranger. Was it the gin? She topped up Zoe's glass. 'Is he married? Is that it?'

Zoe lit her second cigarette then downed her drink in one go. 'Yes, he is. But it's more than that.' She dabbed at her eyes with some tissue, looked over both shoulders and leaned towards Kate. 'Promise you won't tell a soul what I'm about to—'

'No, of course not. Tell me.'

'Ross bloody Kershaw is not only an adulterer, he's also into—'

The doorbell went. Kate decided to ignore it for the time being. '*What's* he into?'

'Well . . .' Ring, ring, ring 'Um . . . don't you think you should get that?'

It was Bronwen, carrying a bottle. 'I've brought some elderflower cordial.'

'Oh good.'

'Gracious,' she said, stepping inside and unwinding a large hairy shawl, 'what's that noise?'

While I was munching on a samosa during the break I flipped through Kate's paintings; about twenty in all, stacked against a wall in three piles. Landscapes in vibrant colours. Portraits. Mostly fairly conventional stuff compared to her polka-dot coffee table, and as far as I could tell, quite good. One guy seemed to feature a lot. Naked. I stared long and hard at one particularly graphic pose.

'My ex,' said Kate, suddenly beside me.

'Charlie's dad?'

'Uh-uh. More recent.'

I looked again, and found myself hating him, which was odd. 'Where is he now?'

She checked her watch. 'Probably in the Pig and Whistle.'

'Right.'

'Bit of a drinker.'

'Ah. Speaking of which,' I said, lowering my voice, 'is it me or is Zoe completely plastered?'

Kate took my hand – nice – and led me to a quiet corner of her large knocked-through living room. 'I gave her a G and T and now she keeps helping herself,' she whispered. 'Bit upset. Been having an affair with that Ross Kershaw MP chap. For three years. I've been sworn to secrecy.'

I too whispered. 'Then why are you telling me?'

'Oops. Anyway, she was about to dish some dirt on him when everyone arrived.'

'Bummer.'

'Yeah.'

Bronwen, who'd nominated herself Elderflower Cordial Monitor, approached us with a large jug. 'Top up, Ed?'

'Thanks,' I said. How come I didn't get gin and tonic?

Kate wandered off and I stood gingerly sipping at Bronwen's insipid sugar-free drink, taking in the scene before me: a slightly swaying Zoe whispering something in Donna's ear; Bob, frowning and turning one of Kate's more abstract paintings this way and that, then this way again; and Gideon, casually slipping a large chunk of pork pie into his sports jacket pocket.

Up on the landing I opened the wrong door and, instead of the toilet, found two boys in a stuffy, dimly lit, black-walled room, engrossed in a silent and grotesque-looking computer game. 'Oh, sorry,' I said.

'It's next door,' mumbled one of them without taking his eyes from the screen.

'Thanks. Sorry again.'

'Oh yeah,' he said, now turning to look at me. 'Can you tell Mum she'll have to give us another tenner if she wants us to stay quiet after nine o'clock?'

'Um . . . who's your mum?' I asked.

'Duh. Kate, of course.'

They were both staring at me now. Two shaved heads. Four ears, glowing from the light of the computer screen.

'You're *Charlie?*'

She gave me a round of applause. 'Oh yeah, and we need some more samosas and Coke.'

At the bottom of the stairs Bob asked where the WC was. 'Second on your left at the top,' I told him. 'Whatever you do, don't take the first.'

'Got Bertha Mason up there, has she?'

'Something like that.'

At mother and toddler group the following afternoon, Donna – sitting next to Suzanne, who was rabbiting on about her new kitchen – thought back to the reading group, and how, during the break, Zoe, who'd looked dead pissed, told her she was having an affair with an MP. Donna had always thought Zoe a bit of a stuck-up cow, but maybe she wasn't so bad. She'd definitely been crying when she said, 'He likes girls even younger than you, you know, Donna. Pays them for it. Threesomes. Drugs. Kinky stuff. You name it.'

Donna hadn't quite known where to put herself, but really wanted to know more. It sounded like something out of her dad's Sunday paper. 'What's his name?' she asked, and Zoe whispered it in her ear, adding, 'Have you seen him on television? Fucking gorgeous.'

When she'd taken her place again and got her pen out and waited for Gideon to say something clever, Donna wrote 'Rosh Kersha' in her spiral notebook, thinking maybe he was Indian or something.

Zoe had woken at 10.15 feeling like death, sworn when she'd seen the time, phoned the office to say she'd be working at home today and gone back to bed.

At one o'clock she came to again, and as her brain slowly cranked itself into action over a strong cup of coffee, she tried to recall exactly how she'd got to be in this state. She remembered arriving at Kate's house. Hadn't Kate had some builders in? Gin and tonic and . . . nothing. Had the group discussed *Middlemarch*? OK, she'd got drunk. Very drunk. How had she got home? She'd woken in bed this morning in her boots and all her clothes, with a note from Gideon beside her saying, 'Don't worry, I'll be gone as soon as I've found somewhere.' What was that about?

Shit, it wasn't Friday, was it? She started palpitating. Reading group, Tuesdays. 'So, today's Wednesday,' she said with relief. God, it would have been awful to have missed her lunchtime session with Ross. Lovely man.

Bob had gone into town early to look for *White Teeth* by Zadie Smith. A blinkin woman again. Zoe's choice this time. If it was another Victorian novel for Gideon to spout endless garbage about, he'd give up the reading circle, that was for sure. They'd be meeting at Zoe's again next week. An hour and a half sitting on those old pine floorboards, a draught whistling round your nether regions through the gaps. This time he'd get her to think about a bit of laminate flooring in her front room. All the rage these days, for some reason. He couldn't think what was wrong with a nice fitted Axminster himself, though he'd never say that at Plus Floors, where they'd all but given up on carpets.

He spent some time wandering aimlessly around Blackwell's. Well, his aim was to find *White Teeth*, but his hunt through the maze of a shop took him via Mathematics, Antiques and Self-help before he happened upon the coffee shop, a Danish pastry, and a welcome sofa. Two student types came and joined him, talking about some teacher they couldn't abide and spooning chocolate-covered foam into their mouths while their phones rang out annoying little jingles. Bob thought back with longing to the old Kardoma on Cornmarket Street. Tenpence for a frothy coffee and an iced bun.

'Oh, excellent!' the long-legged, scruffy-trousered girl beside him said as she stared at her pink phone. 'Hugh says he's got his parents' yacht next week if we can all get to Marseilles.'

'Excellent!' said the lanky, pale-faced lad opposite, who looked as though half an hour on a yacht might kill him.

On his way out of the shop, Bob thought he'd just ask the comely young woman at the counter. '*White Teeth* by Zadie Smith, if you please.'

She pointed to some shelves a few feet away. 'You'll find it over in the S section, sir.'

'Excellent!' said Bob, trying it out. 'Er, ta very much.'

By 1.30 he was behind his own counter and helping a customer choose between a pre-finished hardwood and a non-slip vinyl laminate. Not for the first time, he found himself wishing he'd opted to work mornings, as he could feel that afternoon sleepiness creeping up on him already. Still, it was only three afternoons a week. If he'd been at home now, he and Christine would be settling down for *Neighbours* and a light nap. At ten past two he phoned her for a natter – and to stop her dozing when he wasn't able to – but there was no answer. Probably nodded off.

Christine was wide awake and in Currys looking at televisions. In exchange for a Lancashire hotpot, she'd got her retired neighbour to run the aerial through to Gideon's room, as well as help her with the desk and some picture hooks. Now, she wondered, would he like a television with an in-built video player? Oh, why not? She chose one, asked if it could be delivered and paid with the money she'd siphoned off from her housekeeping over the years.

OK, so that was desk, bookcase, rug, two duvet sets, mirror and TV all taken care of. All she needed now were one or two decorative bits. And, of course, Gideon himself.

Bronwen was working on Returned Fiction, putting all the male authors back on their shelves and leaving the female ones where they were. People almost always perused the returned books first.

It was these little subversive acts that kept her from going insane in the conservative atmosphere of her small branch library. Although forever under the watchful eye of Jim, she had this week managed to slip a poster about a phone mast protest on to the notice board and hide *The Downing Street Years* under a display stand. Not all female authors got preferential treatment. Just as she was pushing her trolleyful of men towards the A section, she spotted Gideon looking through a book in Crime Fiction and was surprised at the jolt it gave her.

He looked up as she approached, quickly closed the book and said, 'Aha, you've discovered my secret vice.'

'Lawrence Block?'

'The whole genre, I'm afraid.'

Well, no one's perfect, thought Bronwen. 'You could always make one of these your choice for the reading circle?'

He laughed at the very idea, and Bronwen joined in, until Jim shot them both a quiet-in-the-library-please look.

'Must dash, actually,' whispered Gideon. 'Lecturing on Mrs Gaskell's *North and South* at three thirty.'

'Wonderful book.'

Gideon plucked an Elmore Leonard from the middle shelf – 'Mm, yes it is,' – and a Chandler from the top one. 'See you next Tuesday,' he said, and wandered off with a hanky dangling from his jacket pocket.

Bronwen ignored the handkerchief, and the fact that he hadn't chosen a Sue Grafton or a Patricia Cornwell, and tried to calm the flutters in her tummy with some yoga breathing. Not since Roger from 'Stop the Newbury Bypass' had she felt quite so unsettled by a man.

Two hours later, Gideon was summing up to a quarter-filled lecture theatre, '*North and South* is, therefore, a novel which, more so than *Mary Barton*, seriously questions the status quo.'

He looked up at his audience. Apart from the five mature women students sitting in the front rows and eagerly taking notes, they were all so depressingly young. One or two were clearly sending text messages. To one another, no doubt. And not, he'd wager, about the plight of the discontented millworkers in *North and South*. One girl was asleep on her friend's shoulder. He thought he could hear the tinny beat of a Walkman.

One thing he'd learned was not to issue assignment titles orally, after one female student heard, 'Give a Marxist response to *Wuthering Heights*' as 'Give Marks's response to *Wuthering Heights*', and handed in a page and a half on how they'd probably recommend lined curtains to keep the winds off the moors out, and a makeover for Heathcliff – a nice linen suit and some loafers maybe. Gideon had scrawled, 'And surely some microwaveable dishes to make the housekeeper's life easier?' and given her a generous twenty-five per cent.

He began to gather his books and notes together on the podium, then looked up again and saw everyone had gone, even the girl who'd been sleeping. Good, he thought.

Outside in the corridor a familiar woman approached. She was somewhere in her fifties and wore a belted camel coat and court shoes. Her hair was part blonde, part grey, and was in that pageboy style so popular when he'd been a post-grad at Leeds.

'Hello, Gideon,' she said with a lovely warm smile.

'Hello there.' Where did he know her from? He frowned at her. 'I'm sorry, I . . .'

'Bob's wife?' she reminded him. 'Christine?'

He was aware he was staring blankly.

'Bob from the reading group?'

That was it. 'Ah yes, of course,' he said, the memory of jam-and-cream-filled sponge cake tickling his taste buds.

Christine fiddled nervously with her patent handbag. 'I just wondered if I might have a word? If you're not too busy, that is.'

'Certainly,' said Gideon. 'Let's go to my office, shall we?'

He guessed immediately what this was about. She'd had a basic education, got married at eighteen, never worked, and was thinking of studying. He'd encourage her, of course. He found those who'd left school at fifteen, lived on post-war rations and never touched a Gameboy tended not to hand in essays on chain stores.

'Ed Adams,' I typed. It was Friday and Georgia and I had done the week's shopping. She now slept, and in the kitchen a ratatouille gently simmered. Clothes had been washed, the kitchen floor mopped and the living room hoovered. I'd paid outstanding bills over the phone and had given my parents their weekly update on Georgia, and it was only 1.30. I still hadn't got round to buying

White Teeth, so obviously couldn't read that, and there was little more I could do to the thesis bar wreck it. Might as well get this out of the way, I thought.

Right. *I grew up in a village in the Cambridgeshire fens, where they said if you faced east on a clear day you'd see the Urals. Apparently, when my twin brother, Will, and I were shown the Brecon Beacons at the age of five we screamed and cowered in the car and the holiday was aborted.*

Someone knocked at the door. I hoped it was Kate and it was. She was in a suede jacket that went well with her hair. A knee-length black skirt and black tights. She looked about eighteen.

'Hi,' I said. 'Come in.'

'Busy?'

'Uh-uh. Just writing my little biog for the group.'

'Can I see it?'

'Sure.' I led her to the computer. 'But I've only done two sentences.'

She read from the screen and said, 'Oh, wow, you're a twin?'

I nodded.

'So is he as handsome, charming, witty and intelligent as you?'

She didn't *sound* as though she was being ironic, but instead of telling her I had the hots for her too, I played it safe. 'We're not identical,' I said. 'Cup of tea?'

'Yes, please. I've brought my lunch, is that OK?' She took a baguette from a bag. 'Miles is doing an hour in the shop.'

Handsome, eh? 'Would you like a plate for that?' I asked.

'No, it's OK.'

I kind of insisted though, as I'd just hoovered and everything. Out in the kitchen, while I waited for the kettle to boil, I closed my eyes and thought about kissing her.

'So do you like mountains now?' Kate asked after she'd enquired about life in the fens. How nice he looked in his dark blue shirt, but how strangely he'd reacted when she threw all those compliments at him. Embarrassed and shy? Deeply committed to Bernice? Or maybe she'd just got the signals wrong. Cambridgeshire and mountains seemed like safe subjects.

'Love them. I trekked in the Himalayas a few years back. Fantastic.'

'I bet,' said Kate, unable to imagine a worse way of spending a holiday. The idea of being more than four minutes from shops and cafés and other human beings filled her with a strange dread. Always had.

'I'll show you where,' he said, getting up from his chair and going over to a neat bookshelf. He pulled out a world atlas and came and sat beside her on the sofa. 'Here.'

Kate found it hard to concentrate on the route he was describing, what with his cheek being an inch and a half from hers. She pondered on whether his legs were as nice as his chest, how his skin felt . . . 'I have to get back soon,' she said. 'Miles's hour is almost up.'

'Oh, don't go.' Ed's hand fell on hers. 'This is so nice.'

She smiled. 'Mm.'

'Do you really find me handsome, charming, witty and erudite?' he asked.

'I think I said intelligent.'

'Right.'

'Well . . . I'd really better . . .'

'Yes.'

On Sunday, Zoe placed the vacuum cleaner in front of Gideon and asked if he'd mind running it around.

'Ah, yes, well,' he said. 'To be honest, I've never actually used one of these machines.' He stood back with his chin in a hand and frowned, as though viewing a perplexing piece of modern art for the first time.

Zoe sighed, not totally surprised. 'Put your foot on this button to switch it on, then aim the nozzle bit at the floor, being careful to avoid the big cushions, the floor-length curtains and my collection of unusual shells and driftwood in the hearth. OK?'

'Right you are,' said Gideon, and with a press of the switch he was off. Zoe watched while he sucked up a week's worth of his crumbs and three of the smaller shells. 'Sorry,' he shouted as they clonked their way up the tube. She'd get them out the bag later.

Next came a washing machine lesson. 'Clothes in there. Soap powder in there. Conditioner in there. Close door. Turn dial to three. Push this button. OK? Now you try.'

Zoe discreetly turned her head while Gideon put his smalls

in the drum. 'How have you managed in the past?' she asked him.

'Mm? Oh well, Penelope always saw to that side of things. And then after Penelope there was always a rather accommodating lady in the launderette. Six pounds and it would all be done for you by the end of the day.'

Zoe wondered what Penelope had been like. They were married for eight years, he'd told her. No children; Penny preferred Labradors. They'd taught at the same school, but she eventually decided she'd rather spend her life with the head teacher.

Gideon managed to elicit a combination of pity and fury from Zoe. At that moment mostly fury, as he spilt powder and slopped conditioner and tried to press the 'on' button before shutting the door.

'Have you got a photo of Penelope?' she asked while she got the machine going.

He looked mildly stunned, but said he believed he had and disappeared upstairs for a while.

'Here we are,' he said when he returned. 'Our wedding day.'

Zoe gasped. Surely that wasn't Gideon? So handsome. So slim. Penelope wasn't really in the same league. Moon-faced, fat ankles. 'She looks nice,' she said.

'Ah yes. A good woman.' He looked at the photograph and sighed. 'Shouldn't have let her slip away, I suppose.'

Now Zoe was veering towards pity again. 'Shall I get a pizza delivered?' she asked, and Gideon flung Penelope to one side and cheered up enormously.

*   *   *

On Monday morning, Donna caught the bus into town and found herself queuing behind Ed in the bookshop, both of them with *White Teeth* in their hands.

'Hey,' she said. 'I'm glad I'm not the only one who hasn't read it yet.'

'Me too. Do you think Bronwen'll give us detention?'

Donna laughed. 'They've got a nice coffee shop here,' she said. 'Do you fancy a quick cuppa? Or are you busy?'

Ed hesitated briefly. 'OK, why not?'

'I just feel like I've got nothing in common with them, even though I have? Do you know what I mean?'

Ed had been following closely, so he did know what she meant. He just wished she wouldn't make every sentence a question. 'Just because you didn't finish your education and you're a single mother on benefits, doesn't mean you're not a bright individual with aspirations.'

This was the best conversation Donna had had in years. No one she knew used words like 'aspirations'. Mostly they said, 'Hiya. Alright?' to her in the street and the corner shop. And, 'He's growing, isn't he?' as if that was an amazing thing for a two-year-old to be doing. 'Yeah,' Donna would say. 'He's gonna be like his dad.' Next time she'd say, 'Yeah, *and* he's got aspirations,' and see if they thought it was some breathing problem.

75

'Well, I want to go back to school,' she told Ed, 'and make up for my GCSEs, and then on to college.'

'Really?'

'Mm. Only I don't know if I'm clever enough. My spelling's crap.'

'So's mine and I'm writing a thesis. Thank God for spellcheck, eh?'

Donna laughed and asked what a thesis was.

'Well,' said Ed, and he went on to explain the different tiers of higher education.

She nodded thoughtfully. 'So let me get this right. You'll be a doctor but you won't like be treating people?'

'No,' he said, laughing, 'although I believe there are some who've tried it.'

Donna looked at her watch and panicked. 'Got to collect Ryan in fifteen minutes. The old battleaxe who runs the playgroup throws a right wobbly if you're late.' She got up and put on a big padded jacket and a black beret. 'Thanks for the advice. See you at Zoe's tomorrow?'

'Yep. See you then.'

'Bye.'

Quite a nice kid really, thought Ed. He gathered his various bags and hooked them on Georgia's buggy. On his way out he spotted Kate at the till, buying a copy of *White Teeth*. He went over and said, 'Not in the shop then?'

'Oh hi, Ed. No, I close on Mondays. It's supposed to be my furniture-buying day.'

She took her book in its little carrier bag and thanked the assistant. 'There's quite a nice coffee shop here. Have you got time for one?'

'Um . . . yeah. Sure.'

Zoe was at her desk. She had stacks to do, but just couldn't get into anything. She yawned, took her laptop out of its bag and plugged it in. *Zoe Langton* she typed, *aged 31, born in Leicester but lived absolutely everywhere. Jack-of-all-trades, alcoholic father took up and dropped jobs and always wanted to be somewhere else. I went to around twenty different schools, and had one or two spells without school when it was clear Dad wasn't going to like his new employment, or the area, or something.*

She thought back to being asked if her family were gypsies when she told a new friend she and her family were living in a caravan till they found a house to rent. The girl was called Rebecca, she remembered, and although she'd said no, certainly not, Rebecca had gone and spread it around that Zoe was a dirty gypo and for the full three months she was at that school no one played with her. She swallowed hard and fought back the tears. *When I was fourteen, my father was hit by a lorry on the hard shoulder of the M4. One of his millions of clapped-out cars had broken down and he was trying to fix it. Mum and I weren't with him. By the time we got to the hospital he was dead. Mum screamed and sobbed and I just thought, Good, now we can go and live with Gran and Granddad, which we did.*

Oh dear, she thought, and blew her nose.

I went to the local secondary school for the next four years, made some

*good friends, worked very hard and to everyone's amazement managed
to get a place at Oxford, where I've lived ever since, although I now work
in London. I joined the reading circle because I get lots of time to read on
trains and couldn't bear another God-I-really-want-a-husband book.*

'There,' she said, before changing the bit about being glad when
her father died, and printing it out.

After a slightly more productive afternoon, she met up with Ross
in a themed pub just off the North Circular. They had nasty wine
and jacket potatoes, then out in a dark corner of the car park made
upright love on the back seat.

At 8.15, Kate bashed the living-room ceiling then heard the rumble
on the stairs.

'I thought we'd all eat together this evening,' she told Charlie
and Jack.

They looked bewildered. Hands in pockets, shoulders hunched.
'Like *why?*' asked Charlie.

'Like because it's a civilised thing to do. Now get the Dijon mustard out, would you? It goes nicely with this salmon en croute.'

'But I *hate* fish.'

'Tough.'

Jack remained hunched while Charlie stomped to the cupboard
and back. 'Couldn't find it,' she said, slamming the ketchup on
the table.

'Try again.'

*   *   *

'So anyway, the woman said she'd come back tomorrow with her husband. But I'm pretty sure she'll buy it.'

'Oh good,' said Jack, making an effort, as he had all the way through the meal, telling Kate about his brothers and sisters and all their pets. He placed his knife and fork at six thirty on his completely empty plate. 'That was nice.'

'Thanks. Finish your pie, Charlie.'

'I can't.'

'You've barely touched it. Or the broccoli. If you waste food, I'll have to cut down on your allowance.'

'Oh, for f—'

'And there'll be fifty p off every time you swear.'

'Am I allowed to say "up yours"?'

'No. Now eat your salmon. And when you've finished I'd like you and Jack to fill the dishwasher.'

Jack was nodding and saying, 'Yeah, sure,' when Charlie scraped her chair back, picked her plate up and took it to the sink.

'Come on, Jack, I've got Doritos upstairs.'

'Oh . . . um, well . . .'

Kate closed her eyes, nodded and gestured for him to go. After throwing away most of Charlie's meal and filling the dishwasher she picked up her book and reread the 'Show Them Who's Boss!' chapter.

FIVE

We were all in Zoe's minimalist front room. Bob and Bronwen had nabbed the two director's chairs and the rest of us shared three big floor cushions. Although I'd headed for the one Kate was on, Donna got there first and I now found myself sitting bottom to bottom with Gideon. We all had our *White Teeth* out and Zoe, with a cushion all to herself, said, 'OK, who wants to kick off?'

Everyone suddenly found their books very interesting. People flicked through pages, chewed on nails and pursed their lips, as though about to say something profound. But we all stayed silent.

'Ed? asked Zoe, and they all looked my way.

I leaned forward, elbows resting on my knees. 'I haven't got round to reading it, I'm afraid. Georgia's been ill and . . .'

Zoe turned to Kate, who started blushing. She's so sweet. 'Um . . . Sorry.'

Bronwen and Bob were examining their laps; picking bits of fluff off, scratching at knees.

Zoe said, 'Gideon?'

'Well . . . ah,' he said, and opened his book.

'Donna?'

'Uh-uh. But I saw it on the telly, if that's any help?'

'I think not.'

There was a bit of a silence, then Donna said, 'How about you, Zoe?'

'God, no. Been way too busy.'

Bronwen asked if she could make a suggestion and we all raised our eyebrows. 'Perhaps weekly reading-circle meetings are overly ambitious,' she said. 'Why don't we gather fortnightly from now on? It'll give us more time to read the books.'

Donna put her hand up. She still did this despite our telling her she needn't.

'Yes, Donna?'

'I definitely want us to meet every week,' she said, with a trace of desperation in her voice. She looked at me for support.

'Me too,' I told the group. Tuesday evenings with Kate or Bernice? No contest.

Kate shook her head. 'Fortnightly would be much better for me,' she said, leaving me mildly gutted.

'I reckon I need a good two weeks to get through a book,' said Bob.

Zoe was chewing on a nail and looking anxious. 'No, no. Weekly's much better. But perhaps we should vote on it?'

'Good idea,' said Bronwen. 'Hands up for continuing with weekly meetings.'

Now I was torn. Would Kate think me overly keen on her if I voted 'weekly'? I took one look at Donna's face and stuck my hand up. Zoe was the only other 'for'.

'That's three,' said Bronwen. 'And those for fortnightly?'

Kate, Bob and Bronwen put their hands up.

'How about you, Gideon?' asked Bronwen. 'Gideon?'

His bottom wiggled beside me and he looked up from his copy of *White Teeth*. 'Well . . .' he said, lifting the book in the air. 'A promising start. Most promising. However, I am having a bit of a problem with the authorial voice.'

'But are you voting "fortnightly"?'

'Ah,' he said, looking around at the group. 'Mm. Fortnightly?'

I thought he was mulling over the question, but Bronwen took it as a yes.

'So fortnightly it is,' she said. 'However, should any of you feel the need to discuss some aspect of a book between meetings, you'd be most welcome to drop in on me. Have a chat over a cup of tea and a slice of something home-made.' Her gaze fell heavily upon Gideon and I heard him swallow.

'So,' said Zoe, reaching to a corner cupboard. 'Anyone for Taboo?'

I was so pleased I wasn't in Bob and Donna's team.

'An *mm* calls,' Gideon told them for the third time, gesturing crazily and trying not to say the prohibited words on his card. 'Name of a play.'

Donna shrugged. 'Dunno.'

'The word's "Inspector", of course,' said Gideon, putting the card down and picking up another. '*An Inspector Calls.*'

'What's he on about?' asked Bob, and Donna shrugged again.

The egg timer was halfway through. 'OK.' Gideon held the card aloft. 'You're bound to get this one. *Mm* realism. Isabel Allende.'

'Who?' they asked.

Kate was almost crying with laughter.

'*Mm* realism.'

'Don't know. Next one,' barked Bob.

Gideon shook his head. 'Come on. Come on. *Mm* realism. Isabel Allende. Gabriel Garc—'

'Next one,' said Donna, folding her arms and sighing. 'This is crap.'

Gideon slammed down the card and picked up another. They had no points so far. 'The word was *magic*. You know . . . Magic realism. How could you not get that? OK. Next one. John Hurt. Naked.'

'Civil servant!' shouted Bronwen. 'Oops, sorry. Wrong team.'

'Are you feeling better now?' Kate asked Zoe out in the kitchen. She was helping her fetch the break-time snack of humous and celery sticks, pleased she'd eaten earlier.

'What do you mean?'

'Well, you seemed to be very upset last week. About Ross and everything.'

The plate in Zoe's hand dropped at an angle and several sticks fell off. 'Shit. What did I say?'

'Don't you remember?'

'No.'

'Anything?'

She shook her head.

'You said you and he had been, you know, for three years. And then you . . . er told me some of the things he gets up to.'

'Such as?'

'Well.' Kate moved closer and lowered her voice further. 'About the . . .' She bobbed her eyebrows up and down.

'Young hookers?'

'Uh-huh. And also . . .' She pulled a disapproving face.

'The drugs?'

'Mm. Especially the . . .'

'Cocaine habit?'

Kate nodded. This was far more than she'd hoped for.

'Oh dear. Who else did I tell?'

'No one, as far as I know.'

Zoe looked relieved. 'Well, it's not true,' she said brightly, straightening her back and popping celery in her mouth. 'I was just pulling your leg.' She grimaced and chuckled. 'Got quite pissed, I think.'

'Right.'

Just as they were winding things up, Bronwen asked if she could share her biography with everyone. 'Mm/Yes/Great' they all said unconvincingly. Here goes, thought Kate: born in South Wales, grammar school, almost married Dai but decided to devote her life to librarianship . . .

'My name is Bronwen Thomas and I grew up an only child, here in Oxford, where my father, Thomas, was an English—'

'Not *the* Thomas Thomas!' cried Gideon. 'Who wrote the seminal *Thomas Thomas on Dylan Thomas*?'

'Yes,' she said, her cheeks flushing. 'Actually, he prefers Tom Thomas. Not quite so repetitive. Um, shall I continue?'

'Please do,' said Gideon.

'Well . . . I thought I might follow in my father's footsteps, but after gaining a first at St Hilda's, decided to see something of the world. Little did I know that globetrotting would become a way of life. First I did VSO in Mombasa, which was terribly rewarding, and then I received a grant to . . .'

Kate's mouth fell open and stayed that way while she listened to Bronwen's CV: amazing locations, worthwhile projects. How she'd worked with Mother Teresa. Every few years she'd pop home and get rid of American cruise missiles, or stop a motorway being built. Kate felt very shallow and knew she couldn't now tell the group about her self-absorbed little life. But how boring must Bob be feeling, she thought, as Bronwen moved on to the Eritrean school project.

'So,' Bronwen finished off to the stunned group, 'I found a house-and-cat-sit and took the job at the library to tide me over while I plan my next project. I advertised for a reading circle, because I belonged to one briefly in the States, whilst doing voluntary work with Hispanic children, and enjoyed it enormously, and because, well, I simply *love* literature. Can't get enough of it.'

'It's the genes,' said Gideon, with an admiring expression.

Donna stared at Bronwen's jeans and frowned.

Over at 14 Spruce Close, Christine was adding the final touches to Gideon's room: mirror, a nice pine-scented potpourri, padded hangers in the wardrobe. A hundred and twenty pounds a week. Imagine. Bob couldn't possibly say no to that.

She sat on the bed, trying not to mess it up, and took a proud look around – so different! – then flashed back to how it had been all those years ago, with Keith's teenage mess everywhere: cassettes, socks, tennis rackets, old plates and cups. Her heart filled with a dull ache and tears pricked her eyes. Her baby. Now with babies of his own. She jumped at the sound of a key in the front door lock and waited for Keith to drop his school bag and call out, 'Mum?'

'Christine!' yelled Bob. 'Got any grub on the go? That Zoe must think we're as anorexic as she is.'

Duggie was staying on part time: after school, Saturdays. Having enticed him out of his headwear and trained him not to end every sentence with 'nah'amean?', Kate felt she could happily leave him alone in the shop for short spells. As Miles's hours shrank due to his burgeoning stained-glass business, Duggie was beginning to come in very handy.

'OK, so you'll be all right if I pop out for an hour or so?' she asked him.

'Yeah, of course.'

It was 3.40 and he'd just arrived. She wanted to go and see Ed and bring him up to date on Zoe. Or was it just to see Ed?

'Here's my mobile number again.'

'Cheers.'

He took a music magazine from his bag and plonked it on the counter, then ran a comb through his hair and beamed at her. Kate got the impression he was generally happier to be in the shop than at home. Something to do with the unemployed stepfather – mullet, tattoos, Alsatians – she suspected.

'I'll be fine,' he told her. 'Off you go.'

Ed had his thesis up on screen.

'Oh, I'm interrupting your work,' said Kate. 'Shall I come back another time?'

'No, no. Don't worry. I'm just fiddling about with commas. Putting them in, taking them out again. I'm submitting it in a couple of weeks.'

'Hey, well done!'

'They could fail it, of course. Or I might have a bad night with Georgia and flunk the viva.'

'Surely Bernice would—'

'Maybe.'

They were at the end of the living room, near the kitchen; the computer table and the highchair forcing them to stand uncomfortably close. Ed had one hand in a trouser pocket and looked a little on edge.

'Georgia's asleep, is she?'

'Yeah, just dropped off.'

It really was awfully quiet, Kate noticed, as she waited for Ed to offer her tea or something.

'Um . . .' he said, taking a step forward, his hand coming up and encircling the back of her neck.

Before I knew it Kate was tugging at my shirt buttons. 'Let me see your chest,' she said as she worked her way through them. 'Mmmm.'

We gradually moved into the kitchen, kissing and stripping each other, totally not caring about the washing machine leak all over the floor. I lifted her up on to the work top and pulled her jumper over her head.

'Oh, Ed,' she said.

'Oh, Kate,' I said back.

And there we suddenly were, making love next to Georgia's sterilising unit; Kate with her head wedged under a wall cupboard and me with my socks in a puddle. It was heaven.

'This makes me as bad as Ross Kershaw,' I said over post-coital refreshments in the living room. 'Well . . . it would if you were a prostitute, and this digestive were a Class A drug.' I dunked it in my tea and looked Kate in the eye. 'I think Bernice is screwing her regional sales manager, Clive.'

Kate's eyes widened. 'Is that why you—'

'No, of course not. I'm mad about you. You're adorable.' I leaned over and kissed her. 'You know, I often pray that Bernice will drive off to Sutton Coldfield in Clive's BMW and leave me Georgia. Is that terrible?'

She kissed me back. 'Why Sutton Coldfield?'

I kissed her again. 'That's where Clive's got a four-bedroom, Elizabethan-style executive house with two en-suite bathrooms.'

'Did Elizabethans have executives?'

'Or en-suite bathrooms?'

We could hear Georgia upstairs. Her initial snuffly little whimpers now reaching come-and-get-me-out-of-this-cot-you-bastard wails.

'Duty calls,' I said with a final kiss.

'Me too.'

At 6.15 I was spooning liquidised cauliflower cheese into Georgia's mouth, trying to feel bad about what happened. But it was hard. What was there to feel bad about? Kate is lovely (and willing) I thought, Bernice loathes me and fucks Clive. Probably.

I picked up the phone with my free hand and called Kate's house.

'Lo,' said a gruff voice. In the background people were hammering ferociously, sawing off table legs and howling with pain.

'Hello,' I yelled. 'Is your mum there?'

'Wait.'

The noises died down and Charlie was back on the phone. 'I think she's out.'

'Oh.'

'Yeah, it's her Alcoholics Anonymous night.' I could hear some other person laughing. 'No, wait a minute. She could be at the breast implant support group.'

More giggling.

'Charlie, put the extension down,' I heard Kate say.

There was a click and a sudden silence. 'Kate?' I asked.

'Yes, hi. Sorry about that.'

'That's OK.'

'Kids, eh?'

I chuckled magnanimously and said, 'Yeah,' wondering why we don't ship them all off at twelve. 'Um . . . how are you?'

'Fine. Thinking about you.'

'Really?' Why would this surprise me? Four years of Bernice battering away at my confidence, I suppose. 'That's nice.'

'And obviously you were thinking about me,' she said.

I laughed. 'That's a bit presumptuous of you.'

'Well, you are phoning me, Ed.'

'Good point.'

On Friday, after she'd dropped her youngest off at playgroup, Donna went straight to the Internet Cafe on the Cowley Road, where she asked the bloke who allocated her a computer if he'd help her set up a Hotmail account.

'Sure.'

She sat at her monitor and he leaned right over her.

'Thanks,' she said, when he'd done it. 'Um, now I need to find the House of Commons website?'

'OK. Well, you go to search and then just type House of Commons in that box.'

'Like this?' she asked.

'Yep. Now click on *go* and then on –'

'Hey!' she said, when the page came up.

'Now . . . what was it you wanted to find out?'

She looked up at him and smiled. 'I think I'll be all right now. Thanks.'

'OK. Give me a shout if you get stuck, yeah?'

He stood upright again and sauntered back to the counter. Donna watched him – nice bum – and decided she probably would get stuck.

After a couple of clicks, she found herself looking at an alphabetical list of MPs and scrolled down to the Ks. 'Kersha,' she said to herself. 'Rosh Kersha.' He wasn't there but Ross Kershaw was, so she guessed that must be him. Probably not Indian then.

It said she could email him by just clicking on . . . ah, right. She took a piece of paper from her coat pocket and copied what was on it, word for word, finishing the message with 'Yours truly Donna Blackthorn' and then her phone number and Hotmail address. After she'd sent it, she went back to the home page and found 'Today's Stars'. 'You'll be tempted to go to any lengths to solve a financial problem,' she read, 'but be sure to keep to the moral high ground. Remember, Capricorn, what goes round comes round.'

Donna stayed in the café for a while – had a coffee and messed about with the nice assistant – but she couldn't get the prediction out of her head, so when wandering back down the Cowley Road she stopped at a newsagent's and flicked through a tabloid. 'Capricorn. A spirit of adventure leads you to an enterprising project that bodes well for future finances. Don't hold back!' She put the paper down, relieved. All she wanted was to better herself. Do an Access course next year, then go to university and not run up a humungous debt. Nothing wrong with that.

She bumped into some people she knew and chatted for a while, went round a student-packed Tescos – God, they were so annoying with their red wine and their Switch cards – then got on her bike with a basketful of special offers and pedalled uphill to Back Lane playgroup.

When Zoe jumped into Ross's car at 12.35 and found him in flat cap and shades with his collar up, her heart sank.

'I thought we might go and find a little entertainment first,' he said after kissing her cheek. He pulled out into the traffic and squeezed her knee. 'There's this little club I've heard about.'

'Oh, Ross, no. Can't we just go to your flat? I do have to get back to work.'

'Hey . . . come on, Zo. You know how you get turned on seeing me turned on.'

She sighed and closed her eyes. OK, there was an element of truth in that. Used to be. They'd started off by watching the odd blue video together, but it wasn't long before Zoe found herself being bustled by an incognito Ross into the kind of place they were no doubt off to now. Testosterone-filled, dimly lit places that made her feel sordid and uncomfortable. Sometimes she'd be the only woman in there. Well, the only one not draped round a pole. However, Ross would then take her back to his flat and make love with relish, whispering the most passionate things she'd ever heard, and she'd think, Oh, what the hell . . . Then twice recently, he'd arranged for a 'sweet young thing' to join them. Perhaps he saw it as a natural progression, but she hated it. She definitely needed to talk to him some time. But not in a midday London traffic jam. Would there ever be an opportunity, though? When they ate out he talked endlessly about himself, and in his flat they did nothing but make love. She sighed and looked over at him. Jesus, even in his stupid disguise he looked good, damn him.

'I'm sorry,' she said, as the car crawled towards Soho or wherever. 'I'm really not feeling well.' When they ground to a halt again she opened the passenger door and quickly got out.

Ross whipped off his sunglasses. 'Zoe? What—'

'Have a nice time,' she said with an apologetic smile.

Ross did enjoy himself, though he wondered what had got into Zoe. Time of the month, no doubt. Back in his office he picked up his emails and found one that particularly intrigued him. It was something of a fan letter, from an eighteen-year-old. Five foot seven, blonde, pretty, shapely, she described herself as. Just left school. Said she found him really attractive and would like to meet him next time she was in London. Maybe next week. He smiled at her spelling and jotted down her phone number. Oxford code, he noticed. Bit of a coincidence. Now, he thought, were his outgoing emails somehow screened? He wasn't sure. He wrote a message back saying he was terribly sorry, but his Parliamentary duties in London and constituency work in Scotland meant he was going to be far too busy to meet her, but to contact her local MP should she wish to raise any issues. He signed it formally and tucked Donna's phone number into his jacket pocket for later.

Zoe also picked up an unexpected email.

I'm really enjoying Middlemarch, thank you. I'll return it when I've finished. Perhaps in person? I've been rather hoping to bump into you at Paddington, or on the train. But no luck. I suppose what I'm saying – rather clumsily! – is, are you attached?

He signed it 'Best wishes, Matthew Soper' and added his London work number.

Zoe decided not to respond. Ross was enough for the time being, and besides, he'd go crazy if he thought she was seeing someone else. Bloody hell, he'd probably dump her. She was about to delete Matthew's message – Ross occasionally used her laptop to send emails – but thought back to the good-looking guy on the train, and reread his strangely touching email, and all of a sudden wondered if life would really be so ghastly without Ross Kershaw.

SIX

It was Monday. The shop was closed and Ed was wheeling Georgia into Kate's hall.

'We're a bit early,' he said. 'Sorry.'

He was wearing a black jacket – donkey style, but obviously Gap or something – a soft-looking grey-green scarf and a nice aftershave. His dark hair was tousled and slightly damp. Fresh out the shower. Lovely, thought Kate. They pecked cheeks and she told him lunch would be ready soon.

She had Ella Fitzgerald on the stereo, a quiche in the oven and an army of butterflies in her tummy. Which was silly. He was a man, not a god. Well, maybe a domestic god, she decided, as he got Georgia out of her spacesuit, wiped her runny nose, took two jars of homemade gunk from a bag and asked if he could possibly use the microwave.

'Of course.' She gave him a demonstration.

'Thanks very much,' he said.

How formal and guarded they were with each other, thought Kate.

*   *   *

Upstairs, at three o'clock, with Georgia fast asleep in the corner of the room, Ed and Kate were being neither formal nor guarded on her bed. The bottle of wine they'd decided to have with lunch had sent them into a frenzy of kisses and gropes at the table while they waited for Georgia to drop off. At ten to three, when they were fit to burst and possibly approaching hangover stage, she eventually did.

'I'm nuts about you,' Ed was now saying as he nuzzled her neck.

'You don't think I'm a little old for you?'

'What's ten years?' he said, and gently rolled her over.

Ten?

Now she may have failed O level Maths but she was sure she could take thirty-five from forty-two.

'Ed?' she said later, when they were lying curled up and exhausted under the duvet.

'Mm?'

'What year did you leave school?'

He laughed. 'Are you always this romantic?' He kissed the back of her head. 'I could talk about Black Wednesday if you like.'

Kate felt a sudden jolt from him. 'Seven years,' he said hurriedly. 'I meant seven. Not ten. Years between us.'

She turned and said, '*Ed*,' sternly.

'OK, I'm thirty-two.'

Thirty-two! Four years younger and he'd be equidistant between herself and Charlie. Would she want to go out with a man ten years or more older than herself? Probably not. Al Pacino excepted, of course.

'But, so what?' he asked.

'Well . . . I just think—'

There was a sudden and loud hammering at the bedroom door. 'Who's in there?' shouted Charlie. She tried the knob and knocked again. 'Mum?'

'Hi, love,' Kate called out, while Ed bolted upright and held the duvet over his chest. 'Um, I've got someone here.'

'A man?'

'Ye-es.'

'Ugh, gross.'

They went for a walk on Port Meadow; to clear their heads and give Georgia some fresh air, but mostly to get away from Charlie and Jack's racket. It was misty and darkening as they took it in turns to push Georgia over the gravelly path towards where they might just be able to show her a duck if the light held out.

Kate stopped and scanned the vast flat common. 'Have you noticed that Port Meadow looks different every time you come here?'

'Er . . . no, not really.'

'There are so many varieties of tiny wild plants that the whole common keeps changing colour. Then sometimes you're tripping over cows and horses and other times there are none in sight.'

'I've tripped over fifteen-year-olds and their bongs.'

'Right.' It takes an artist to notice these things, she guessed. It was getting late and the place was almost empty, for a change. Being just a short stroll from the city centre, it would fill up on a pleasant Sunday with pre- and post-lunch groups of amblers, lone dog walkers and silver-haired Americans trying to find one of Morse's pubs. 'Just follow this path,' Kate had told one particularly ancient and frail-looking couple, forgetting that the Trout's a good mile-and-a-half walk, and then, of course, they'd have to get back. The next day she'd checked the *Oxford Mail* for a 'Towpath Tragedy' story.

They showed Georgia some ducks and then had a kiss and a cuddle on the little wooden bridge. Thirty-two, thought Kate. Bloody hell. But then Barbara Windsor, Liz Taylor and Joan Collins came to mind and she decided, heck, what's good enough for them . . .

'What the blazes!' said Bob. He stood in the middle of Keith's old room, hands on his hips, eyes taking in all the changes. 'Have you had that chap with the frilly shirts in?'

Christine laughed off the compliment. 'I thought . . . just for a little bit of extra income . . . um, we could, you know . . .'

'What?'

'Let the room.'

'You mean have a lodger?'

Christine didn't like the word 'lodger'. It reminded her of a widowed aunt in Portsmouth, forced for years to take in sailors who missed the toilet.

'Paying guest,' she said. 'Actually, I've found one. Willing to pay a hundred and twenty pounds a week for full board.'

Bob's eyes lit up. 'Oh aye?' Perhaps he could whittle his job down to two afternoons, or none. On his way downstairs to put the kettle on, he slowly got his head around the idea and pictured someone like Carol Vorderman living with them. A good sport and a picture to look at. One thing you could say about his missus, she was full of surprises!

No, that wasn't true, he'd decided by the bottom stair. Christine never took him by surprise. That was what he liked best about her.

Bob put three lumps in his tea. Christine wished he'd use the tongs. 'So . . .' he said, popping one more in. 'You reckon you've found someone that wants the room?'

'Mm. Nice chap.'

Ah well, he thought, putting Carol out of his mind.

'Younger than us,' added Christine.

Bob stirred his tea. Someone he could introduce to the pleasures of fishing, perhaps. Take down the pub of a Sunday while Christine organised the roast. Might not be so bad. He said, 'You told him I'm a breast man, I hope?' and chortled.

Christine laughed at her husband's tired old joke. 'You do get *two* breasts on a chicken, you know, Bob.'

A car drew up outside the house and idled for a while. It sounded like a taxi. Christine went over to the living-room window and pulled back one of her nets. Gideon! She smoothed down her apron, tried to cool her flushed cheeks with the back of her hands and walked calmly past Bob and into the hall.

'Caroline!' roared Gideon, lugging two suitcases towards her. 'Hello.'

'It's Christine, actually.'

'Christine, yes. A few days early, I know. Zoe and I came to blows over the washing machine.'

Doing his own washing, thought Christine. There'd be no more of that.

'Gideon?' said Bob behind her.

'Ah, Bill.' Gideon heaved a tatty suitcase over the threshold. 'Jolly decent of you to offer a port in a storm.'

'You wha—'

'It's just for a while,' Christine lied in her husband's ear when Gideon went back for a third piece of luggage. 'He's having a dreadful time at that Zoe's. You know, sometimes she's only got coriander in her fridge. In you come, Gideon. I'll show you to your room.'

Bob wasn't sure he knew what coriander was. In something of a state of shock, he found himself picking up a case and following Gideon's muddy-bottomed trousers up the stairs.

They were missing *Emmerdale*, which was upsetting Bob more than he'd ever admit.

Gideon was eyeing the last custard slice on the coffee table, saying, 'Of course, once I've found a publisher for *Wuthering Lows – The True Story of Haworth*, I intend to buy my own place.'

'Would you boys like to halve the last cake?' asked Christine. 'Let me fetch a knife.'

'I don't suppose you fish, do you?' said Bob, more to fill the ensuing silence than because he wanted to spend a day on a riverbank with Gideon. Perish the thought.

'Yes, I do enjoy a little coarse fishing. I find it clears the mind. You know, far from the madding crowd. Silence and solitude.'

Silence and solitude? Where Bob went on Saturdays, there were literally dozens of blokes lining the riverside. A friendly bunch they were; all avoiding the big Saturday shop or having to strip the washing machine to get at a mischievous five p. Or just their wives and kids, really.

'Don't suppose you've got rods and everything?' he asked Gideon. 'You need all the equipment these days, you know.' Bob sometimes wished he could hire a small horse and a Sherpa to carry his. Christine regularly tutted at the expense, but she didn't understand that you had to keep up.

'Not *with* me, no.'

There is a God then, thought Bob.

Just as Christine walked in with a knife and fresh plates, Gideon leaned forward and scooped up the last custard slice. Bob watched his wife turn and slip quietly back to the kitchen and wondered if life would ever be the same again.

'Of course, Faulkner was a great fisherman,' said Gideon. He'd taken a large bite and was talking with his mouth full. Something Christine couldn't abide, noted Bob. 'Or am I thinking of Hemingway?'

*   *   *

Bronwen left the library at six with two well-reviewed detective novels by women writers in her bicycle basket. It began to rain heavily as she cycled, so she unwound her scarf and threw it over the books to protect them. She arrived at Zoe's east Oxford house with her hair plastered to her head and rain dripping off her nose – rather distressed that she wasn't looking her best – and rang the doorbell.

'Oh,' said Zoe, immaculate in suit and heels. 'Bronwen. Hi.'

'Hello. Um . . . I've just brought something for Gideon. Is he in?'

'Actually, he moved out. Today.'

'Oh?'

'Wasn't really working.'

'I'm sorry to hear that,' said Bronwen, thinking how difficult Zoe must be to live with. 'Do you know where he's gone?'

Zoe chuckled. 'He said he was moving in with Bob and Christine. Can you imagine?'

Bronwen tried. No, she couldn't. 'Gosh, how odd,' she said, and got back on her wet bike.

After shutting the door, Zoe returned to her screen and reread the message from Matthew Soper.

Thought I'd try you at this email address. Almost finished the book. I'm hoping for a happy ending, being something of a soft-hearted romantic. I'd love to hear from you. Matthew

She chewed on a thumb. She was supposed to have been having dinner with Ross this evening, but he'd cancelled this afternoon. Again, the bastard. She'd been too miserable to carry on working, so had caught an early train home. Oh well, here goes, she thought. **Hi Matthew, I'm glad you like Middlemarch . . .** She went on to tell him about her job, her house, and even about the reading circle. She gave the impression she was unattached (which, let's face it . . . she thought) and suggested lunch at a French restaurant close to where she worked.

After she'd sent it, she changed into jeans, took a deep breath and went to tackle Gideon's room.

It was Tuesday evening and I found myself quite missing the reading group. However, Bernice was home early for once and being nice to me. She even bathed Georgia.

'Mmm, that was delicious,' she said of my fairly average pasta dish. 'Lovely. Thank you.' She insisted on washing up, and afterwards said, whoops, she'd forgotten to give me the present she'd got me.

Bernice? Present?

'Here.'

It was a shirt – pale blue, synthetic, dull – the kind I'd imagine Clive has dozens of. How far apart Bernice and I had grown, I thought. And had she always had that rather ugly nose? I thanked her limply.

'I thought you could save it for your viva.'

Actually, she had a point. Georgia had puked and peed over

every shirt I had, and besides, they were all getting on now. 'Good idea.'

'Um,' she said, settling on the sofa and curling her legs up. Bernice was never this relaxed in the evenings. She'd stride around, and she'd click things open and snap things shut and make loud business-speak phone calls, but she wouldn't kick her shoes off and look me in the eye. 'Did I tell you about the course the company wants me to go on?'

Ha! Another mini-break with Clive in a Cotswold hotel. I said, 'No?'

'It's for a week. In Cumbria. I thought I'd told you?'

Liar. 'No, I don't think so.'

'Actually, it'll be ten days in all. From Friday.'

Ten days? I couldn't help thrilling to this news, but tried to look concerned and put upon. 'Well, I suppose I'll be able to manage . . .'

'Good!' she said, and was up off the sofa, grabbing her briefcase and in front of the computer in five seconds flat. 'Spreadsheets,' she explained, and was silent for the rest of the evening.

'Is that Donna Blackthorn?' asked the man on the phone.

'Yes,' she said wearily. More double glazing? She kept telling them she had three pounds in the Halifax and lived in a council house but they never gave up.

'This is Ross Kershaw. You sent me an email?'

Donna stopped in her tracks halfway across her kitchen. What a time for him to phone! Jake was yelling for his after-school snack and the washing machine was on its final spin. 'Oh, hello,' she said, aiming for the cupboard under the stairs.

'Hi. How are you?'

She slipped in and pulled the door shut, tugging at the phone lead underneath it. 'Fine, thanks.' Fuck, it was dark. But a lot quieter.

'I was wondering if you'd like to meet up? Whenever you're next in London.'

'Yeah, that would be nice,' she said, her voice sounding weird. This was partly because she was putting on a posh accent, and partly because she knew there were spiders in the cupboard. 'How about the day after tomorrow?' she asked. No point in wasting any time. Get some money in the bank by Christmas, maybe.

'Friday? Sounds good. Lunch?'

'Yeah, OK.'

He said where he'd meet her at Paddington. 'I'll be carrying a *Financial Times*, just in case you don't recognise me. People can look very different in the flesh.'

Donna didn't like the way he said 'flesh'. Definitely an old letch. 'Is that the pink newspaper?'

'Um . . . no, orange, I'd say.'

'Right.' She didn't want to contradict him. Her dad was colour-blind too. Insisted he had a grey car when the whole world could see it was green. 'What time?'

Ross suggested one o'clock and Donna hurriedly agreed, keen to get out of the cupboard before she ran out of oxygen or a spider landed on her. She couldn't decide which would be worse.

They said their goodbyes and as she hung up she pushed open the door to find two puzzled faces in front of her.

'Where's my samwidge?' asked Jake.

It had been a busy week in the shop and Miles had gone down with flu. Kate had taken lots of money but hadn't got much work done, so when Ed pushed Georgia through the door at eleven on Friday morning she begged him to man the shop while she worked out the back.

'Sure,' he said, slipping out of his coat.

Kate was surprised he was so willing, but as she got her paints out and heaved a horrible 1950s dressing table to the middle of the floor, she remembered Ed telling her that being a stay-at-home dad can get a bit lonely. That you don't really have the network women have. The health visitor had put him on to another guy, Stuart, who he'd popped in on only the once; Stuart being conversationally unable to get past the contents of his daughter's nappies. Ed said the mothers at his local baby clinic were always trying to include him, but he'd had to give up the coffee mornings as he just got too turned on by all the bare breasts.

Halfway through base-coating the dressing table, Kate went to check on him. Well, just to look at him really. He'd be quite a bonus to the shop, she thought. Could draw more women in. If she moved the counter and had him sitting almost in the window . . .

'Everything OK?' she asked.

'Yep. No ram raiders. Just a guy with a bin bag and a string belt.'

'That's Harold. He comes in for a sit-down. Don't let him near the yellow chaise longue.'

'Ah, sorry.' He got up and went over to it. 'It's not too bad,' he said, brushing hard at the seat with a hand. 'Well, maybe a damp cloth . . .'

'Don't worry. No one's ever going to buy it. Oh, you might get Mad Pat in. She'll tell you about her cataract operation. You just have to listen, really.'

'Right. No normal customers then?'

'They tend to come in on Saturdays.'

Ed thrust his hands in his pockets and jiggled his loose change nervously. 'Oh yeah, by the way,' he said, 'Bernice is away for ten days. On a course.'

'Really?'

'So she says. If you like we could, you know, do something. Over the weekend. But only if you feel like it. I expect you've got other plans.'

'I'm here all day tomorrow, but after that—'

'Why don't you come to dinner tomorrow evening? Bring Charlie, if you like.'

'But she's foul!'

'Don't worry, I'm good with kids. I can get through the Charlie test.'

'Well, if you're sure,' said Kate, thinking maybe she'd have her daughter come down with something.

* * *

Kate and I were having an awkward snog in the back – bodies not touching owing to the paint on her shirt – when someone came in the shop. I hurried through before they had time to kidnap Georgia, and found an elderly woman wandering round picking up small items and peering at them. She held up an ornate hand mirror and waved it at me. 'How much is this then?' she asked, squinting at the price tag. 'Only I haven't had me second one done yet.'

'Sorry?'

'Cataract. They done the one, only I've got to wait for me left eye.' She winked at me and cackled. Hence the 'Mad', I thought.

I went over and told her the price.

'It's ever so clever what they do,' she said. 'Once you've had the anaesthetic, they—'

'No!' I screamed, being a touch squeamish about blood and gore and all things medical – as everyone at the John Radcliffe maternity unit would verify. 'Sorry,' I said, hurrying to the buggy. 'Got to feed my daughter.' I lifted up the floppy, deeply comatose Georgia, sat at the counter with her and got a bottle out of my bag. Eye operations have to be the worst, I thought, dizzy and perspiring. I pretended Georgia was sucking ferociously at her lunch and broke into something of a lullaby.

While Kate and Ed were sharing sandwiches at the shop counter, Zoe was in Covent Garden telling Matthew Soper all about her nomadic childhood over a goat's cheese starter. 'My father just couldn't settle to any place or any job,' she said, waiting for his eyes to flicker off to some distant woman as Ross's would have by now.

'Really?' asked Matthew. 'Where did you live then?'

Bloody hell, he seemed genuinely to want to know. She hoped she wouldn't break down and sob with gratitude. 'Oh, everywhere. London, the north, Dover, Cornwall. I had a zillion schools. Which was fine if I didn't like a particular school. I knew I wouldn't be there long.'

'But not so good if you'd made friends and really liked a place?'

Zoe felt her eyes welling up, her throat thickening. 'No,' she said, and swallowed hard. Oh hell, what must he think? Ross always told her to find a shrink and get rid of her bloody baggage when she was like this. Was her nose going red?

Matthew patted her hand. 'It sounds a lot more fun than eighteen years in Peterborough with a father who painted tool outlines on his shed wall.'

Zoe laughed and blew her nose.

'*And* I loathed my secondary school,' he continued. 'Got bullied for a while. I prayed my dad would get transferred to a National Westminster branch in a distant city, but it never happened.' He smiled and gave her hand a little squeeze. 'You see how lucky you were?'

'Mm.'

The waiter came up and asked if they'd decided on a main course yet, but Zoe was full.

'Me too,' said Matthew. 'Shall we just have coffee?'

Ross hated it when she couldn't cope with a main course; told her it was embarrassing to have to eat alone, and that she could at least make an effort.

'Coffee would be great.'

She excused herself and repaired her makeup in the Ladies. Matthew was too good to be true, she thought, clicking the top back on her lipstick. She almost wanted their lunch to end now before she found out he had a beermat collection. She fluffed up her hair and checked her back in the mirror, then strode through the restaurant to their window table.

As she sat down she spotted Ross in a black cab, right outside the restaurant. There seemed to be some kind of traffic hold-up, and he was sitting there, just feet from her, talking to a youngish-looking woman on the far side of him. It took her a while to register what she was looking at, then she said, 'Shit,' and ducked down so that Matthew was shielding her. Earlier in the week, she'd told Ross she had a dentist's appointment this Friday lunchtime.

'Zoe?' asked Matthew.

'Fuck. Sorry. Excuse my language and don't move.' She counted to ten and took another look. The taxi was still there. Ross normally fumed in traffic jams, but he was obviously wrapped up in his young distraction. As the girl leaned forward, chatting and laughing with Ross, Zoe tried to get a better look at her. She had masses of blonde hair and a large black beret. She couldn't tell if she was pretty or not, but of course she would be. For the thousandth time, a painful jealous pang shot through her. The taxi pulled away and Zoe sat up. 'Sorry,' she said again. 'Someone I wanted to avoid.'

Matthew laughed. 'I kind of gathered that.'

At 6.40, twenty minutes before they were due to close, Gideon walked into the library and set Bronwen off. 'Deep breaths, deep breaths,' she whispered, and waved nonchalantly. There was something a bit different about him, but she couldn't make out what. A haircut, maybe? No.

Her hand shook as she scanned three CDs for a young woman and found her change for a twenty. He was over in Crime Fiction again. Should she go and chat or play it cool? There was a bit of a queue, so she stayed put.

'Hello there,' he said eventually, sliding two Lawrence Blocks towards her. 'They keeping you working late this evening?'

'Only another ten minutes,' she whispered. She'd be out of there on the dot tonight. They all would.

'How are you getting on with *White Teeth*?' he asked.

She date-stamped his inside pages. 'I love it. And you?'

'Still having a bit of a problem with the authorial voice, I'm afraid.'

'Oh dear.'

'Mm.' He collected his books, put them in his briefcase and flicked his scarf over one shoulder. 'If you feel like discussing it, I'll be next door in the Bricklayer's Arms.'

Bronwen's knees buckled, just slightly. 'Love to,' she said hoarsely. 'See you in about ten minutes.'

When he'd gone she realised what was different about him. His clothes were all clean and pressed.

'I'd like a pint of Guinness, please,' said Bronwen.

'Right you are.'

Gideon grabbed some change from his pocket and headed for the bar. By the time he got back Bronwen had run a comb through her wild hair and lost the high colour from her cheeks.

'I always recommend trying the real thing,' he said. 'A pint of Guinness in a rustic Irish hostelry.'

'I have. Daddy took me on a literary tour of Ireland when I was eighteen. Oscar Wilde's birthplace, Yeats's tower . . .'

'Joyce's tower?'

'Oh yes . . . Swift, Beckett, Shaw. It's amazing that such a poor, tyrannised country produced so many great writers.'

Gideon leaned back in his seat and rested his pint on his stomach. 'Well, you know, I've often thought that great literature tends to come out of emerging societies. I believe it to be part of their process of self-definition.'

Bronwen frowned. 'Um, didn't V. S. Naipaul say that?'

'Ah,' said Gideon, eyeing her with a mixture of respect and wariness. 'No doubt.'

Three of them made their way into my tiny living room.

'This is Jack,' Kate told me, then mouthed a 'Sorry'.

It was the guy from Charlie's bedroom; a long string-bean of a boy. Looking at Jack was like someone had adjusted the vertical hold in your head.

'Hi, Jack!' I said, pointing a two-fingered gun at him. Kate and I laughed.

'Yeah,' he nodded. 'Everyone does that.'

'Oh. Sorry. Well, what kind of pizzas do you like?' I handed them a menu. 'I was just about to order some.'

Charlie said, 'Mum *never* does this,' and pointed to the everything-we-can-think-of-we'll-chuck-on deluxe. 'That one.'

'Please,' said Kate.

'*Please.*'

'Er, yeah, same for me,' said Jack. 'Please.'

'Got any good games on your computer?' asked Charlie as I headed for the phone.

'Only chess, I'm afraid.'

She turned to Jack. 'Do we know that?'

Jack scratched his head. 'It's not the one where the Americans infiltrate the Russian chess tournament and—'

'That was *Killing Commies.*'

'Oh, yeah. Crap game.'

'*Really* crap.'

While we waited for our delivery, Charlie spent two minutes on computer chess, then flicked through the CDs – 'Nevererdovem, nevererdovem, oh yawn Radiohead, nevererdovem,' and eventually settled down in front of *Blind Date*.

'Wotta wanker!' Kate and I kept hearing as we stood chatting in the kitchen.

When the pizzas arrived we ate in front of the television, Kate and me with wine and the kids with the cans of Coke I'd stocked up on.

'OK,' I said when I'd cleared everything away. 'I've got *The Mummy*, *Shrek*, *American Pie* and *Ali G in da House*. What do you fancy?'

Two interminable videos later, they left.

'I think you passed,' whispered Kate, as she pecked my cheek goodbye.

'Cheers, mate,' said Jack.

Charlie nodded at me. 'That was good. Thanks . . . er, Ed.'

'My pleasure.'

She pulled an enormous hood over her head, and with a scary twinkle in her eye said, 'Does anyone call you Eddie?'

'No. I'm not really that keen on—'

'I think I will.'

'Fine.'

SEVEN

Donna kept a diary for when she sold her story. 'Lunch with R,' it said for the previous Friday 'His place. Two Sps. SS.' She'd devised a code. R – Ross. Sp – spliff. H – harder stuff. SS – straight sex. KS – kinky sex. T – tarts.

He was much better-looking than she'd been expecting. Well, for an old geezer. They'd had lunch in some dodgy dark basement bar in God-knows-what part of London. Nice food, though. She told him she'd just done her A levels and was interested in politics, and had applied to study it after her gap year. 'I saw you on the telly,' she said. 'And thought I'd like to meet you and learn more about—'

Ross was sliding a hand up her arm. 'Life?'

'Yeah,' she said, giving him a sexy look. She knew she didn't really have to flirt with him. He was obviously as randy as hell.

They got a taxi to his place, which turned out to be all right, but nothing special. A one-bedroomed flat in a block. A kitchenette that looked like it was never used and a bedroom that looked like it was – too many mirrors. Mirrors everywhere, she noticed, as he

115

was slowly peeling her clothes off and kissing every bit of her. When she looked up at the ceiling tiles she could see he had a small bald patch. Still, he was what her magazines called a considerate lover – warming her up nicely and being dead clever with his tongue. She hadn't had anything like that with Carl for those three years – selfish and always pissed. Nor with Mark. But then you expect sixteen-year-old boys to be in a bit of a hurry.

Ross told her not to phone him. He'd call her, he said, and he already had. Talking for twenty minutes about what he'd like to do to her while she made the boys' tea. She told him the kids in the background were her younger brothers and had to slap a hand over Jake's mouth when he came up and said, 'Muu—'

She closed her diary, put it back in the shoe box, then slipped the box on to a shelf in the wardrobe and chuckled to herself. Maybe she'd nip up to Matalan tomorrow and get some nice lacy thongs.

Monday and the shop was closed. Kate was at home making soft, fluffy, zebra-stripe cushions for an old art-deco sofa she'd upholstered in lime green. She had a little sewing room upstairs, and when Charlie was at school, Radio Two had something good on, the sun was out and the birds were pecking at the feeder she'd put at just the right height, it was probably her favourite place in the world. She was humming to something she didn't really know the tune of, happy as Larry – whoever he was – wondering whether to ask Ed along to her Monday-afternoon trawl through the junk shops. He might enjoy it, she thought, but on the other hand, as a five-two-and-a-half waif, trying, bless her, to run a business all on her own, she did tend to get things for good prices. The men who owned these cold and dingy businesses, with their two or three hangers on and a fug of cigarette smoke, would trip over themselves to help carry things out to her camper van, or knock an extra fiver off if she pointed out a chip or crack. Kate had become a regular customer and they'd learned early on that she knew the true value of veneered, ugly-looking pieces of furniture that made you think of mutton stew and a bath once a week. Oh, what the hell, she decided, and picked up the phone.

'Hi, it's me,' she said.

'Bernice?'

'No, me. The other one.'

'Er . . . sorry?'

'Oh, stop mucking around. I was wondering if you want to come and look at second-hand furniture shops with me this afternoon? Alternatively, we could have a lovely long shag while Georgia sleeps?'

'Well,' he said, clearing his throat, 'it's very nice of you to offer, but considering we haven't met . . .'

What the . . . ?

'I'm Ed's brother.'

His twin! She froze.

'Hello? Are you still there?'

'Sorry, wrong number,' she said and put the phone down.

Shit.

A few seconds later it rang. 'I did one-four-seven-one,' he said. 'I'm Will, by the way.'

'Right.' Her face was aflame. 'Look, I was only kidding just now. Bit of a running joke.'

'Yes, of course. Anyway, Ed's out getting his thesis bound. I'm baby-sitting.'

He sounded so much like Ed, she still couldn't be sure it wasn't him. 'Oh, I'll call back later then. Thanks.'

'Who shall I say—'

'Bye.'

In the end, her curiosity got the better of her and she took a sudden sharp right on her way to the junk shops and wove the VW down Ed's cluttered street.

The man at the door was good-looking and Ed-like, but clearly not him. Will was around the same five ten, five eleven, but stockier, and his hair was shorter and darker. This was something of a relief. All the way there she'd imagined one day slipping her tongue in the wrong man's mouth. Or worse. He said Ed was due back any minute and did she want to come in and wait.

'No, I . . . yeah, OK.'

He was born first by eighteen minutes, he told her. He was quite a chatterbox. Ed had been better at schoolwork and he, Will, had been better at making friends and, later, girlfriends. They'd gone to different universities, and Ed had diligently studied Politics and Economics while Will had done Sports Studies and worked his way through lots of girls. 'I've never had a problem on the woman front. Bernice was my girlfriend first, you know. Five years ago. Came to my Oxford gym and couldn't resist my charm. Terrific figure.'

Hers or his?

'She fell back on Ed after I . . . after we split up,' he said, pouring Kate some filter coffee.

'Really?'

'Ed was sympathetic and there for her, and I suppose she thought she was getting back at me. Before anyone knew it they were setting up home together. No grand passion. Ed's just a much nicer person than me.'

'Right.'

'Bernice, on the other hand, is a self-absorbed control freak. Vindictive as hell.'

Kate saw graffiti on her walls and a letter bomb exploding in her hand. Her palms grew damp and she wished Ed would come back.

'Yeah,' he said. 'She and I are very much alike.' He seemed to find this very amusing.

'Ah, you've met then,' said Ed when he finally arrived. Kate had Georgia chewing on her finger with her tiny emerging teeth. It was beginning to hurt. 'How's she been?' he asked his brother.

'Georgia or Kate?' said Will, who tended to laugh, alone and at length, at his own jokes. He went to the kitchen and came back with coffee for Ed. 'So you two are having a fling, eh? Playing with fire in the Bernice department, aren't you, Ed?'

Ed shot Kate a what-the-heck? look, and she inevitably blushed.

'Kate thought I was you on the phone,' explained Will.

She grimaced. 'I'd better be going,' she told Ed. 'I'm having a buying afternoon, going round the junk shops.'

'Sounds like fun.'

'Yes, it is. Anyway . . . I just popped in to say hello. See if you wanted to—'

A key turned in the lock and all their heads shot round as the front door flew open. In walked a tallish woman with an auburn French pleat and a tissue over her nose. Her eyes were pink, wet and swollen and her bottom was a shade large for cream-coloured trousers. She dragged a suitcase behind her, dumped it on the living-room floor and kicked the door shut.

'What are you doing here, creep?' she said to Will. 'Haven't you got a chain of tacky gyms to run?'

'Lovely to see you too,' he said, and kissed her soggy cheek. 'Are you all right?'

She emitted a short undignified animal-like sound. 'Fine,' she said, picking up the suitcase and heading for the open staircase. 'Hay fever.'

Will said, 'In October?'

As her bottom made its way upwards Kate thrust Georgia at Ed. 'Bye,' she whispered, tiptoeing to the door.

Bernice told me the course had been cut short. I wouldn't have thought this would cause her to curl up and howl under a duvet for an entire afternoon, but when will I ever understand women?

After taking her up a plate of dinner and catching her thumping the pillow and telling it she hated it, I went to the end of our dark, cold and compact garden.

'I think Bernice and Clive have had a tiff,' I said quietly into the cordless phone.

'Excuse me,' said Kate. 'Who am I talking to?'

'Ed, of course.'

'Prove it.'

'What? Oh, I see.' Was I going to have to do this every time? 'OK. Um . . . you've got a small birthmark in the shape of a banana on your left upper buttock.'

'A banana! Now who's being unromantic? OK, tell me about Bernice. She wasn't what I was expecting at all. No horns or anything.'

'Well, she seems unduly upset about her course coming to an abrupt end. What's more, she said if her fucking regional manager phones, I'm to tell him to go fucking fuck himself.'

'Mm. One would deduce . . .'

'Yes.'

'Can't you phone him?'

'Who?'

'Clive. Tell him she's falling apart, and not to be such a cold-hearted, two-timing swine.'

'But how do we know he is?' I asked innocently.

She tutted. 'God, why are men so hopeless at reading the signs?'

'How can I read the signs when I've never met him?'

Kate sighed and said she gave up.

'And besides,' I added, 'I *am* supposed to be the naïve and cuckolded partner.'

'True.'

I made my way towards the house and some warmth and asked Kate what she thought of my brother.

'I don't know,' she said. 'He talks about himself a lot. And he's not as nice-looking as you.'

'Really?'

'Mm.'

'Oh, by the way,' I whispered, now inside the kitchen. I switched the gas rings on to warm myself up. 'I didn't mean banana, I meant crescent moon.'

'Too late.'

Following an email vote, they were gathered at Bob's house again.

'I grew up in a council house in north Oxford,' said Donna, reading from her notes, 'so me and my mates from the estate went to school with all these rich kids from like Woodstock Road, whose parents were all scientists and lecturers and things. Anyway . . . now I've got my own place on the other side of town, where I live with my two kiddies who are five and two and three-quarters. My dad's up the car factory, but my mum's got a really good office job in an accountant's. Part time. When I was fifteen, I started going out with Mark. He was a year above me and everyone was after him, only I got him. When I fell pregnant, Mark and his family suddenly moved to Cardiff. My dad didn't speak to me for ages because I wouldn't get rid of it, but he came round when he saw little Jake, and now him and Mum baby-sit the boys whenever I want. My ambition is to get an English degree. If Kelly Forester, who was a right slacker and a slag, can do it, I can. So, soon I'm going to do this course that if I pass can get me into a college. Maybe Molefield College or somewhere.'

Gideon let out a long audible sigh, while Bronwen said, 'That's terrific!'

'Anyway,' continued Donna without her notes, 'that's why I joined the reading circle. Sort of get some practice?'

'Jolly good idea. Well, thank you for sharing your story with us, Donna. Perhaps you'd like to tell us how you got on with *White Teeth*?'

'Yeah, OK.' She picked up her pad again and twirled her ponytail round a finger as she read. 'I think *White Teeth* is a very ambitious first novel,' she said, 'which manages to be both epic and intimate in its approach.'

'Ah yes, very good,' said Bronwen.

'Smith illuminates the difficulties of life in an alien culture, and although she has many serious themes – for example, the immigrant's fear of dissolution – the book is sprinkled with amusing examples of cultural quirks.'

Gideon sat up and crossed one ironed trouser leg over the other. This girl could get a First, he thought. Not that hard at Molefield.

'I must admit,' said Ed, 'I was pleasantly surprised. I was expecting a calories, fags and shags novel.'

'Oh, I knew it wasn't that,' said Kate. 'But I was still very impressed. She can write from the perspective of a range of characters, and they're all fully rounded, don't you think?'

'Yep, definitely,' chipped in Zoe, who'd only read the first few pages, what with having two men on her mind.

Donna glanced at her notes. Mustn't let all that time on the Internet go to waste. 'I thought it had a deliciously farcical . . . er . . .' she looked down again, 'dee noo ment.'

Gideon smiled. 'I think you mean denouement.'

'Right.'

Bob said the book had been a bit of an eye-opener for him, not really knowing any darkies himself.

Bronwen bit her tongue.

During the break they all enjoyed vol-au-vents, a variety of things on sticks, and a home-made chocolate éclair each. Christine had done an extra one and put it aside for Gideon's bedtime snack.

Gideon was talking to Bronwen about her father, gently tugging at the waistband of his trousers and wondering if Christine might let it out a bit.

'Let's just say he's lost some of his intellectual acumen,' said Bronwen. 'He is eighty-one, after all. And then there's the . . . um . . .' She didn't really want to mention creeping senility. Last week she'd found three books in his fridge. 'He hasn't been well.'

'Ah.' Blast, thought Gideon. How exciting it might have been to thrash some ideas around with *the* Thomas Thomas. Still, might be worth meeting, just to be able to say he had. He began angling for an invitation, when Christine approached with a plate and his mind swiftly turned to the last two vol-au-vents.

*   *   *

'Well!' exclaimed Bronwen. 'I think that was a very productive session. I do feel we've covered *White Teeth* now, don't you?'

Everyone agreed.

'Let me see . . .' she continued, 'the week after next we should be gathering at—'

'Oh, do meet here again,' shouted Christine from behind the five coats she was carrying through. 'It's no trouble, is it, Bob?'

'No trouble at all,' said Bob from his Parker Knoll recliner.

Gideon – slippered feet on a poof – told them it was fine by him too.

Kate said, 'Perhaps we should have a bit of a whip-round for the food. It hardly seems fair . . .'

Christine was about to object, but Bob shot her a look, and everyone delved into their pockets and purses. Bronwen suggested three pounds each and quietly whispered to Donna not to worry, she'd pay hers.

'Oh, ta,' said Donna, pulling the hairband off her ponytail and shaking her long blonde hair around her shoulders. 'The benefits don't go far, you know. If I'm left with a pound on Sunday night, I think I've done well.' She pulled her hat from a coat pocket. 'Pay you back when I'm rich.'

Shouldn't be too long, she thought.

'Can I borrow a couple of quid?' Ed asked Kate.

'Sure.'

'Only Bernice hasn't given me my housekeeping yet.'

'Very funny.'

Ed laughed and thought: But true. Bernice really wasn't functioning very well.

Zoe was feeling flush, so chucked an extra pound into the dish. After zipping up her purse she looked over at the others and caught her breath. Donna had plonked a big black beret on top of her loose blonde hair. She was chatting and joking with Bronwen. Bronwen suddenly turned into Ross, and Bob's living room turned into a black cab. Zoe shuddered. Bloody Ross. So many things triggered off painful memories. She shook away the image and decided she'd call Matthew when she got home.

Donna watched Zoe and wondered what Ross saw in her. All skin and bone, as her mum would say. And he obviously preferred his women much younger.

'I like your hat, Donna,' called out Zoe. 'Are they the latest thing?'

'No, not really.' Only someone ancient would say 'the latest thing'. 'Used to be my mum's.'

Zoe frowned. 'Oh.'

Bronwen pulled on her bicycle helmet. 'Right! See you all next time with *The Beach*.'

'Yes,' they all said.

Bob hadn't heard of *The Beach* by Alex Garland, but imagined it to be a bit of a wartime thriller. The Normandy landings, perhaps.

EIGHT

Early Friday morning on her way to find a copy of *The Beach*, Kate
saw what looked like Ross Kershaw coming out of a college. Surely
not. He was with a very don-like middle-aged man in tweed, and
they turned to walk the way Kate was going. She doubled her
pace to catch up, and was practically running by the time she
overtook them and hurriedly glanced back. Yes, it was definitely
Ross Kershaw. Those film-star looks. Lovely. No wonder Zoe was
hooked. Where had he got that tan? Unseasonably good weather in
Scotland, perhaps. She slowed down, completely out of breath, and
let them pass. Ross, giving off the aroma of something expensive,
was checking his watch and looking decidedly bored.

'And *ninth*ly . . .' said his companion.

She called on Ed on the way home. Will was upstairs with some
therapeutic exercises for Bernice.

'Are you sure that's what they're doing?' she asked, as the
floorboards creaked, creaked, creaked above them.

Ed was practically whispering but there was no need. 'Will says he wants to make up for the pain and misery he caused Bernice five years ago. Oh yeah, did you know—'

'He told me.'

'If you ask me he's got an overinflated sense of the effect he has on women. She wasn't that depressed about it. Jumped straight into bed with me. And Mick Rayworth.'

'You mean an orgy?'

'Well, no. I've never really gone for men in cagoules.'

'Hey, speaking of debauchery, I just saw Ross Kershaw in town.'

'Yeah?'

'Coming out of Trinity.'

'His old college, maybe. He was at Oxford back in the seventies.'

The creaks stopped and more than two feet were making their way towards the stairs. 'Better go,' she said, with a quick peck.

Will had dumbbells under each arm and a radiant Bernice behind him. She glowed with perspiration and was fluffing up her reddish brown hair with all ten fingers. At the bottom of the stairs she said, 'Fancy a coffee before you go, Will?'

Would she know where we kept it?

Will patted her bottom and said, 'OK, just a quickie,' then looked my way. 'Ah, Ed! You're back.'

'I only popped out for a paper,' I said.

He turned and watched Bernice wiggling off to the kitchen in Lycra. He'd always been a plump-bottom man. 'Did I tell you I've lost my Oxford manager?' he asked me.

'No?'

'Gone over to Oxfit for five K more.'

'Oh dear.' I didn't really care but tried to sound interested.

'Anyway, just got myself a replacement.' He nodded towards the kitchen. 'Now that Bernice has quit her job . . .'

'She *has*?'

'Did I hear my name?' she asked from the doorway.

'But you know nothing about running gyms!' I cried.

She raised her eyes to the gods and went back in the kitchen.

'You just need managerial skills,' said Will. 'Bernice has certainly got those. Look at how she organises work and family.'

I could hear lots of banging and cursing. 'The cupboard above the kettle,' I called out.

Back in London for his lunchtime session with Zoe, Ross was standing naked at his open bedroom window, exhaling dope smoke into the cold November air. 'Sorry, Zo,' he said.

Zoe looked over at his body: slim, tanned, broad-shouldered; legs she wouldn't mind herself. She wanted him to come back to bed, tell her she was beautiful and that he adored her. That she was the sexiest woman he'd ever known. She wanted their usual hungry, hurried, Friday-lunchtime lovemaking. Messy and satisfying and full of sweet words. It was what had kept her going for three years. She clasped her fingers together under the duvet. *Please God make him come back to bed. Please . . .*

'It's been a ridiculously busy week,' he told her, turning and smiling apologetically. 'I suppose I'm just knackered.'

He walked across the room and picked up his boxers. As he stepped into them, Zoe willed herself not to get tearful. These things happen, she thought. But twice in a row?

'What are you doing this weekend?' she asked, and held her breath.

'I'm not sure.'

When Ross disappeared to the bathroom, Zoe got up and peered into one of his dozen mirrors. No makeup mistakes or food between her teeth, so it wasn't that then. 'Not your fault,' she whispered to her reflection, then dressed, slipped on her low-heeled shoes and ran a comb through her hair. By the time Ross returned she had her coat and scarf on and her bag under an arm.

'Oh, are you off?' he asked. He padded down the hall on bare feet and held open the door for her, kissing her cheek as she passed, then running the back of a finger down it. 'Love you.'

When she'd gone, Ross lay on the bed and called Donna. 'What are you doing?' he asked. He could hear water in the background.

'Oh . . . um, just running myself a bath.'

She swished the washing-up water in the sink. Jake was at school,

Ryan was watching cartoons in the front room and she was about to tackle the previous night's pans.

'Mm, tell me what you're wearing,' said Ross, his right hand making its way downwards.

Donna was in combat trousers and an old hooded top of Carl's. It was in two shades of grey and had baked bean sauce splattered on it. 'I'm down to my stockings and suspenders,' she said, and tacked on a giggle. 'Oh, and my shoes, which are really really high with ankle straps.'

Through the window she could see fat Naomi pegging things on her rotary washing line. Pink sweatshirts and stretch denim jeans. Mini skirts. Someone should tell her.

Ross said, 'Take your shoes off.'

'OK.' She counted to seven. 'There, they're off.'

'Now get into the bath.'

'In my stockings?'

'It's a lovely image,' he said, breathing faster.

Donna stirred up the water in the washing-up bowl. 'I'm just stepping in. Sinking down. Ooo, that feels nice.' She picked up Ryan's plastic beaker, filled it and let the water pour out, a bit at a time. 'I'm splashing myself. Mm . . . the bubbles are tickling my breasts.'

God, she thought, this beaker's a right mess. Chewed to bits. She'd maybe get him another one this afternoon. She needed to go to the supermarket for some things before they collected Jake, who hated shopping and was a right pain these days. Throwing things in the trolley when she wasn't looking. Running round and bashing into old people.

'Touch them,' said Ross.

Donna blinked. 'Sorry?'

'Your breasts.'

'Oh, right.'

Concentrate, she told herself.

When it was over – didn't take him too long – she got out her diary and wrote 'PS' for 'phone sex' next to the day's date.

'Come on, Ryan,' she said, switching off the TV, hauling her drowsy son off the sofa and shoving his arms into a quilted jacket. 'Got to go to Kwik Save.' She stared dreamily at the space above his head for a while and smiled. 'Maybe Mummy'll buy us all some nice bubble bath.'

Zoe feigned a migraine and went home. The further from London she'd got the better she felt, but in the bath she still hurt inside. It was ridiculous, she knew, to rely on someone like Ross for affirmation of her attractiveness. After wrapping herself in towels she rang Matthew and got his voicemail. 'Call me?' she said, trying to sound breezy.

She lay on the sofa trying, unsuccessfully, not to think of Ross. She needed him but did she love him? He said an old girlfriend had once called him lovable but not likeable. Zoe had laughed along with him at the time; however, 'lovable but not likeable' had regularly popped into her head over the years. She certainly didn't see him as a good friend. She wasn't herself with him, he was available only on his own terms, and he rarely enquired about her everyday life. She should just swim away from the whole horrible scene, but . . . well, that would be hard. What started off as an infatuation had now become a scary addiction. He was like an evil drug, she thought, and was wondering if there were people-addiction clinics, when the phone rang.

'Oh hi, Matthew,' she said, suddenly feeling she'd stepped back into the warm bath.

'Are you ill?' he asked.

She smiled for the first time in hours. Such a nice voice. Soft and cheerful, with not a trace of arrogance. 'No, no, just working at home today.'

When Zoe and Matthew were arranging a theatre date, Gideon was sitting in his tiny office drumming the desk with his fingers. Students were welcome to come and see him between three and five o'clock for one-to-one tutorials. He looked at his watch. Four fifteen and only Lynne Hopcroft so far. Or was it Liz? He sighed, tucked Elmore Leonard in a drawer and created a new document on his computer. *Biog.*, he typed and underlined it. *Name: Gideon Entwistle.* Oh, for a name like Wilde. *Occupation: College Lecturer. Subject: English Literature. The nice thing about Molefield College is that one can still call the subject that, rather than the all-encompassing, let's-deconstruct-sauce-bottle-labels 'English Studies'. Background: My father had his own painting-and-decorating business.* He deleted this and typed, *My father was a successful entrepreneur and my mother was a housewife. I grew*

up in Kent, where I passed my eleven plus and went to the boys'
grammar school in Tunbridge Wells, then on to Keele University and
an MA at

'Come!' he shouted to a half-hearted knock at the door. In walked
a large boy in an anorak. Why couldn't they make an effort to look
like students – grow their hair, wear tight trousers? Gideon attempted
a smile and told him to take a seat. 'What can I do for you?'

'Yeah, right,' said the student, a battered A4 pad on his lap. 'It's
this essay on Pin'uh what you give us.'

Had he seen this one before? They all looked alike. Gideon
guessed this chap was taking his 'Twentieth-Century Playwrights'
module and said, 'Yes?'

'Only I don't understand.'

'Ah.' Gideon rifled through a pile of papers, pulled one out and
quickly read the essay title. 'How are Pinter's audiences made to feel
uncomfortable?' Could he have put it more simply? 'What don't you
understand?'

'Er . . . well, I was wondering if you mean like their seats are hard
and the heating ain't bin put on. That sorta fing.'

What would be the penalty for slapping a student, wondered
Gideon. Imprisonment? Might be worth it. He clasped his hands
tightly in his lap and explained in primary-teacher mode exactly
what he'd meant. After ten minutes, and several A4 pages of
frantically scribbled notes, the boy said, 'Cheers,' shoved his biro
in a pocket and lumbered off.

'Shut the— Oh, never mind.' Gideon tutted and got up and
popped his head into the corridor to see if anyone was waiting to

see him. A little way off stood the boy. He had his back to him and was on his mobile. 'Yeah, worked a treat. But listen, I want a fiver off everyone who copies it, right?'

They closed the library at 12.30 on Thursdays. Hooray for spending cuts, thought Bronwen, as she whizzed down Headington Hill on her big black bicycle, hair and scarf trailing behind her. She made it to St Mary's with time to spare, so lingered over lunch in the Convocation Coffee House for a while, trying not to make eye contact with the attractive man in the long coat who'd been behind her at the last lunchtime recital. Tall, thick and wavy fair hair, cherubic face. Mid-forties? A freelancer of some sort, perhaps. Obviously had time to spare during the day. Musician? Writer? A rather ethereal aura, she thought, compared to Gideon. Their eyes met and Bronwen formed a brief smile. He responded with the same before they both returned to their quiches.

She chose a pew across the aisle and slightly behind for a good view of him. She noticed delicate little ears through his curls and thought they indicated a sensitive nature. On four occasions during the organ recital he turned his head and glanced at her, fleetingly.

'Most enjoyable,' he said to her on the way out.

'Oh, yes,' she replied and they somehow found themselves back in the Convocation Coffee House, sharing a table and a slice of date and walnut cake.

*   *   *

Duggie was about to wrap up a sale. 'She really wants a hundred and fifty for it,' he was telling a fairly wealthy-looking woman. 'But, as it's obviously going to a good home, I'm prepared to let it go at one forty.'

The woman said, 'Oh, really?' and got out her cheque book.

Duggie watched her eyes wander over to a large mirror. 'It's lovely, isn't it?' he said. 'But reserved, I'm afraid.'

The woman took a closer look and shook her head. '*What* a shame. It would have gone fabulously in my dining room.'

He stroked his chin. 'Well . . . let me just check with the boss.' He went through to the back and winked at Kate. She gave him a thumbs-up, and he returned to the shop. 'She says as no deposit was left it's yours if you'd like it.'

The woman was delighted, as was Duggie, who was now working on a basic-wage-plus-ten-per-cent-commission basis. He punched the air when she'd gone. Twenty quid. Not bad for ten minutes' work. He jotted some figures down in 'Duggie's Dosh' book and went back to reading *Guitar* magazine.

It's funny how things turn out, I thought. Was it only eight years ago I was wallowing in a Tatopani hot spring, stoned out of my mind and trying desperately to impress Laura, a stunning American who'd hooked up with us in Kathmandu. Ha! I moved Georgia over to the other knee and wiped dribble from her mouth.

'She's teething, then?' asked a plump mum beside me. She had the ugliest baby you ever saw,

'Yes.'

'Have you tried—'

'Dentinox? Yes.'

'I find it works wonders.'

'Yes. It's very good.'

Laura got together with Pete in the end. Pete with his when-I-was-hitching-round-South-America anecdotes I'd heard a million times. Laura had also 'done' South America, so they had lots to talk about. Before Nepal I'd only 'done' Norfolk, having been a completely skint undergraduate, then MA student at UEA. I suppose I could have told Laura about our end-of-year parties on Cromer beach.

'Georgia Adams?' called the nurse, as though waiting for Georgia to reply 'Yes!' close her newspaper and take herself through to be weighed. I gathered my daughter and our various bits and made my way to Nurse's room, where Georgia and I would enjoy excessive patronisation for the next five minutes.

'Gosh, we *are* looking bonnie!' the sturdy, freckled, anywhere-between-thirty-and-fifty nurse exclaimed to Georgia as she put fresh paper towelling into the scales. 'Daddy's obviously doing a super job!'

I glowed with pride. If only Bernice would talk to me this way.

Later, we called into Kate's shop, where Duggie was explaining the mechanisms of a drop-arm sofa to an attractive young woman in vaguely hippie gear. Laura came to mind again.

'It works on a ratchet system,' he was telling her. He pulled a small metal hook and the arm fell by degrees. 'Like this.'

'Oh, I see,' said the girl. 'Great when friends want to crash.'

'Yep. It's late Victorian, I'd say.'

'Wow.' She stroked the velvety seat. 'And this deep plum's really cool.'

Kate came in from the back. 'Mm, it's very Biba, isn't it? I used to love their colours.'

'Me too,' said the girl. 'My gran's got all their old catalogues.'

'Your gran!' Kate stopped abruptly, just as I was pushing Georgia past her.

'Yeah, so's mine,' I said, and she thumped me.

It was only when Kate hid a yawn behind her hand that I realised I'd been talking for, well, quite a while about the Himalayas or Him*aal*ias as we who've scaled them like to say. She'd been rubbing down a chest of drawers and occasionally throwing in a 'Really?' or 'Sounds great.'

'Oh God, I'm sorry,' I said.

'No, no. It's just my sleepy time of day. Perhaps I'll make a pot of tea. Would you like some?'

'Please.'

'I'm out of yak's milk, I'm afraid.'

I laughed. 'Actually, that reminds me of one time when we were close to the Tibetan border and—'

'Earl Grey or PG?'

'What? Oh, PG please.' I followed her through to the kitchenette. 'I wish you hadn't chosen *The Beach*, you know. It's giving me terrible wanderlust.'

Duggie popped his head round the door. 'Kate, she's offering six hundred.'

'She's still *here?*'

'Yeah. I think she might be after my body.'

'In that case say six forty, then accept six twenty.'

'Right.'

'He's a godsend,' said Kate when he'd gone. 'I just hope he's keeping up with his schoolwork.'

When Ed said, 'Talking of schoolwork . . .' and started telling her about a village school, eight miles from the nearest road and run by mountain goats – or was it Tibetan monks? – Kate threw two extra bags in the pot for added caffeine, then gave Georgia's buggy a sharp nudge to wake her up. Which worked.

'How's Bernice?' she asked, as Ed heaved Georgia on to his lap and unzipped her spacesuit. 'Still exercising with Will?'

'Probably. She's managing his Oxford gym. Starting today.'

'No!'

'That's what I said. They've got very pally again.'

'Really? Maybe they'll . . . you know.'

He grinned. 'Fingers crossed.'

Kate couldn't help wondering what Ed might do for money if Bernice went. Male escort for the older woman, perhaps? *I'll have to bring my daughter along. But don't worry, she's very discreet.'* She could offer him work in the shop, but Duggie wanted to be full time in the holidays.

'Have you got any plans?' she asked him. 'You know, now you've finished your thesis?'

'Well . . . I was thinking at the clinic today that I might write a novel. Something like *The Beach*, only it takes place in—'

'Nepal?'

'Right! Guy in his thirties sets off with his young daughter to revisit old Himalayan haunts. Gorgeous women flock to him and his cute baby. Bit of sex. A murder mystery, perhaps. You know, when we were passing through Nagarkot, we heard about these unexplained—'

'Sugar? Oh no, of course you don't.' She swallowed a yawn, lifted the teapot lid and popped another bag in.

'Hurry up, you two,' called Gideon from Bob's Parker Knoll. 'It's about to start.'

Bob dried the last of the plates and put it in the cupboard, while Christine hoisted the tea tray and said, 'Coming!'

By the time the *Emmerdale* theme tune started up they were in their places – well, Bob wasn't actually in *his* place – and Christine was pouring them each a nice strong cuppa.

During the ads, Bob popped out for a leak he didn't really need, so as to avoid listening to Gideon's analysis of part one. Christine had always been a patient listener but Bob could tell Gideon's verbals went straight over her head. He took as long as he could in the cloakroom, checked the thermostat and straightened a picture in the hall, but still caught Gideon saying, '– you know, according to

Propp there are thirty-one generic narratemes in a story, whether folk tale or soap opera.'

'Well, I never,' said Christine, casting off a sleeve at a rate of knots.

Bob took the remote from his trouser pocket – Christine told him it would give him cancer if he kept it there, but no way was he letting Gideon get his hands on it – and turned the volume up three notches. 'It's good, this Toyota ad!' he shouted.

'Ah yes,' Gideon yelled back. 'A fine example of Western phallicism, wouldn't you say?'

WINTER

NINE

'Happy New Year, Ed!' sang Bronwen.

Cold air emanated from her as I wished her a Happy New Year back and took her coat. 'Do go on through. We've got a nice fire going.'

Like Zoe and Bob before her, Bronwen gasped when she saw Kate's living room. 'Goodness, what a transformation!'

I could see this was beginning to really piss Kate off. For the third time she said, 'All Ed's doing.'

I had to admit I'd done a pretty good job. Soon after Georgia and I moved in, I'd filled a large skip with Kate's accumulated crap. I thought she'd cry, 'No, I beg you, not my seventy-four empty jam jars!' – but all she said when she got back from work and peered in the skip was, 'Good riddance. What's for dinner?' I went on to do the downstairs floorboards with a deafening industrial sander. 'Do you *have* to, Eddie?' Charlie shouted from the doorway, and I grinned an evil grin. After some agonising, I decided on an Amish colour scheme: off-white, pale blue and lots of warm wood.

'Fuckin 'ell!' said Donna, walking into the room in big wet boots

I wish she'd taken off. 'Have I come to the wrong place?'

When I let Gideon in the house I was about to ask him not to comment on the home improvements, but then thought: Nah, he'll never notice. And he didn't.

It wasn't that I didn't trust Charlie to be kind and caring to Georgia and not break each of her tiny fingers for something to do, but I thought I'd pop upstairs before we got going and check things out. 'Won't be a tick,' I told the group.

'She's having a great time, aren't you, George?' said Charlie. She was bouncing her on her knee, just centimetres from the computer screen. I wasn't sure what I was more worried about, the microwaves slowly cooking Georgia's brain or the long-term effects of seeing Nazis having their heads shot off. But how to get her away? It wasn't wise to say anything critical to the highly reactive Charlie, but inspiration suddenly struck.

'Would you like to change her nappy, Charlie? Or shall I?'

'I think it's terribly exciting,' Bronwen was saying as Georgia and I entered the living room, 'having a little love match in the circle.'

Gideon wriggled in his seat, cleared his throat and shot Bronwen an embarrassed look.

'I'm talking about Ed and Kate,' she told him.

'Ah,' he said, his eyes darting between Kate and me. 'Well . . . yes, jolly exciting. Anyway. Down to business, what? How have we all got on with Conrad over the holiday period?'

*　　*　　*

Kate hadn't got on at all with Joseph Conrad, what with having to organise a particularly festive and present-packed Christmas for Charlie in order to bring her round to the idea of nuclear family life. It had been a bit of a shock to Kate's system too.

'Bernice has made up with Clive and wants to go and live with him,' Ed had told her one evening.

They'd opened a bottle to celebrate, then another, and after lots of drunken sweet nothings, a quickie on the sofa and Ed saying he wasn't sure how he was going to manage the rent without Bernice, Kate invited him to move in with her.

She'd then staggered home, fallen into a deep sleep and woken the next morning with a start; staring, unblinking, at the ceiling for a while. Had she really done that? Would he remember saying, 'Yes, I'd love to move in but I might have to tidy up a bit'? She'd looked around at her bedroom. She quite liked living in a mess. Didn't all artists? No, no, living with Ed would never work. She thought back to the afternoon she'd turned up at his place with a hot, flaky pastry Cornish pasty and he'd followed her with a dustpan and brush until her final mouthful.

But move in he did, and renovate he did and . . . well, maybe she wasn't such a naturally untidy person, she decided now, scanning the living room and taking in all the lovely changes while Gideon rambled on about *Heart of Darkness* and Donna took notes and everyone else checked their watches and shot hungry looks at Ed's splendid buffet. He was such a treasure.

*   *   *

147

Kate noticed Zoe had a hangdog expression and black circles under her eyes, so during the break she poured them each a gin and tonic in the kitchen while the others were digging into the tapas.

'Oh, thanks,' said Zoe. 'Just what I needed. Better take it easy this time though!'

Kate laughed and said, 'Happy New Year.'

'You too.' She downed her entire drink then looked around the room and sighed. 'I think yours is going to be better than mine, though.'

'Oh?'

'Mm,' she said, trying to drain more from her glass. 'Man trouble.'

Did Zoe only have to sniff gin to start pouring her heart out? 'Ross?' asked Kate, tentatively.

'Yep.' Her eyes welled up.

Kate unscrewed the bottle top. 'A drop more?'

'Thanks.' She sat at the table and thrust her glass forward. Kate filled it while Zoe sniggered and flicked her hair back. 'He can't get it up these days.'

'Oh dear.'

'Funny, eh? Mr if-it-hasn't-got-a-hairy-chest-screw-it Ker-shaw.'

'Well, you know, it can happen to men in, er . . . mid-life. Especially if they've got stressful lives.'

Zoe began laughing hysterically and crying at the same time. Which must be quite hard to do, thought Kate.

'You know,' Zoe said with a strange sob, 'I didn't get one call, email, anything, from him at Christmas or New Year.'

'Well, I suppose he was with his family up in Scotland?' said Kate. Why did she keep making excuses for him? 'All the same . . .'

'Matthew rang me every other day from South Africa. He and his parents were visiting his sister.'

'Matthew?'

'Oh . . . he's someone I met recently. Nothing's happened. He's just a really nice man.' She blew her nose noisily into some kitchen roll.

'Attractive?'

Zoe nodded and blew again. 'Very.'

'Well, then . . . why don't you . . . you know?'

'It's not that easy, Kate,' said Zoe. 'Could I have another gin?'

'Sure. Give us your glass.'

'You see, Ross has kind of got into my soul. Do you know what I mean?'

'Oh yes,' said Kate. Flash had done that to her all those years back. How she'd let herself be manipulated. She'd never quite got to Zoe's state of helplessness, though. She handed over the tonic.

'Thanks.' Zoe's eyes welled up again. 'He's such a bastard.'

Ed came in, saw the gin bottle and shook his head. 'Make her some coffee, quick.'

'No,' hissed Kate out the side of her mouth. He was putting the kettle on and they had their backs to Zoe. 'She's fine, believe me. It's all under control.'

'I'll bugger off then, shall I?' he whispered back.

'Please.'

'But why does she put up with all that shit?' Ed asked. They were sitting up in bed in their nightwear, like a couple of long-standing rather than a couple of six weeks. 'She could get anyone. She's absolutely gorgeous.'

Kate scowled. 'Oh yes?'

'Well, you know. In a skinny, nervy kind of way.'

'Hm, beats me. She doesn't strike me as the eager-to-please type, but people tend to behave differently in a relationship. Look at how you love to be browbeaten by your women but won't put yourself out for anyone else.'

'Not true.'

She turned and stared at him while he pretended to read *Heart of Darkness*. 'What?' he said, lowering the book.

'I forgot the *Oxford Times* crossword. It's on the kitchen table.'

'Get it yourself.'

Kate sighed and rubbed her temples and Ed went and got it.

After the meeting, Bronwen had whipped up the Woodstock Road on her bicycle, arriving at her father's house with aching thighs and frozen cheeks and a bag of ready-made meals. He so obviously hadn't been feeding himself recently.

She showed him what she'd bought – fisherman's pies, cottage pies, nothing spicy – 'Just put them in your new microwave, Daddy. I'm sure Mrs Cornish will help you out.'

By ten to midnight, after a bit of a battle, she'd got hot milk and pills inside her father, and had him tucked up under the shabby quilted eiderdown he refused to part with. She stood and watched for a while as his eyelids grew heavier, and whatever he was muttering about – some horse he'd once put a bet on? – became more and more indistinct. He fell asleep with his mouth open and his now scrawny neck quite lost inside his pyjama top, and as a large tear dropped on to her chest, Bronwen believed she'd never seen anything that made her feel quite so sad, not even on her forays into the Third World.

She swallowed hard, wiped at a cheek and headed for the disarray in the kitchen. A sopping wet towel on the floor. Dozens of saucepans left to soak. Rancid milk in a jug. Really, she thought, as she tied the apron behind her back, what on earth did Mrs Cornish do here for two hours each day? She'd call her tomorrow; give her a bit of a talking to. She must phone Malcolm too, she remembered. Tell him she'd got those tickets.

She popped into the living room and put Mendelssohn on the record player – Overture to *A Midsummer Night's Dream* – and hummed along as she emptied the bin and scrubbed at pans and thought about how unsettling it had been to see Gideon again this evening. Colour flooded her face as she thought back to her New Year's Eve *faux pas*. Oh dear. And they'd had such a wonderful time, circle dancing. Gideon had struggled to pick it up, which had somehow added to the evening's jollity. 'No, no, Gideon,' Oscar had gently chided him. 'This is a rural Russian dance. Imagine you are on the ice, wearing heavy clothes. Now, hand on my shoulder . . .

and glide . . . glide . . . experience community and joy. Whooaaa, back you come, Gideon. Would bare rather than stocking feet be better for you?' In the end they'd placed him in the centre to partake of the circle's energy, which he'd seemed much happier with. Such fun. But why had she gone and ruined the evening by trying to turn Gideon's chaste, 2 a.m., New Year's kiss into something rather more? Too much of that innocent-looking punch, perhaps?

She flashed back to Gideon prising himself off her, leaping from the sofa and reaching the front door before she'd even recovered her breath. Oh, the shame. How had she not realised how unappealing she was?

She rubbed vigorously at all the surfaces, filled the washing machine for Mrs Cornish and double locked the front door, before tugging on helmet and gloves and cycling off into the night.

On Thursday, at the top of South Parks, Donna thought about seeing Ross next week and was surprised at how excited she felt.

'Very good, Ryan,' she called out when he said, 'Look, Mum!' for the hundredth time. He was at the top of the slide, waving. She waved back. 'Hold on, there's a good boy!'

She wasn't sure if things were really going according to plan. Like, she wasn't actually supposed to fall for the guy and get jealous and all that. Was he still going out with Zoe? Would she make Zoe suspicious if she asked her? Would Zoe even remember what she'd whispered to her all those weeks ago? After all, she had passed out on the settee shortly after. Had to be carried out to Bob's car.

Donna felt a pang of guilt about maybe seeing Ross behind Zoe's back, but then shook it off. It must have finished between them. He'd told Donna loads of times she was the only woman in his life. That him and his wife hadn't done it for years. 'Careful, Ryan!' That when the time was right, he'd leave Fiona and marry Donna. Imagine being an MP's wife! That would be one up on Kelly Forester with her degree.

Back at home, she checked to see if he'd left a message. Then tried 1471 and just got her mum's number. Oh, well. She hadn't heard from Ross for ages, but then he had been up in Scotland. Mind you, one little call would've been nice over Christmas. Still . . . never mind, he'd be back in London soon.

She got out last year's week-to-view diary and flicked through. She read R for Ross, Sp for spliff, H for harder stuff (cocaine), or SS for straight sex on every single page from late October onwards. Three times she'd written in PS for phone sex. No KS for kinky sex, or T for tarts. She reckoned Zoe must have been making that stuff up. Sad cow.

She picked up the new diary she'd bought with the WH Smith voucher her gran had given her for Christmas and tapped her long blue fingernails on it. Was there any point in keeping a record? It wasn't like she'd ever use it. Not now that they were in love. She popped it in the box with the old diary and went downstairs to where Ryan had made something with his Duplo.

'Look, Mum,' he said, holding it up. 'Daddy.'

'Oh, yes!'

'See Daddy soon?'

'I expect so, darlin,' she said with her fingers crossed. No way was she taking her son to Bullingdon prison. Maybe you'll have a new daddy before long, she wanted to tell him. And a nice big house.

She picked up Joseph Conrad, and the dictionary she'd also got with her Smith's voucher, and took them through to the peace of the kitchen. She'd almost finished the book, and she wanted to say to Ross, quite truthfully, 'I've just read Joseph Conrad's *Heart of Darkness*,' next time she saw him. As she went along she looked up words she didn't know – conflagration, inscrutable – just so she'd know what people were on about when Ross took her to posh parties, like at Number 10 or wherever.

The following week, Zoe and Ross were having an early lunch in a Beefeater in the far west of London. Ross kept checking the time, and twice he'd watched the waitress's rear all the way to the kitchen.

'I just decided I didn't want to . . . to *do* that kind of thing any more,' Zoe was telling him. Since she'd stepped out of his car that day, she'd turned down another invitation to a tacky joint and told him she was no longer going to take drugs, just have the odd joint perhaps.

Ross sat back in his chair and looked bored and pissed off. 'Fine,' he said, then raised an arm and waved it. 'Could we have the bill, please?'

Zoe willed herself to think of something else to talk about.

It was never easy to initiate conversation with Ross, but she wanted to salvage something from their lunch. 'I've just finished Conrad's *Heart of Darkness*,' she said shakily. 'Have you read it?'

'When I was eighteen,' he sighed. 'Like everyone else.' He slipped his coat on and tapped the table with his credit card. 'Come on, come on,' he murmured, looking the waitress's way. When the girl finally approached he produced that devastating smile Zoe hadn't seen in a long while.

Back at the office, after her two-hour lunch break and a filthy look from her boss, Zoe called Matthew and said, yes, she'd love to come and stay this weekend. She'd been avoiding anything physical with him, not wanting to rush into a serious relationship, and also, unbelievably, not wanting to be unfaithful to Ross. Now she thought she never wanted to see that callous self-absorbed peacock again. Before getting on with some work she scribbled a list – 'Clammy hands. Noisy nose-blower. Says "nucular" instead of nuclear. Tartan socks' – and stuck it to her computer for times of low resolve.

Ed was minding the shop till Duggie arrived at 4.30, so Kate cycled into town to look for inspiration. She'd found a fabulous old commode in a skip at the Council dump – the things people throw away! – which she felt inclined to go Japanese with. After flicking through several art books, she was walking down Broad Street to the Ashmolean and its Oriental rooms, when she saw

Bronwen arm-in-arm with a man. She stopped and blinked, then started following them, mesmerised. Occasionally, Bronwen and her man would linger by a shop window; pointing at things, laughing. She looked quite girlish, with her long wild hair and happy expression. Almost pretty. Kate was fascinated. A less nosy person than herself probably wouldn't have sneakily taken a left, then a right, and a right, then another right at breakneck speed, in order to accidentally bump into them.

'Bronwen!' she then puffed with a startled expression.

'Oh hello, Kate,' said Bronwen, unhooking her arm from her friend's. 'How are you?'

'Fine, fine.'

'Um, this is Malcolm. Malcolm, Kate.'

Kate said, 'Hi,' with a nod.

Malcolm – blond curls, black calf-length coat, multi-coloured hand-knitted scarf – said, 'Hello,' and offered her a cold hand. 'Pleased to meet you.'

Bronwen looked a little uncomfortable, as though expecting Kate to say, 'Now wait a minute, Bronwen, we all thought you and *Gideon* were lovers.'

'Not at the library today?' asked Kate.

'Half-day.'

'Oh.'

'And your shop?'

'Ed's there.'

'Ah.'

That was conversation more or less exhausted, so Kate told them she was just on her way to the Ashmolean, said goodbye and dashed off, horribly aware that she was going in completely the opposite direction.

'Hot gossip,' she told Ed from her mobile. 'Bronwen's got a man and he's not Gideon.'

'Yes, we do still have the yellow chaise longue,' said Ed, all businesslike. 'In fact, a gentleman's just considering buying at this very moment.'

A bus roared by.

'You want to offer seven two five?' he asked her.

Then another bus.

'Well, if you'd like to come into the shop and . . . Oh, sorry, I've just been offered seven thirty. And as the other customer is actually here . . .'

Kate couldn't believe it. The yellow chaise longue! After all these months. She hung up and let Ed carry on talking to himself, then turned round and went back towards the museum.

While Kate was sketching vases, Gideon was in his office trying to come up with a quote for Bronwen. She'd almost certainly made a pass at him after her circle-dancing group's New Year's Eve party, and he'd almost certainly hurt her feelings with his clumsy excuses and his rush towards her front door. Perhaps, he'd felt, it might be a good idea to put a few apt words into an appropriate card and pop it in the post. He crossed out the Shakespeare he'd taken from his book of quotations, scratched his head, then remembered a bit of George Herbert.

Love bade me welcome: yet my soul drew back
Guilty of dust and sin.

Perhaps not. He didn't want to sound like a pervert.

If only Penelope hadn't been so candid about his failings on the bedroom front, he wouldn't be in this situation now. He chewed on his pen, wondering if women always throw these things at men when they're on their way out the door, or if he really was hopeless. He'd grown terribly fond of Bronwen, and since the New Year's Eve débâcle he'd missed her and found that fondness growing, day by day. In addition, her as-yet-unseen and almost certainly splendid breasts were taking up a good deal of his thoughts when he should be writing that paper on Smollett. But how he'd hate to disappoint. His only hope was that as a woman gets older and, well, more desperate, she'll place less emphasis on a man's ability to provide her with previously undiscovered sensual heights.

He took up his book of quotations and searched on. 'Alas! the love of women! it is known / To be a lovely and a fearful thing!' Fearful? Hm. And would Bronwen appreciate something from the rakish Byron?

This was all too tiresome, he decided, and took a book of true crimes and Christine's packed lunch out of his briefcase.

*　　*　　*

When Kate walked in the shop, Duggie and I were discussing music. I thought he'd be into garage or bike shed or whatever, but his tastes spanned the decades and he was obviously *au fait* with any Muddy Waters, Pink Floyd or Clash album you could throw at him. 'It's what I spend all my money on,' he told me. 'If I didn't have my mini disc player I'd probably do myself in, having to sit around listening to my mum's music. Like, you know, *Titanic* soundtrack.'

'And *Fifty Love Songs You Never Wanted to Hear in the First Place*?'

'You got it. My stepdad's almost worse. Got every Iron Maiden album.'

'He looks like someone auditioning for *Doctor Who*,' said Kate.

'Duggie's stepfather?'

'No, Bronwen's man.'

'Oh, right.'

She pulled some sketches from her bag and said, 'I think I'll have a go on the commode now.'

'We promise not to look,' I told her, and Duggie and I fell about.

It was Friday and Ross was keeping an eye on the digital alarm clock over Donna's shoulder. She had her back to him and was chattering on about going to university, while he was thinking about his early evening flight to Inverness.

'Anyway,' she was saying, 'it's going to be *really* hard financially, being a student. Even though my parents are both high-class lawyers they're dead tight with their money.'

Donna paused, waiting for him to say not to worry, he'd help her out, but Ross was now concentrating on her left thigh, running a hand up and down it and wondering if he might be up for a second round. She certainly did it for him, young Donna. He'd recently considered introducing her to the pleasures of a threesome, but wanted her well and truly on the hook first. 'You could take out a student loan, you know?'

'And end up with a big debt? No thanks. Anyway . . .' she said with a big sigh, 'not your problem.'

No, he thought. Things were stirring down below, but did he have the time? He buried his face in her abundant locks and gently chewed on her shoulder. Shouldn't take more than ten minutes.

'I've just read Joseph Conrad's *Heart of Darkness*,' she said. 'Do you know it?'

Ross jumped and surfaced from her hair. How extraordinary! 'Yes, I do,' he told her when he'd got over the shock. 'Read it several times. It's all about man's vulnerability and corruptibility.' He laughed and turned her round to face him. 'Of course I wouldn't know anything about that.'

Afterwards, he lay on his back, arms behind his head, and said, 'I've written a novel, you know.'

'No!'

'Mm. A lot of politicians do. Came out last year.'

'Blimey. What's it about?'

'Oh . . . political thriller . . . bribery, back-stabbing . . . quite a bit of sex.'

Donna giggled. 'Now there's a surprise.'

'Here,' he said, lifting her head from his chest and turning to his bedside table. 'Borrow it if you want.' He handed her a paperback.

Donna sat up. *Out for the Count* it said on the cover, *by Ross Kershaw.* It showed a man lying on his front next to a ballot box, blood pouring out of his head. Most of the picture was dark and sinister-looking, while the lettering was red like the blood. 'Thanks.'

Ross tucked a strand of Donna's hair behind her ear and chuckled. 'Might be a bit light for your taste, of course.'

TEN

Matthew and Zoe walked through a pretty Cotswold village he'd driven them to, then up a country lane and into a wood. It was a cold but crisp and sunny day that made even the bare winter trees and scrappy ground look appealing.

'But then I came to my senses,' he was telling her, 'gave up on the pipe dream, got a proper job and bought a house.'

'But you still play, do you?'

'Oh yeah. The odd function, the occasional pub gig. Actually, I'm supposed to be playing in the local tomorrow lunchtime. I said I had a guest and probably wouldn't—'

'Oh no, you must!'

'You wouldn't mind?'

'Not if you don't mind me being there.'

'I'm pretty awful.'

'Liar.'

He laughed and took her hand and they walked in silence for a while, both of them trying not to think about the previous night's awkward lovemaking. Matthew had been tense and Zoe had shivered in the Arctic temperature of his bedroom. Later, he'd got up and thrown another bedspread over them – 'Sorry. Haven't got round to central heating yet' – then fallen asleep hugging her, while she listened to a thousand distressed cows in a distant shed and wondered if the house had mice.

They emerged from the wood to a glorious view: the village they'd come from nestled in a valley; beautiful undulating hills with little patches of last week's snowfall glistening in the sunshine. Zoe turned to Matthew, still holding her hand, and had an overwhelming desire to kiss him.

'Come here,' she said, leading him back into the wood, away from the public footpath and towards a small clearing hidden by a clump of trees, where she took off her big waterproof jacket and laid it on the ground. After looking over both shoulders Matthew took his off too.

It was quick and exciting, and the sound of chatting ramblers just yards away added a certain frisson. 'I can see you like an element of risk,' said Matthew afterwards, trying to get his breath back.

'Don't you?'

He laughed and helped her on with her jacket. 'I think I could get to like it.'

In the pub the next day, Matthew introduced the other members of the jazz band. 'Kim, Jeff, Ritchie.'

She nodded at them. 'Hi.'

'This is my girlfriend, Zoe,' said Matthew.

Girlfriend! It was all she could do not to fall to the floor and kiss his nice brown lace-ups.

I was cooking Sunday lunch for Kate's horrible mother and her equally horrible boyfriend, Eric, over here from France and doing the rounds. They kept breaking into French with each other, which, when people were plying you with wine and making sure your parsnips were roasted to perfection, seemed rather rude. I took a break to phone Sutton Coldfield.

'How's Georgia?' I asked Bernice.

'I just wish she'd eat something. She turned her nose up at the tandoori chicken last night, now she won't even look at the Mexican pizza we've just had delivered. I thought children lived on pizza and chips?'

It was where to begin with Bernice, really. 'I left you some plastic tubs of food I made especially.'

'Really?'

'In with the disposables.'

'Ah. Oh, that.'

'Yes, it's lamb and vegetables in one, chicken casserole in another and fruit and toffee yoghurt in the round blue one. All home-made.'

'I, er . . . threw it all away. Thought it was poo.'

Well, an easy mistake to make. 'Has she eaten *anything*?'

'She's quite keen on the liqueur chocolates left over from Christmas. Had quite a few of those. Also, I'm a bit worried about—'

'What?'

'Well, she keeps doing this weird thing.'

My pulse began to race. One weekend with Bernice and Georgia was developing abnormal behaviour. 'What weird thing?'

'You put her down, on say, the table.'

'Don't put her on the table, she'll fall off.'

'Oh, all right. Anyway, she then rolls on to her front and starts doing this strange wiggly thing. Like a seal or something.'

I relaxed. 'She's trying to crawl, Bernice.' If she wasn't my daughter's mother it would be quite endearing.

'Ed!' I heard from the kitchen. 'My gravy's gone lumpy!'

'Sieve it!' I shouted. 'Better go,' I told Bernice. 'You'll get her back by five, won't you?'

'Or maybe earlier?'

'Please.'

Kate had warned me about her mother. 'It'll be one small gibe after another until you think you can't take any more, then she'll come over all sweet and flirty and adoring and win you round.'

Not me, I'd thought, the moment she walked in the door and said, 'Ah, Kate's toyboy, I presume.'

An ancient, jowly, pot-bellied guy with a straggly grey ponytail, white T-shirt and Wrangler top and bottoms stood behind her with a large rustic pot in his hands. I'd been hoping they'd bring a saucy French wine, myself. 'One of your mother's,' said Eric, handing it over to Kate then kissing her cheeks three times. Kate quietly pulled a face. Eric's kisses, or the pot?

After half an hour or so, Daphne asked where Charlotte was, as though suddenly remembering she had a granddaughter.

'Charlie!' Kate called up the stairs. 'Granny and Eric are here!'

'Oh, for goodness' sake, Kate,' bristled Daphne. 'You know I prefer the French *Mamie*.'

When Charlie bounded down the stairs and into the living room Daphne let out a quiet shriek and said, 'My, you've . . . changed.'

'How are you, Granny?' asked Charlie, standing awkwardly by the door, tapping one hand with a CD ROM and making it clear she wouldn't be staying long.

'*Mamie*,' said Daphne.

'Oh yeah, forgot.'

As we ate, Daphne and Eric criticised my cooking; well, I guessed that was what they were doing as they pointed at their food, pushed it around, shook their heads and mumbled to each other in French. Next came my choice of paint. 'Pale blue *is* rather passé,' pronounced Eric.

And a total denim look isn't?

Daphne told me I should grow my hair a little longer to soften my angular face, and to never, but *never*, wear that particular shade of green. I was on the verge of picking up my dessert bowl and telling her she should *always* wear lemon sorbet, when she put her hand on my knee under the table and said, 'Kate's done so well to find such a charming, handsome and accomplished person as you, Ed. I hope you'll both be very happy. A toast, I think, Eric.'

'To Kate and Ed! A delightful couple,' cried Eric, and we all clinked glasses.

'Thanks,' I said, a trifle puzzled. Were they on drugs?

Later, when everyone was occupied filling the dishwasher or – in Eric's case – dozing in front of the football, I sneaked to the phone and rang my parents. 'Just wanted to tell you how wonderful you are,' I whispered.

'Have you been at the sherry, Edward?' asked Mum in her East Anglian posh.

'Only a bit. Tell Dad I think he's great too.'

'He's at Vic's, moving a wardrobe. In other words watching the football. How's my adorable granddaughter?'

'Still adorable, and very well.'

'And how's Kate?'

Mum liked Kate, to roughly the same degree that she'd detested Bernice, or 'that woman', as she tended to call her. I rather liked Kate too, which was fortunate. OK, she was culinarily challenged, she watched mind-numbing TV programmes and she had a ladette tendency to drool over attractive men, but she loved Georgia and – as far as I could tell – me, and, unlike Bernice, she let me play my Radiohead albums when she was within hearing distance. Kate's friends mainly visited her in the shop, so, contrary to my fears, I didn't have Sarahs and Claires and Rachels streaming through the house, drinking all our coffee and weighing me up.

'She's fine,' I said. 'Her mother and stepfather are here for a few days.'

'Oh, that must be nice for her.'

'Yes.'

'Your dad and I would love to come down again soon.'

'That would be great,' I said, and meant it. They'd spent Boxing Day and the one after with us, arriving with a pillowcase full of presents for Georgia – the kind Will and I had woken up to every Christmas – a bathrobe for Kate, a record token for Charlie and a Nigella Lawson book for me. 'We know how you like to cook, Edward.' 'Thanks!' I'd said, genuinely delighted. I rarely used recipes, but loved Nigella on the cover.

'. . . and your dad's making Georgia a little doll's house,' Mum was now telling me.

'That's impressive.'

'Well, at the rate he's going it'll be ready when she leaves for university.' She laughed at her joke and I joined in. She was so laid back and easy to talk to, my mum. In fact, she was a lot like Kate, I suddenly realised. Only tidier, and, as far as I knew, less inclined to tear her partner's shirt off at the drop of a hat. The number of buttons I'd sewn back on! Still, a small price to pay for wild, other-worldly, sweat-laden sex.

'And how's Charlie?'

'Fine.'

'Still got that . . . hairstyle?'

'She's thinking of growing it.' Ever since I'd promised her five pounds for every centimetre.

'Oh, good,' said Mum. 'Such a lovely face she's got. Anyway, your Auntie Kathleen's on her way round with a zip for me to put in, so

168

I'd better run the sweeper round quickly. Lovely to hear from you, Edward.'

After hanging up, I passed by the kitchen door. 'There's no excuse for slovenly vowels,' Daphne was saying quietly to Kate. 'Where on earth was he dragged up?'

'Near Ely,' sighed Kate. 'You know, the Fens.'

Daphne laughed, 'Oh dear, say no more,' then asked if there was any chance of a decent cup of coffee. 'I've drunk nothing but filth since we took off from Nîmes.'

After they left, just before four, I paced up and down nervously until I spotted the BMW pull up down the street, then hurried out to gather my daughter into the arms of a competent parent. Bernice handed her over with a relieved-sounding, 'There you are,' while Clive emptied the back seat.

'Well,' I said, 'anytime you want to have her . . .'

Bernice smiled. She was quite nice to me now we weren't shackled. I suspected Clive went through it, though. They'd kissed and made up shortly after their mini-tiff. Bernice got her old job back and one evening announced her intention to move to Sutton Coldfield, as the strain of keeping their affair a secret at work was getting to them. Not the strain of keeping it from her partner, apparently. She said she'd try to see Georgia as often as she could, but after a brief Christmas visit to us, this was their first hands-on go.

'We thought she could come and stay some time in April, after our spring push,' Bernice was telling me.

'April would be good,' I told her. 'Or May . . . June.'

At this point, Kate came flying from the house and hugged both myself and my daughter. 'Thank God she's home safely,' she said, kissing Georgia, then taking her from me and heading for the house. 'Georgia's back!' I heard her call out in the hallway.

'Wicked!' came Charlie's reply.

An odd look – something vaguely like envy – flickered across Bernice's features, before she snapped, 'Clive!' just as he was closing a door. 'You've left that revolting changing mat in there. Try not to be such a prat.'

When Bronwen arrived at work on Monday morning there was an envelope waiting for her with her name written on it in a flamboyant hand. (Gideon hadn't known her full address so borrowed Bob's car and delivered it the evening before, counting on there being only one Bronwen Thomas on the library's staff.)

'Goodness,' she whispered, tugging off her helmet, unwinding her scarf and changing into her work shoes. She found a quiet corner in the Large Print section and ripped open the envelope. From it she pulled a greetings card with a pink and yellow bouquet on the front. The card had glitter scattered all over and Bronwen thought it truly awful. (The choice in Gideon's local newsagent's had been somewhat limited, and he'd considered going into town. But on a Sunday? And besides, Christine had been on the last stretch with the roast by then.)

Bronwen opened it up and read: 'Love's like the measles – all the worse when it comes late in life. (Douglas Jerrold)'

It was signed 'Gideon'.

'Goodness,' she said again. 'What can he mean?'

All morning she thought about the quotation. Was he in love with her and suffering? Judging from his behaviour on New Year's Eve, no. Was he sympathising with her for making a fool of herself? Was he calling her old? It all went round and round her head until, at 11.45, he appeared in person with a pile of books, and she almost yelped out loud.

Having realised the ambiguity of his chosen quotation, which had seemed so pertinent and nicely jocular at the time, Gideon decided on a damage-limitation course of action, cancelling his morning lecture and catching the college minibus into town, then a double-decker up to Bronwen's library.

'Did you receive my . . . er,' he whispered while she checked in his books.

'Yes,' she said. 'I, um . . .'

'Didn't really understand?'

'No.'

'I thought not. So I've, well . . .' He pulled another envelope from his pocket and handed it over.

She took it from him, slipped it in her cardigan pocket and said, 'That's eighty p, please.'

'Sorry?'

'Eighty pence fine. Twenty per book.'

'Ah.'

Out in the cloakroom, she opened the second card and read:

'Absence is to love what wind is to fire. It extinguishes the small, it inflames the great. (Comte de Bussy-Rabutin)'

Bronwen sighed. She felt none the wiser, particularly as the front of the card showed a group of semi-dressed young people drinking, smoking and dancing in a strobe-lit room. 'Working hard at Uni!' was written across the top. (Gideon had grabbed it from the rack in the college bookshop; it being the only one without 'Birthday' or 'Valentine' on it.)

Had Gideon's fire gone out? Oh dear, this was all so difficult. In some ways Malcolm was far more straightforward, but there wasn't the chemistry. Gideon had such a warm face and a certain animal magnetism. On the other hand she and Malcolm could talk for hours about music, her second-greatest love after books, and they'd so enjoyed the Brandenburgs at the Sheldonian. Plus, he was far more available, not living as Gideon did with a woman who procured slavish adherence to her mealtime schedule.

She washed her hands and looked long and hard in the mirror. She thought she was probably what they'd have called a 'handsome woman' in Victorian literature. A few too many grey hairs these days but it didn't seem to be handicapping her in the men stakes. It was just trying to fathom them when you got them.

While Bronwen was feeling confused by Gideon, Christine was ironing his socks.

'There,' she sighed contentedly, placing all six pairs on top of his cotton/wool mix vests. She unplugged the iron, unhooked the coathangers of shirts and took them up to his room.

'What a pickle,' she said with a chuckle. It was almost like having Keith back again!

She made his bed, picked up discarded clothes and popped them in the Ali Baba, gathered assorted bits of crockery and placed them out on the landing, then turned her efforts to his desk. He'd spent several hours working in his room yesterday and there was paper everywhere. Dear, dear. Lots of crossings out, she noticed, as she gathered up half-crumpled sheets. She stopped to read some of his notes. 'If this be not love, it is madness, and then it is pardonable.' A line was dashed through it. Underneath was some other saying about love, then another and another. She picked up the next sheet and it was the same. Gideon had never mentioned he was a poet. Why were they all about love?

After a sharp intake of breath and a weakening of the knees, she sat down on the swivel chair. Was there a woman in his life she didn't know about? Just as Keith had kept quiet about Cath, until they'd turned up one day and announced their engagement. 'Sorry, Mum,' he'd said, 'only I thought you might try and put her off me.' He was twenty-six and Christine had begun to hope he'd never leave the nest. She'd then spent months making him all his favourite meals and keeping his room spick and span, but he'd still gone ahead with the wedding and ended up with a girl more concerned with her local government job than her husband and children. And now Gideon was probably about to go off with some floozie.

Perhaps tonight she'd do the borsch he'd enjoyed so much. She smiled to herself, wondering if he'd talk about that Dustiesky chap through all three courses again.

ELEVEN

Donna was a week and a half late. What with falling in love and going up to London and organising the boys with her mum or Naomi, she'd forgotten to take the pill a couple of times. She'd bought a pregnancy testing kit with her spare travel money. Ross gave her the train fare each time she went to see him, but she caught the bus and saved a tenner. The test came up positive and she locked herself in the bathroom for a while to recover, Ryan bashing at the door and wanting squash.

'In a minute, darlin.'

It was Ross's, of course. She wouldn't go anywhere near the jerks who'd been sniffing around since Carl went inside. Blokes who have to belch halfway through their pints. She'd never even *seen* Ross with a pint. Oh dear, how was she going to explain this to her mum and everyone? And how would Ross take the news? She thought if she decided to keep it, she wouldn't tell him for a while. Just so he couldn't talk her out of it.

'Hang on, Ryan.'

She flushed the toilet and let herself out and decided to look at things differently. What were those positivity things she'd memorised from that magazine? She scooped up Ryan and kissed his fat cheek. 'I am *positive* and my life is *positive*,' she said over and over as they went down the stairs, until Ryan started joining in and she laughed and kissed his cheek again.

Hey, it seemed to be working already! There in her head was a picture of her and Ross and the three kiddies in one of those four-storey houses with fancy balconies that the bus always crawled past on its way to Marble Arch. They might even have an au pair. Not one that was too pretty, though. She wouldn't mind if Ross's kids came to stay, only it could be a bit hard being a mum to them, what with his girls being only two and four years younger than her.

'I now see problems simply as opportunities,' she said as she stood and looked around her kitchen, with its horrible fake-wood units and that door the Council hadn't been round to fix yet. She'd ask Ross for a dishwasher, definitely.

Kate was pondering on the turn her life had taken. Well, *their* lives. Far from being the evil-stepfather figure, Ed was turning out to be a kind of best friend-cum-fairy godmother to Charlie. He'd slip her an extra pound in the mornings from the paltry maintenance he got from Bernice, so she could buy something nice for lunch. 'A wholemeal sandwich,' he'd tell her. 'Make sure it's got salad in it.'

'Yeah, I will, thanks,' she'd say, and go off with saveloy and chips written all over her face.

He'd arranged for someone to tune the old piano, on which she'd had those three years of painful lessons, then enticed her out of her room to play simple duets with him while Jack carried on ridding the world of evil. 'Oh, I used to love this one,' Kate heard her say, the old Michael Aaron book open in front of them. She couldn't recall Charlie loving anything about the piano. When her grandfather gave her a chemistry set for her tenth birthday, it was the first thing she tried to blow up.

Kate noticed Charlie's hair was getting a little longer, and one day found the electric head shaver in the flip-top bin. She told Ed and he said, 'Ah, it worked then,' and smiled enigmatically and wouldn't say what.

Jack was pitching up less often and Charlie was joining them for meals and communal telly watching, playing with Georgia on the rug. Also, she'd started dropping into the shop in a smattering of makeup, chatting and flirting with Duggie and flicking through his music magazines. In spite of herself, Kate felt relieved. She'd often imagined having to tell everyone her thirty-year-old daughter lived with her 'friend' Roberta.

'Charlie's just been through what we called yearnineitis,' said Ed, 'when I was teaching at Thomas Cranmer.'

'You taught at Charlie's school?' exclaimed Kate.

'Well . . . I was a classroom assistant for a while, thinking I might like to go into teaching. But I found it knackering and demoralising and the pay was an insult.'

'When were you there?'

'Nineteen ninety-five.'

'Oh, right. Well before Charlie's time then. How long?'

'September the fifth to September the eighth.'

Yes, it was all going incredibly well, Kate thought, as she wove her way on foot through Oxford's early-evening gridlock. She and Ed never seemed to row, and, what's more, she came home to a warm and tidy house, nice food and a relatively upbeat Charlie. If Ed only had an income things would be totally perfect.

Once home, she called out 'Hi,' from the front door and could hear murmurings in the living room.

'OK,' Ed was saying to Charlie at the dining table – Georgia over one shoulder, lovely smells coming from the kitchen – 'if the cube root of pi plus zero is nine, then x will be the square of the hypotenuse divided by four over y minus the radius.' (Or similar.) He got up. 'See if you can do the next one on your own.'

When, at times like this, Kate felt she should walk around with 'Inadequate Person' flashing on her forehead, she had to stop and remember that Ed was incapable of transforming a chucked-out ghost of an armchair into something that would pay three tele-phone bills.

'Had a good day?' he asked.

'Thirty-five.'

'Better than yesterday, then.'

'Mm.' Yesterday's answer had been, 'Minus two fifty.' The amount she'd taken from the till for lunch. 'And you?'

'Got some writing done while Georgia was asleep.'

'Oh, good. How much?'

'A paragraph.'

'Oh.'

'It's a good one, though. Want to read it?'

'OK.'

He was right. It was great. But over a pot of tea they calculated that at a paragraph a day, Ed would finish his book when he was forty-seven.

'I should be able to speed up once Georgia's at nursery,' he said.

Kate rolled her eyes and said, 'That'll be a while,' then asked what was smelling so good.

'Lemon and tarragon chicken. Free range and organic, of course.'

'Aren't they expensive?'

'We made thirty-five pounds today, didn't we?'

'We?' Kate was about to say, but held back, remembering Ed had just added ten thousand to the value of her house.

My central character, Rickie, cut quite a dash. I'd decided, midway through the first chapter, not to encumber him with a young daughter: one, because she was being subjected to high-altitude oxygen deprivation; and two, because I found Rickie having masses of sex in tents and tea houses. It was all taking place in 1970, so the free love was totally plausible. With all references to little Olivia removed, I set about creating a character with Morse's intellect,

Sherlock Holmes's powers of detection, Sherpa Tenzing's stamina and Che Guevara's looks.

'He's loosely based on yourself then,' said my brother before laughing a good minute down the phone.

After that I decided not to talk about what I was writing. It's like opening the oven door on the soufflé, someone once said. I started taking Georgia off to a wonderful steamed-up east Oxford café with highchairs and toys to bash and toddlers to hold her attention, where I sat J. K. Rowling-like, scribbling away in a large notebook. After school, I'd pay Charlie to amuse Georgia for an hour while I typed everything up, printed it out, read it again and said, 'Bloody brilliant,' quietly to myself.

By the end of January, I had three chapters and a synopsis ready to send off to one or two lucky agents.

At the end of January, Donna was still throwing up every morning, Zoe and Matthew were spending weekends together, and Ross was forming an attachment to a 'dancer' from Romford.

Bronwen and Gideon had reconnected, meeting up regularly after work for a pint and a bar meal. Bronwen was delighted that he chose to wrench himself away from Christine's cuisine to spend time with her, but the truth was, Christine was suffering from a prolonged bout of flu and Bob had taken over the cooking. Both Bob and Gideon had endured gippy tummies for a night and a day after one particularly chewy chicken omelette, and a limp, bed-ridden Christine had ticked Bob off for not cooking the diced chicken first. He'd know next time, he said. The days Gideon phoned in to say he wouldn't be back to eat, Bob made himself cheese on toast, which he was quite good at.

'I'm afraid the missus is still poorly,' Bob was telling Ed over the phone.

'Oh dear.'

'So I reckon we'd better meet at your house next Tuesday, seeing as how you've got all that space now.'

'Yeah, OK. I'm sure it'll be fine with Kate.'

'What's the name of the chap you wanted us to read? Hang on – I'll write it down this time.'

'Farley Mowat,' Ed said slowly. '*Never Cry Wolf.*'

'Right. A thriller, is it? Whodunnit?'

Ed wondered if Bob would give it a miss if he heard it was a true story about a man watching a family of wolves in northern Canada, and he did so want them all to read it. 'More a passionate tale of survival with an animal-interest element.'

'You mean like a Dick Francis?'

'They've often been compared.'

Bob put the phone down and went back to Gideon's shirts, fresh out of the tumble dryer and, as far as he was concerned, in no need of ironing. He put them straight on to coathangers, took them up to Gideon's tip of a room, then went downstairs and crossed 'Wash and iron G.'s shirts (spray starch on collars)' off Christine's list.

'Right,' he said, reading glasses halfway down his nose, list at arm's length. 'What's next? "Dust and polish living-room ornaments".' Didn't sound too arduous. He grabbed the can and a duster from the cupboard under the sink and went through to the next room.

'Bloomin eck,' he said, as he stood before a legion of rabbits, squirrels, snoozing cats and little glass deer. Had Christine always had this many knick-knacks? He rolled up his sleeves, yanked the top off the aerosol and gave the first of Christine's hand-painted wall plates a good squirt. No, not quite right, he thought as a mass of white foam splattered the plate and the surrounding wallpaper. And oh eck, what a stench . . .

He coughed his way back to the kitchen, put his glasses back on and discovered he had oven cleaner in his hand. Soon remedied, he thought, fishing the dishcloth out of the washing-up bowl and dripping it through to the living room.

Fifteen minutes later, Bob heaved a three-foot cheese plant on to the sideboard to cover the damage to the wallpaper, and, rather than risk another aerosol disaster, went around the room blowing dust off the ornaments until lightheadedness forced him to put his feet up for a while in front of Gloria Hunniford.

'Why don't you come to town Friday evening?' Ross was asking Donna. 'I might have a little surprise for you,' he added seductively.

Donna's heart did a flip. He'd left Fiona! He had a gorgeous ring for her. From the West End in a little velvet box. 'OK.'

'Come to my flat at nine?'

His flat? 'Oh,' she said, disappointed. But hang on, maybe he was planning to take her out to a smart restaurant from there. Propose to her over a candlelit dinner.

'Donna? Hello?'

'Um, yeah, nine o'clock's fine.'

'And dress up. I want you to look spectacular.'

'Oh right.' She laughed. They would be going out after all. 'We're gonna do something special, are we?'

'Very special.'

She put the phone down and panicked. It was late Wednesday and all the shops were about to shut. That left her one and a half days to get a sexy but sophisticated outfit, plus new undies and a trim at Sandra's. She called Naomi and organised the next day's childminding, then rang her parents and arranged a small loan and some more childminding. They said yes, being happy to help her out and look after the boys while she went off to learn computer skills in Reading.

'It's a special weekend course,' she told them, thinking Ross would probably want her to stay till Sunday. 'Like compulsory.'

She didn't like fibbing to her mum and dad, but when she and Ross Kershaw MP were married they'd all look back and laugh.

Back in Marston, Christine lay in bed fretting about the dust building up, but didn't have the energy to do anything about it. Bob said he'd given everything a good going-over, bless him, but men never think about the corners and crevices. She had to say she was a bit disappointed in Gideon. Her Keith would have been popping in and out of the bedroom with cups of tea and the *Oxford Mail* and bits of news. Straightening her bedding and saying, 'Hurry up and get better, Mum. Dad's cooking's killing us.' But Gideon was out a lot, according to Bob. A woman, just as she'd suspected, but Bob didn't know who.

She shivered and pulled the duvet right up. If Gideon moved out she'd get someone a bit younger for the room. A nice lad who was fed up with living on those noodle pots and sniffing his socks before putting them on. Yes, that's what she'd do, she decided, turning herself slowly over and drifting back into sleep. 'So hot,' she whispered. She was suddenly burning up again and began dreaming that she was trapped in a house fire. Flames were leaping around her; she could smell the smoke. Acrid smoke.

'Damn and blast!' said Bob. He put the mini-extinguisher down and looked at the mess it had made everywhere. All to put out a measly little frying pan fire. Well, and the tea towel he'd thrown over it and half the curtain. Men weren't cut out to cook, he thought, wheezing and opening all the windows, just as women weren't put on this earth to lay carpet. They might be training up young Tessa at Plus Floors, but wait till she found herself alone on a job with a tricky alcove and a blunt Stanley knife.

Bob cleaned everything up, took the burned curtain down, said a silent but urgent prayer for Christine's rapid recovery and made himself cheese on toast.

As Gideon still hadn't taken the bed plunge, Bronwen was keeping Malcolm on a back burner. On Thursday they met up at their usual place then decided to take a stroll through University Parks. Malcolm was talking about the foreign student he gave conversation classes to in his Osney home. Bronwen had never been invited there. He'd been to her house once for a pre-concert sherry and she'd sat looking at him, rather puzzled by the lack of desire on her part to take his glass off him and lead him up to her noisy brass bed.

'It's only three hours a week but it's totally exhausting,' he was saying.

As far as Bronwen could make out this one student was all Malcolm did. He'd mentioned a well-to-do mother, so she gathered he must have a private income.

'Teaching can be very tiring,' she sympathised. 'I've often had to do it to support my travelling.'

'Oh, to travel,' sighed Malcolm as they entered Pitt Rivers museum with its collection of artefacts from all over the globe.

'Well, why don't you?' suggested Bronwen, and when he shrugged and said, 'Mm, one day, perhaps,' she wondered if she might ask him to join her on her next trip – back to India, perhaps.

They wandered round the wonderfully dark and cluttered room, admiring the enormous totem pole, pulling faces at the shrunken heads and giving silly names to the Egyptian mummies. Yes, he'd make a jolly nice travelling companion, thought Bronwen.

Afterwards, they had a cup of tea in Little Clarendon Street, then when they were walking back into town they heard, 'Malcolm!' and a man on a bicycle screeched to a halt beside them. Between the helmet and the scarf, Bronwen could make out he was in early middle age. Beautifully clear skin, she noticed.

'This is Larry,' said Malcolm. 'Larry, Bronwen.'

Larry pulled off his glove and shook Bronwen's hand. 'I'm glad I've bumped into you, Malc,' he said, panting. 'I'm just on my way to the covered market. Thought I'd get us rainbow trout for tonight. What do you think?'

'Trout would be lovely.'

'Right.' Larry put his glove on, adjusted his scarf and leaned over and kissed Malcolm's cheek. 'See you back at home.'

On Friday evening, Donna found herself with an hour to kill, so went into a sandwich bar run by foreigners and ordered a cup of coffee. When it arrived she was told, 'Please to drink up quickly. Café close in five minute.' She could *never* live in London, she thought, then remembered the four-storey house and the au pair and decided of course she could. She had butterflies, and wondered exactly what surprise Ross had for her. Would tonight be a good time to tell him about the baby? A double celebration?

When all the chairs but hers were up on tables, Donna paid and went out into the cold February air. Twenty-five past eight. She'd borrowed the big navy coat her mum got from her catalogue, but still shivered as she walked around peering in closed shops and checking her watch every two minutes. Maybe she should have worn a cardie over her thin clingy dress with a slit. She had flimsy strappy shoes on and by the time she buzzed Ross's doorbell at nine on the dot, she'd lost the feeling in most of her toes.

'Wow,' he said when he took her coat. Down in the foyer she'd fluffed up her thick hair, applied another layer of lipstick and sprayed more Yardley on. 'I've just opened a bottle of Margaux I've been saving for a special occasion,' Ross told her. 'Do you like it?'

'Er . . . yeah.'

He took her hand and she could hear romantic music coming from the living room. 'This is Kirsty,' he said as he led her through.

'Sorry?'

Sitting on the sofa was a dark-haired girl in a short skirt and extremely high boots. Kirsty? Wasn't that a Scottish name? This was the special occasion then. He wanted her to meet his eldest daughter! Better create a good impression she thought, holding out her hand. 'How do you do?'

The girl laughed and got up. She took Donna's hand and kissed it, leaving a big smudge of lipstick behind. Donna was a bit surprised but thought maybe that was what they did in Scotland.

'Kirsty was about to do a little dance for me,' said Ross.

Donna said, 'Oh, yeah?' and wondered how on earth she could do a Highland fling or whatever in those boots.

Ross turned Marvin Gaye up, then sat on the sofa and patted it. 'Come here,' he told Donna.

When Kirsty was down to a G-string and rotating her arse just inches from Ross's face, Donna felt like all the walls of his flat had fallen on her. Only she wasn't in pain, just completely numb. She remembered drunk Zoe. Threesomes . . . kinky stuff. Ross had hold of her hand and was moving it slowly towards his lap while he undid his flies. She looked at his face: smirking, eyes glued to the girl's bum.

'Rub me and suck me,' he told Donna.

She stared in a blank, disbelieving way at him, and slowly bent over, took him in her mouth and dug her teeth in. She let go and quickly sat up again, and while Ross screamed and doubled up, Kirsty stopped gyrating and Marvin carried on singing about sexual healing.

'Bitch,' Ross was saying between groans. 'Bitch.' He heaved himself up and slapped Donna's face. It stung like mad and brought tears to her eyes.

'Total bastard,' she yelled, and he hit her again. This time harder.

Before she got on the bus at Victoria, Donna went into the railway station and found a photo booth. She had just enough money for this and a taxi once she got to Oxford. After sitting on the stool and seeing her reflection she began sobbing uncontrollably. Swollen and bruising already. When the developed photos dropped down into the slot she picked them up and in a quiet wobbly voice said, 'Every day in every way I feel more positive and optimistic.'

TWELVE

At least this one had bothered to put fingers to keyboard. 'Dear Dr Adams,' it said,

> Thank you for sending us the opening chapters of your novel *CLIMB AND PUNISHMENT*. Although you have an assured, easy writing style, we do feel that the Kathmandu trail has had its day in both the fiction and non-fiction fields, and would suggest that you turn your considerable talent to subjects which strike a chord with today's 25–45 male readership – relationships, personal grooming, cookery, DIY, new parenthood, etc. Although we are unable to . . . *blah blah* . . . wish you success with . . . *blah blah* . . .
>
> Best regards, Rupert Jones-Bellingham.

I read it a third time then flung it on the dining table. I wasn't sure I wanted someone called Rupert telling me what to write, but quite warmed to him for the 'considerable talent' comment.

Kate read the letter before going off to the shop and said, 'If that's what they want just send them your diary.'

I kissed her goodbye and thought: Hey!

It was Saturday, so Charlie would sleep till mid-afternoon. I busied myself with housework and shopping and Georgia all morning, then when the vision of unloveliness finally plonked down the stairs and covered my newly hoovered house in toast crumbs, I asked nicely if she'd baby-sit while I did a bit of work.

She yawned, stretched, went horizontal on the sofa and switched the television on. 'Three fifty an hour.'

'It's gone up!'

'Weekend rate.'

'Two fifty and I'll help you with your Fifties Britain essay.'

'Alright.'

Diary of a Homebody I typed upstairs, *by Ed Adams.*

Thurs 17th: Got up and made us all breakfast. In our kitchen you can wash a plate, fry an egg and let the cat out without moving from one spot. Small isn't the word. Come to think of it, small *is* the word.

I sat back, not totally convinced that people wouldn't rather be reading about sex, drugs and Tibetan prayer wheels. The diary was pure fiction, of course. Our kitchen was big enough to play table tennis in, as Charlie and I had done just the day before. I completely thrashed her and she sulked, so we played again and I managed to lose 6-21.

OK.

Went to the supermarket, where sixty-something 'Ray' on checkout scanned all my two-for-ones and said was I planning a trip on Noah's ark. I laughed and said, 'Ah yes, good one,' even though he'd asked me the same question last week. Once again I made a point of avoiding 'Debbie' two tills down, who never fails to sneeze into a mangled tissue, obliging you to wash every single item when you get home.

I felt tempted to have my hero snatched and bundled into a large van in the supermarket car park, but, aware that abduction hadn't featured in Rupert's criteria, I sent him off to Do-It-All for a shower curtain.

My brother came for dinner. Kate was exhausted, Charlie was morose and I had my mind on the new novel. Luckily, Will had the ability to hold an entire dinner-party conversation by himself and managed to cover dietary supplements, slimming aids and the damage cheap trainers can do to your feet, while the rest of us chucked in only the occasional 'Mm'.

'So have you found an agent, Ed?' he asked during dessert.

I'd been miles away. 'Er, actually, I'm working on a new project at the moment.'

'They rejected it then?'

'Well, yes. But I only sent it to three—'

'Ha!' he let forth with unalloyed delight. How he hated it that I'd got a doctorate while he had a Third in Sports Studies.

'I thought it was dead good,' said Charlie through a mouthful of raspberry crumble.

'What was?' I asked.

'*Climb and Punishment*. Read it on the computer when you were out.'

Oh Jesus, all those sex scenes.

'Only I didn't understand all the stuff about the gasman.'

'Sorry?'

'You know . . . they kept saying, "it's a gasman. What a gasman." I mean, like what would the gasman be doing in Africa in the first place? Didn't make no sense.'

I was torn. Should I teach her the 1970 equivalent of 'wicked', give her a geography lesson, or tick her off for using double negatives?

'Must be good to know fourteen-year-olds rate you,' said Will with a hearty laugh.

'Fifteen,' Charlie told him. 'I had a birthday last week.'

Will smacked his brow. 'Oh *God*, Ed told me but I forgot. I'm so sorry, Charlie. Here . . .' He took his wallet from a back pocket and counted out two twenty-pound notes and a tenner. 'Buy yourself something nice, eh?'

Charlie's eyes were as big as her dinner plate. 'Wow. Hey, Mum look at . . . Oh.'

Will and I turned to find Kate fast asleep, head lolled, spoonful of crumble in her hand. She'd had a long hard day at the shop. 'Twelve hundred and fifty-five!' she'd announced when she got back. I took the spoon from her, closed her mouth and lifted her from her chair.

'God, I *never* wanna be old,' said Charlie.

On Sunday morning, Zoe and Matthew were wandering hand-in-hand around Habitat, Matthew having said that he loved coming to stay with her but probably couldn't endure too many Saturday evenings on a director's chair. Zoe wanted to buy every sofa in the place, but didn't even have the money for one, what with her colossal mortgage and the cost of commuting. Still, it was nice just being out shopping together.

'I haven't done anything this couply for years,' she told him with a hug, and he stopped, turned her round and kissed her long and hard in the lighting section.

'Marry me,' he said.

'Marry you?' she cried as a bit of an audience gathered.

'I love you so much. Be my wife?'

'Aaahh,' said a woman with two spotlights in her basket.

Zoe stroked Matthew's hair. 'And I love you too.'

'So . . . what do you say?'

'Say yes!' someone called out.

'Well, um . . . OK, *yes*,' said Zoe and they kissed again.

Eight shoppers, two assistants and the store manager clapped and whistled. Habitat had never seen such spontaneity.

Zoe drew back. 'But . . .'

Everyone held their breath and Matthew said, 'What?'

'I don't think I can be Zoe Soper. Sounds like a Japanese prime minister.'

He laughed and twirled her round and somebody said, 'Anyone got a camera?'

'Tell me about this guy you were seeing before me,' said Matthew over a pre-lunch celebratory gin and tonic. They'd laid her little kitchen table and were sitting waiting for the pasta to cook.

'Oh, nothing to tell. He was a complete . . . not very nice. And not very available.'

'Married?'

Zoe nodded.

'Did you love him?'

'I thought I did.' She put a hand on Matthew's knee and squeezed. 'But now I know I didn't. He's . . . um . . .'

'What?'

'Oh, nothing.'

'Tell me.'

'Let's just say he's in the public eye.'

'Really?' He winked at her. 'Go on. It won't go any further. Promise.'

Zoe finished her drink. Her breathing quickened and her eyes began darting here and there. She felt her stomach tighten.

Matthew stroked her hair. 'Hey, it's all right. You don't have to tell me.'

'Ross Kershaw. The MP.'

'Christ,' he said, staring into space for a while then looking back at her. 'No, Zoe, don't cry. Please. Here, have my serviette. Oh, shit.'

Bronwen had nothing against gays, she just didn't want to be going out with one. She'd focus on Gideon now, she decided, although she might consider the odd concert with Malcolm. She picked up the phone and tapped out Gideon's number. Bob answered so she put on a strong Welsh accent until Gideon got to the phone.

'Fancy lunch at The Trout?' she asked.

'Ah, um . . .' said Gideon. 'Bit of a trek, what?'

Bronwen shook her head and tutted to herself. So much for taking him to the Canadian north, her latest idea since reading *Never Cry Wolf.* 'Shall I come to the Victoria Arms in Marston? Can't be more than a three-minute walk for you?'

'Splendid,' said Gideon, his stomach rumbling, the thought of a pub roast making him salivate.

'Give me half an hour to cycle there.'

Gideon pulled a face. 'Really?' At least an hour until they'd eat then.

Upstairs, Christine was making an effort to drag herself out of despondency and get back to the helm. But what was the point? They were all managing quite well without her, thank you. Bob said he'd been doing a grand job with the cooking for himself and Gideon. Everything he cooked smelt like cheese on toast to her, but that was probably her virus. Anyway, she was sure Gideon would be off soon. That Ed seemed to be taking over all the reading group catering. And when was the last time Keith or Heather turned up for one of Mum's Sunday roasts?

She picked up her magazine and scissors, but when she got to the recipe page she loosened her fingers and let everything flop on to the duvet. Let's face it, she just wasn't needed any more.

'Thought I'd do us a nice Welsh rarebit for our lunch!' she heard Bob call from the kitchen.

'Ah yes, just the ticket!' replied Gideon.

'I think I'll have the roast beef,' said Bronwen twenty-five minutes later. The fast bike ride had given her quite an appetite.

Gideon said, 'Me too.'

After ordering, they took their drinks over to a recently vacated table, where they settled themselves in and talked about Thomas Hardy. Gideon liked his novels but Bronwen thought his poetry wonderful. 'Such depth.'

Damn, thought Gideon, if only he'd known that a few weeks ago. 'One has to admire him for pushing the boundaries, as it were.'

'You mean sex out of wedlock and so on?' asked Bronwen.

'Yes,' said Gideon, whose eyes, with an apparent will of their own, started darting back and forth between Bronwen's breasts.

Bronwen, aware of their appeal to Gideon, had taken to wearing fine-knit, tight-fitting jumpers that moulded themselves to her cleavage. She arched her back for maximum effect and dared to wonder if this might be the day he finally got to see her appendix scar.

When they'd finished their lunches and three glasses of wine and were sitting back with their coffees, she sat up very straight, pulled her sweater down, tucked her tummy in and pushed her chest out. 'Why don't we take a taxi to my place?'

She smiled and put a hand on his arm, and Gideon raised his eyes to hers. 'But what about your bicycle?'

'Bugger the bicycle.'

When Kate got home on Tuesday, Ed had everything organised for the reading group meeting: chairs, lighting, a small buffet that she helped herself to. She showered and changed and arrived downstairs just as Bronwen was removing her cycle helmet and saying, 'Terrific book, Ed. Well done!'

Ed wobbled his head proudly and said, 'Thanks,' as though he himself had written *Never Cry Wolf.*

'Although you've rather naughtily broken our fiction-only rule,' Bronwen added, wagging a finger at him.

Ed hung his head in mock shame. 'Sorry,' he said.

'Ah, well . . .'

Next came Bob who had it clutched in his hand, a bookmark showing that he'd got to about page eight. Then Gideon, smelling strongly of Lenor, and Zoe looking absolutely radiant.

'It's been a *lovely* day, hasn't it?' she said.

'Er . . . yeah.' It had rained from ten onwards where Kate had been.

Zoe smiled. 'Mmm, something smells delicious, as usual,' she said, and beamed all the way into the living room.

Ed fussed with the cushions, making sure everyone had one, then looked around at the group. 'So, it's just Donna to come then?'

She told them she'd fallen down the last couple of stairs and bashed her face on the telephone table.

'Gosh, Donna, how dreadful,' said Bronwen. 'Have you tried arnica? It works wonders on bruising.'

'Just frozen peas.'

Nobody could actually see too much of Donna's bruising, although it was obviously there. She was wearing her foundation thick and had her hair down so it dangled over her cheeks as she sat looking at the book on her lap.

'Well,' said Ed, waving his Farley Mowat in the air, 'who's managed to read it?'

Donna shook her head and Bob said he'd only made a start, what with running around for Christine.

'Fabulous, fabulous book,' cried Bronwen. 'Doesn't it just make you want to go and study these darling creatures in their own habitat?'

'Perhaps not with the gusto of Mowat,' chuckled Gideon. 'The chap lived on nothing but mice for a while in his endeavour to understand wolf life.'

Ed said, 'That was pretty amazing, wasn't it?'

Bob was looking a bit blank so Kate thought she'd fill him and Donna in. 'You see the Canadian government saw the wolf as a terrible threat to the caribou population, and also inclined to prey on any humans in their vicinity. Farley Mowat set off to prove them wrong.'

'Oh aye?' said Bob, rather unenthusiastically.

'You know,' chipped in Bronwen, 'after *Never Cry Wolf* was translated into Russian, the Soviet government banned the killing of wolves.'

Bob nodded, and Donna – head still down – murmured, 'Right.'

'Can I read a passage?' asked Zoe. 'He's quite a witty writer, isn't he?' She laughed and flicked her hair back and Kate thought she'd like some of whatever Zoe was on. 'I absolutely loved this bit on page twenty-seven!'

During the break, Kate noticed Donna wasn't milling around Ed's buffet with the others, and found her in the kitchen getting herself a glass of tap water.

'Oh no, don't,' she said. 'We've got bottled in the fridge.'

'Is it fizzy?' asked Donna. 'Only fizzy's giving me wind at the moment.'

'It's OK, we've got both.'

'Oh, ta.'

Kate got some out of the fridge, poured a glassful and handed it over. When Donna looked at her, just inches away, Kate could see her face was quite lopsided with swelling. Her eyes were red-rimmed and sad. 'Are you going to be all right, Donna? Maybe you should go home and take it easy.'

'That's a laugh,' she said, pulling a chair out from the table and sitting down. 'You haven't met my boys.'

'No. I bet they're great, though. I sometimes wish I'd had a boy as well as a girl.'

'They're a bit of a handful.'

'I can imagine.'

'Especially Jake, my oldest. Little devil he is.'

'Well, I think you should be very proud of yourself, bringing up two children on your own.'

'Er . . . three, actually.'

'Really? I thought you—'

She leaned back and patted her tummy.

'Donna!'

'Yeah, I know. It's a right mess.'

Kate joined her at the table. 'Are you sure you'll be able to manage? I mean, have you thought about, you know . . .'

'Getting rid of it?'

'Mm.'

'Don't think I could do that.'

'What about the father? Is he likely to be supportive?'

'Uh-uh.' Donna's eyes became watery and she pulled a wad of tissue from her sleeve. By the time it reached her nose, tears were forming lines in her foundation. 'No one knows. Not my mum even. They'd never believe me anyway.'

'What do you mean?'

Donna wiped her eyes with the back of a hand. 'It would be like: oh yeah, Mum and Dad, you know I told you I was doing a computer course in Reading? Well, I was actually seeing this violent married bastard drug-addict MP in Shepherd's Bush. I tell you, Kate, if this kid starts talking in a stupid Scottish accent, I'll—' She stopped and looked up. Ed had wandered in with an empty orange juice jug.

Kate cried, 'No!' and flew at him. As he reversed out of the door she was pushing shut, she whispered, 'You are *not* going to believe this.'

'Sorry, out of orange juice,' I told the others. 'Plenty of apple left. Coffee in the pot.'

'Got anything stronger?' whispered Bob. 'Only I'm a bit out of sorts.'

'Well, there is, but it's in the kitchen and I'm barred from there. Bit of a heart-to-heart going on.'

'Ah, right you are. Never mind. It's Christine, you see.'

'Oh yes?'

'Very worried about her, I am.'

I steered him over to a corner. 'Is she still ill?'

'Oh, the flu's gone. She just won't get out of bed. Keeps saying nobody needs her any more. I tell her I do, but that's not enough, it seems. Anyway, it was a dreadful blow, our Keith moving out. That was a long time ago, mind you, and it's helped that Gideon's been there for her to pamper, but now he's got this girlfriend.'

'That would be Bronwen,' I said, and Bob's head spun towards his lodger.

'Well, I never!'

I lowered my voice. 'Are you saying that if Christine had someone to nurture, perhaps a very little person – say three or four hours a day at, oh, five or six pounds an hour – she'd get better?' I pointed at the ceiling and could see the penny drop. Bob raised his eyebrows and asked to use the phone.

Two minutes later he wandered back in looking decidedly happier. 'She said to tell you she doesn't want paying.'

'*No!*' I kept saying.

'Yes, *really!*' Kate kept saying.

'Can you believe it!' we both kept saying.

Everyone had gone and we were slumped in armchairs staring into space. After a small silence I said, 'You know you had that trip to London two weeks ago, supposedly to buy fabric in the East End . . .'

'OK,' she said, throwing up her hands. 'I had sex with Ross Kershaw and six lap dancers.'

'Huh! I knew it.' I tapped my glass for a while then looked up at her. 'I wonder if we should warn Bronwen?'

THIRTEEN

'Choo choo, choo choo . . . here comes the train,' said Christine. 'Wheeere's the tunnel?'

Georgia obviously had no idea what she was talking about but nevertheless opened her mouth and let the plastic spoon in.

'Good *girl*.'

Bob looked on from the other side of the dining table. It was grand having Christine back to her old self. The house somehow squeaked and sparkled again, and had an altogether nicer smell. The downside was that Gideon was around more, but not, he'd noticed, getting those larger portions at mealtimes.

After lunch, Christine put Georgia down for an hour's nap while she cleared up and rinsed out the towelling bib and wiped the old wooden highchair. Lucky they'd hung on to it. Keith's children had used it in the days when they regularly trooped over for lunch on Sundays. Christine had also kept the old cot and one or two mobiles, so it was a bit of a home from home for Georgia really. Our Georgia, as she and Bob were now calling her. 'What time's our Georgia coming today?' Bob would ask. Or, 'I reckon our Georgia's going to be a real cracker when she's older.'

'Oh, she's perfect now,' Christine would insist. 'Children shouldn't be allowed to grow older.'

Later, they all went to the park and stopped at the playground where Christine went gently back and forth on a swing with Georgia chuckling away on her lap.

'Eh up, this takes me back!' shouted Bob next to them, swinging himself energetically. 'We'd get so high we'd do what we called the bumps. Wheeeee . . . almost there!'

After they'd all had enough of swinging, Bob sat on the little wooden roundabout with Georgia while Christine pushed. Round and round they went. Christine said, 'Boo!' every time they passed and Georgia chuckled. Push – 'Boo!' – chuckle. Push – 'Boo!' – chuckle.

After a while an ashen Bob said, 'I think that might be enough now, love!'

I collected Georgia at four, as usual.

'Bob's a bit poorly,' Christine explained as we listened to him retching in the cloakroom. 'Nothing contagious, don't worry.' She handed me Georgia and an extra carrier bag I hadn't brought along. 'Just one or two things I've run up on the Singer.'

'Really?' I started to open the bag but thought, What if I don't like them? Would it show in my face? And closed it again. 'That's very kind of you.'

'Oh, I enjoy it. And she's such a tiny tot, I'm able to use up all my little remnants. How's the book coming along?'

'Great, yeah.'

'I expect it'll take you a while, won't it? To finish it, I mean.'

Three months tops, but Christine so looked as though she wanted me to say fifteen years.

'Mm, yeah. A long way to go yet.'

Out in the camper van, Georgia all tied in, I checked out the contents of the bag and couldn't believe what I was seeing. Neither could Kate when she arrived home.

'God,' she said, going through little dresses and dungarees that Georgia would be big enough for by the spring. 'They're amazing. Really stylish and such lovely materials. Just look at that stitching. How much did she charge you?'

'Nothing, of course. It's Christine, you know. I have to force fifty quid a week on her for the childminding.'

'That woman's got so many wasted skills. I wonder if she'd do some sewing for me. Cushions and things.'

'Could you wait till I've finished my book before you offer her another job?'

'What page are you on now?'

'A hundred and three.'

I was actually on page forty-three, but a hundred and three sounded better. The entire story was mapped out in my head, so I wasn't really lying. Rickie was going to start an illicit liaison with a mum, Amanda. They'd met at the baby clinic, where they discovered they both had colicky babies. Sharing tips on gripe water

205

and similar was about to turn into sharing a duvet – all to be conveniently documented in his diary, which I'd get his partner to come across while he's 'at the gym' one evening. I saw the climax as a *Kramer vs. Kramer* tear-jerker of a custody battle, which he wins because his partner spends eighty per cent of her life on planes. Along the way, my hero would strip the fitted pine cupboards, go on clothes-shopping sprees, bake sundried tomato and rosemary ciabattas and cry a lot. Rupert was going to love it.

Kate took Georgia off for a bath – their little bit of bonding time – and I rustled up a roasted vegetable and couscous dish, writing down all the stages as I went along in order to casually drop the recipe into the book. When Kate read the first couple of chapters of *Diary of a Homebody* the other week she said, 'Great, yeah. But you know, if Rickie was Vickie I could never speak to you again.'

Kate hadn't expected Donna's home to be so nice. All done on a budget, obviously, but there were tasteful cream sofa throws and bright cushions, arty mirror frames Donna might have painted herself, the odd interesting poster, oatmeal carpet and quite a few plants. Shelves of books. One or two toys were lying around, but on the whole the place was incredibly clean and tidy. And at nine thirty on a Monday morning! To see Donna in her own home was to see a completely different Donna. Donna the woman. With responsibilities and a remarkable sense of correctness. Her books went in height order, each plant had both saucer and cork mat beneath it. The video player showed exactly the same time as the wall clock. Kate took in the glass-top coffee table and wondered if even Ed could have fanned magazines out quite so perfectly.

'Excuse the kitchen,' said Donna, leading Kate through, then pointing at some nasty brown units. 'I wish the Council would come and replace them. And fix the back door. Still . . . I suppose it's not too bad.'

'You've got it looking really nice, Donna.' The worktops were clear, the cooker gleamed.

'Thanks. I keep meaning to come to your shop. Not to buy anything, of course. Too skint for that. Just to get some ideas. Mind you, haven't got the energy for anything these days.'

'How are you feeling?'

'Well, the sickness has stopped, which is good. Tea or coffee?'

'Oh, whatever you're having.'

'Tea?'

'Yep. Thanks.'

Kate wondered why the reading group hadn't met there, then remembered Donna saying the boys charged around till eight or nine most evenings. 'It's nice and quiet when Jake and Ryan are at school and playgroup,' said Donna, as though reading Kate's mind. 'Course, that'll all change when number three comes along.'

'You're definitely keeping it then?'

'Oh, yeah.'

'Have you told—'

'Bastard Kershaw? No, I'm working on that one.'

'Your parents?'

'Not yet. Though I expect they'll notice soon enough.' She

pulled her baggy top tight against her stomach to show she was already bulging a bit. Poor kid, thought Kate, going through it all a third time when she so desperately wanted to study. Kate had just about managed one child and a career, with the help of friends and, for years, an allowance from her father that covered childminding. She guessed Donna's options were more limited, and suddenly felt like jumping on a London train and cornering Ross Kershaw herself.

Donna made tea in a pot and carried cups and saucers and everything through to the living room on a tray. 'Help yourself to ginger thins.'

'Thanks.'

Kate was dying to know how Donna and Ross met. Such an unlikely liaison. Had Zoe been involved somehow? 'Um . . . I hope you don't mind me asking,' she said.

'Mm?'

'But, how did you meet Ross Kershaw?'

Donna was prepared for this. 'Well, I was having a drink with a friend in London. Last November. Anyway, he came and talked to us and took my number.'

'Oh, right.'

'Then he phoned up a few days later. Wanted me to come and see him. Said he'd pay the train fare. He was a bit ancient, but I was sort of flattered really.'

'Yes. Well, he's very nice-looking.'

'He's a year older than my dad.'

'God.'

'Only my dad's a really nice person.' She bent over and pulled a shoe box from behind the sofa. 'Here, look at this.' From inside the box she took a set of four photos and handed them to Kate. 'That was straight after he hit me. It was worse on the Saturday.'

'Oh, Donna, what a thug. How awful it must have been for you. God, imagine if this all came out.'

Donna grinned and took her old diary from the box. 'Yeah, imagine.' Then her expression changed. 'Only I'm not sure I'd want that. You know, for the baby's sake? And my boys, and my mum and dad. It's all a bit—'

'Bloody hell, has he written a book?' Kate's eyes had wandered over to Donna's pine bookcase and seen 'Ross Kershaw' in bold red. 'May I look?'

'Sure. But I wouldn't bother. Even I can tell it's crap.'

Kate tutted and took it from the shelf. 'What do you mean, even you? You underestimate yourself, you know, Donna. Yuck, what an awful cover.'

She flicked through pages, then stopped and chewed on a finger as she read. 'Jesus,' she said, then laughed. 'This is appalling. Listen to this: "Natalie looked pleadingly at him across her desk, her long auburn hair tumbling over her shoulders and down to her pert breasts. 'Russ, I'm begging you, don't do this to me. No man has ever satisfied me as you do, or as often. You're the best, Russ. If you leave me now . . .'" Oh my God, Donna, I don't believe this! "'. . . it will be like putting my heart through that shredder over there'".'

'Told you.'

Kate read on and laughed so much her stomach hurt. 'Can I borrow it?'

'Yeah. I was gonna give it to my mum for her next car boot sale.'

'Oh no, don't do that. It's a classic.'

'What, like *Jane Eyre*?'

Gideon's students were having a reading week, so enabling him to sit up in Bronwen's bed, dropping breakfast on her lace bedspread. 'A fine satirist,' he said, 'Tobias Smollett. But hugely criticised for the baseness of his characters.' He bit into a slice of wholemeal toast and nodded to himself.

Bronwen had a shawl around her as she was right beside the draughty window. She rarely bothered with breakfast herself. 'I've never read him.'

'Ah, yes, well, not exactly a household name. I'd recommend you start with *Adventures of Peregrine Pickle*. I've got a copy if you'd like to borrow it?'

Bronwen wasn't sure mid-eighteenth-century political satire was her thing, but nevertheless said, 'Mm, thank you.' Should she remove that dollop of marmalade from the pillowcase, or not draw attention to it?

'He's thought to have strongly influenced Dickens, you know. And Scott actually acknowledged his influence on him.'

'Is that so?' Best to leave it. She'd chuck everything in the Hotpoint later. 'I'm just reading Anita Shreve.'

210

'Who?'

'It's contemporary.'

'Ah.' Gideon started on his second round of toast. 'Of course, one thing that didn't help was that Smollett tended to alienate people. Had something of a short fuse.'

'Did he?' Bronwen glanced anxiously at her alarm clock. She'd phoned work to say she had an early doctor's appointment, but didn't want to push her luck. 'Well,' she told Gideon, trying to ease back the bedding without disturbing his plate. 'I suppose I should get going. Mondays can be very busy. People have finished their books over the weekend. Plus we get the OAPs who haven't spoken to a soul since Friday, poor things.'

'Had a bit of a go at some admiral chap and went to prison for libel.'

'Gosh.' Probably better to just shuffle down to the end of the bed. There, she thought, when her feet hit the floorboards. She turned and looked back at her lover and felt a small flutter of elation.

He returned her smile and held forth his empty plate. 'Any more where that came from?'

SPRING

FOURTEEN

Ross Kershaw was heavily disguised as the train pulled into Oxford station: cap pulled down low; sunglasses, despite the dreary damp day. He'd wanted Pritchard to come to London to discuss the Oxford Union debate, but the man had inconveniently tripped and sprained his ankle on his way out of the Bodleian.

The trouble was, there were just too many women to avoid in Oxford. Well, two; but that was enough. Actually, three if you counted that little post-grad he'd bedded the time before last. She still occasionally left him messages, but he thought it best to avoid girls with boyfriends who rowed for England.

He made a beeline for the taxi rank and asked for the Banbury Road, collar right up as he knew Zoe commuted by train. He'd committed himself to this damned debate a couple of weeks ago, but now regretted it. Still, to be seen taking a strong stand on drugs might boost his reputation, particularly with the PM. There was talk of a reshuffle. If he didn't get a ministerial position this time, he might well stand down at the next election. Go back to the salmon farm idea.

'Did I hear you say Banbury Road?' asked a young woman through the driver's window. 'Only that's where I'm going. Perhaps we could share?'

Ross swiftly removed his cap and glasses and opened the door beside him. 'Of course.'

How old, he wondered. Twenty? Slim, but not skinny. Long shiny locks. He took her rucksack off her and placed it on the seat to his right, forcing her to squeeze into a tiny space on his left; his best side. 'My pleasure,' he said. 'Been somewhere nice?'

'Just London. And you?'

'I work in London, actually.' He paused and counted to five. 'I'm an MP.'

'Wow!' said the girl, as though she'd learned he was the Sultan of Brunei. 'Actually, I thought you looked familiar.' She ran a hand through her hair and stared wide-eyed at him. 'You know I've *always* wanted to see the House of Commons.'

'Well,' said Ross, pulling a pen from his jacket pocket, 'I'm sure that can be arranged. Why don't you give me your phone number?'

'He reminded me of my Uncle Steve,' Donna was telling us.

'Oh yes?' said Bronwen.

'Yeah. When Uncle Steve goes to like Minorca or something, he always takes custard creams and Walkers crisps and one of those titchy jars of Marmite. We had this holiday in Lanzarote once and he came too. Anyway, one day we found him in his hotel room eating cold baked beans and a Safeway's malt loaf, reading the *TV Times*. He said, "Bugger, they're repeating *Randall and Hopkirk* tonight," and my mum told him to get a life.'

'He does rather sound like Ma— er, the guy in the book,' said Zoe. 'Some people don't cope too well with change.'

'Mm, that was a nice analogy, Donna,' said Bronwen.

'Yes,' said I.

'Yes,' echoed Kate.

We were all being nice to Donna because she was looking tired, and – barring steroids and a full-time nanny – obviously wasn't going to fulfil her dream of going to college in the autumn. She put her hand up.

'Sorry for being so thick,' she said, arching her back and putting her other hand in the small of it, 'but why was my story about Uncle Steve an allergy?'

Gideon leaped in with, 'Ah, let me explain,' but Donna said could he hang on a bit because she had to pee again.

We weren't getting very far with *The Accidental Tourist*, what with having spent the first ten minutes discussing how to pronounce the central character's name. Macon. Now would that rhyme with bacon, or be Mackon or Mason? Bronwen had chosen the book, but couldn't enlighten us. Both Kate and I had seen the film but couldn't remember. We finally settled on 'he'.

'He's probably Anne Tyler's most memorable character,' said Bronwen.

'Oh, but what about the woman in *Ladder of Years*?' asked Zoe. 'Just wandering off in a totally unpremeditated way. Leaving her family on the beach, catching a bus and starting a new life. I loved her.'

'I liked the young guy in *A Patchwork Planet*,' chipped in Kate.

Zoe said she'd been meaning to read that one, and Bronwen got up and hooked it off one of her shelves. 'And have you both read *Breathing Lessons*?' she asked.

'Of course!' they cried.

Bob and I were giving each other fancy-a-game-of-cards? looks, but then Donna returned and Gideon took five minutes to tell her that analogous meant similar, and before we knew it Bronwen was serving up coffee and banana cake.

I was lurking by the kitchen door, eavesdropping.

'Now I'm like obviously pregnant he couldn't be really shitty to me, could he?'

'You've decided to go and see him then?' asked Kate.

'Yeah. Maybe later this week, or next week. I dunno.'

'And do you want me to come with you?'

'No, I'll be all right, thanks. I wish he was a bit nearer, though. I get knackered just taking the boys to school these days.'

I stepped into the room and said, 'Actually, Ross Kershaw's going to be here at the Union in a few weeks' time. If you want to save yourself a trip to London.'

'You know!' cried Donna.

'Uh, yeah.'

Kate looked embarrassed. 'Sorry. I haven't told anyone else, though. I promise.'

'Good,' said Donna, topping up her water glass. 'What's the Union? Is it that place that Prince and Jon Bon Jovi played at?'

'Well, not exactly played,' I told her. 'It's a debating society, and, yes, sometimes they invite rock stars and supermodels along.'

'And what's Shitface going to be doing there?'

'Oh, I can't remember exactly. I think it goes something like "This house believes the Government is undermining its war on drugs with too much friendly fire".'

'Don't get it.'

'Friendly fire,' I explained, 'is when you accidentally kill some of your own soldiers or allies.'

'Like the Americans are always doing?'

'Exactly. So I suppose what they're saying is that although the Government's trying to eradicate drug use, it's constantly undermining its war by being soft. You know, reclassifying, decriminalising . . . I guess Ross Kershaw will be there to tell them the Government is tackling the subject seriously.'

'Yeah well,' said Donna, 'let's hope no one strip searches him on his way in.'

Kate and I laughed.

'Cos I won't get any child support out of him if they chuck him in prison, will I?'

'Oh, I don't sup—' I began, as the sound of crockery on floorboards made us leap out of our skins.

Zoe had been carrying a stack of coffee cups through to the kitchen when she'd heard the words 'Ross' and 'Kershaw' and 'child support', plus all the words in between, and everything just seemed to slip from her hands. Stepping over the mess at her feet, she shot into the kitchen where Kate, Ed and Donna stood staring at her.

'Are you all right?' asked Kate.

Zoe opened her mouth and tried to speak. She pointed at Donna's swollen middle and mouthed something, and Donna grimaced and said, 'Uh-oh.'

'Are you having Ross Kershaw's baby?' Zoe eventually managed.

Ed grabbed a little stool from under a worktop and placed it behind Zoe's wobbly legs. She slumped down on to it and looked up at Donna. 'Well?'

'Dustpan and brush called for!' sang Bronwen, sailing into the room in her flowery trousers. She opened the cupboard under the sink but then stopped, turned and registered the atmosphere. 'Everything OK? Can I get anyone any—'

'Gin and tonic,' said Zoe.

'Sorry, no gin. I've got some homemade parsnip wine.'

'That'll do.'

'Anyone else like a drop? It's a rather good batch.'

Bob ambled in. 'Wouldn't say no.' He'd left Gideon telling the spider plants about Richardson's *Pamela*.

'Please,' said Kate and Ed.

Donna shook her head and carried on curling hair round a finger and staring at a distant wall.

* * *

We left Zoe and Donna to it, and when we were back in our living-room places I filled the others in. Well partly. Along the lines of: Donna's been seeing Zoe's ex-boyfriend and now she's pregnant with his baby. There was no need to name names, I felt, or mention adultery, drugs, prostitution and physical abuse. By means of the odd don't-you-dare-or-I'll-batter-you look, I managed to keep Kate quiet too.

'Golly,' cried Bronwen. 'Poor Zoe.'

'Never mind her,' said Bob. 'What about that poor kiddie Donna's carrying? Having a hussy of a mother like that.'

'She's a very good mother,' snapped Kate. 'Her house is really nice, and clean and cosy, and she loves her boys.'

'Well . . . all the same.'

'I just thought it must be a dreadful shock for Zoe,' said Bronwen. 'That's all.'

Kate snorted. 'It's going to be more of a shock for the father.'

Bronwen said, 'He doesn't know?'

'Uh-uh. You see he's—'

'Kate!' I shouted, and wagged a finger.

'No. He doesn't know yet.'

Gideon was flicking through his *Accidental Tourist* and rubbing his chin. 'I'm sorry,' he said, looking up at the group with a puzzled expression. 'I'm afraid I don't recall this particular storyline. Of course, I did read it rather speedily.'

'When did you meet him, and how?' asked Zoe, her face pale, the glass of parsnip wine trembling slightly in her hand.

'Um . . .' Donna paused. Should she be upfront and risk being thumped by Zoe as well? She decided to tell her what she'd told Kate.

'You picked him up then?'

Donna didn't like Zoe's tone, but thought she was being dead calm in the circumstances. 'More the other way round, I'd say.'

'Christ, he was still seeing me then. Did he ever mention me? Does he know we know each other? Did you ever tell him about the reading group?'

'Uh-uh.'

'So it's just a bizarre coincidence then?'

'Yeah,' said Donna. 'Weird, eh?'

Zoe suddenly came over cold. 'Oh my God, it was *you* in the taxi.'

'What?'

Zoe finished her drink and shook her head. 'Never mind.' When she stood up to get herself some more wine, Donna went over to the stool and lowered herself on to it.

'Sorry,' she said. 'Do you mind?'

'No, no.'

'Ta. Listen, um . . . like when did you and Ross actually break up?' Donna regretted the question immediately. Please say November, she willed Zoe.

'Middle of January.'

'What!' She knew she shouldn't have asked.

'It dragged on for ages, until I finally decided I'd had enough of him being . . . well . . .'

'A right perv?'

Zoe's eyes widened and she nodded. 'Did he get you to do . . . um—'

'Threesomes? Tried to.'

'God, that's a relief.'

'Not for me, I can tell you. I was really in love with him, you know. Anyway, I bit him where it hurts, he knocked me around a bit, and I haven't seen him since.'

'Jesus. You mean when your face was all—'

'Yeah.' Donna suddenly found herself crying and hugging her big tummy. 'He doesn't know I'm expecting,' she sobbed into her chest, and was surprised to feel Zoe's arm work its way round her shoulders.

'Bastard,' hissed Zoe.

'Total.'

Zoe squeezed hard and said, 'Shall I make us a nice cup of tea, Donna?'

'Yeah, alright.'

The following day, Duggie was supposed to be revising for his GCSEs but was out in the Cotswolds with Kate in a rambling stone house packed with old furniture. Two sprightly sisters, who claimed to be in their eighties, were giving them a potted history of every item. 'And then Aunt Bess decided she had as much walnut as a house could take and passed it over to Mother, who thought it'd go nicely in the blue room.'

Kate noticed they were mostly addressing Duggie, who'd put on a suit for the occasion and consequently looked as old as your average chain-store manager; although most chain-store managers wouldn't have their sock tops and an inch of leg showing, owing to the fact that their suit was bought for their nan's funeral when they were fourteen. Nor would they probably choose to wear grey, red and silver trainers.

'It's a delightful piece,' Duggie was saying with a thoughtful nod. 'What a shame the handles aren't original.' He scribbled something on a pad and moved on to a set of dining chairs. 'Nineteenth century?'

'Late eighteenth, we believe.'

'Possibly. Possibly.'

Kate was only interested in the junkier stuff, and had no desire to rip these sweet ladies off, despite the fact that they'd probably got close to a million for their house.

'We certainly won't need these chairs, or the table,' chirruped the larger sister. 'We're installing ourselves in a darling little nursing home near Gatcombe Park. Nouvelle cuisine, Jacuzzis and a cabaret on Wednesdays.'

'Sounds absolutely marvellous,' said Duggie, overdoing it a bit, Kate thought.

The smaller sister cupped his elbow and led him into yet another room. 'Do tell us what you think of the tallboy,' she said. 'I mentioned it to your assistant on the telephone.' She nodded towards Kate, who pursed her lips and followed.

'We've no one to pass these things on to,' the other one was saying. 'We neither of us married, you see.'

'Hard to believe!' cried Duggie.

They giggled and told him it wasn't for lack of suitors, and Kate wondered if she might just go and wait in the VW.

'Anyway, History's a piece of piss,' Duggie told Kate in the village pub. 'And I took Maths GCSE a year early. Me and the other clever Dicks. Got a B. Some of them are taking it again to try and get an A, cos it looks better on the UCAS form. But not me, thanks. Anyway, I don't think I want to go to university.'

'No?'

'Nah.'

'What else would you do?'

'Entrepreneur.'

Kate laughed. 'Yeah, right.'

'No, no. Got it all planned. I'll start small. Well, once I've got my lottery win.'

'*Right*.'

'I buy a ticket every Wednesday and Saturday, so I'm bound to get lucky one day. Then I'll get hold of a few antiques, nice bits of furniture. I mean, if I'd had five thousand quid I could've bought half that stuff we saw just now, sold it at twice the price and made a wad, yeah?'

Kate couldn't deny it. 'On the other hand,' she pointed out, 'I'll make a four- or five-hundred-per-cent profit on those bits we did buy.'

'But there's all that faffing around you do, tarting them up.'

'I enjoy that.'

'Yeah, well, time is money, you know. A bit of Mr Sheen and a quick turnover, that's what I'd go for. Get some premises in a prime location.'

He could go far, Kate thought, but then reminded herself that Duggie bought sherbet fountains for his lunch and had written, *I would of come in yesterday but* . . . on that note he'd once popped through her door.

'I think it might be worth waiting a few years,' she told him. 'People will take you more seriously when you're older. Get some A levels, at least.'

'Yeah, you're probably right. I don't wanna end up like my stepdad, hanging out in William Hill all day in my best stonewashed jeans. Mind you, if I get that big lottery win . . .'

'Yeah, yeah.'

When Duggie's fresh crab salad with tarragon, rocket and endive arrived, he unwrapped his knife and fork and spread his napkin on his lap. 'This looks *bad*,' he said, to the waitress's consternation.

'He means good,' explained Kate.

'Can I get you anything else?' they were asked.

Kate said no she was fine, and Duggie asked for salad cream. 'But not a cheap one. Heinz, if you've got it.'

'Certainly, sir.'

Bronwen's arms ached. The shears were rusty and made each chop at the brambles much harder than it should have been. Surely Daddy could afford to get someone in to sort out this jungle? She chopped on, then, armed with a sturdy pair of gardening gloves, picked up the prickly strands and threw them into the wheelbarrow. If only the waste heap were a little nearer, she thought, as she grabbed the handles of the barrow and made her way round the old vegetable patch, over the croquet lawn, past the tennis court and gazebo and behind the red-brick shed that would have housed an extended family in many parts of the world.

Time for a little sit-down and some lemonade, she decided, yanking off the gloves and wiping her damp brow. It was late afternoon and very warm, and although she'd planned to work until the light ran out, she now wondered if her poor old bones were up to it.

'Lemonade, Daddy? I made it myself and it's nicely chilled now.'

'Put a ball right through the window this morning.'

'Who?'

'Young Michael. We had to get the glazier in.'

'Ah.' Young Michael, a childhood playmate of Bronwen's, was forty-six. He had once smashed their kitchen window with a ball. 'Well, it's all fixed now,' she told her father, pulling the blanket off his knees. 'Come and sit outside and watch me garden.'

'I told Granger he was a bloody fool.'

'Did you? OK, up you get. Lean on me. Oh . . . where's your other slipper?' She eased him down again and straightened her sore back. 'What have you done with it?'

'A stroll down to the beach after supper, Anthea? Eh?'

'I'm not Mummy, I'm Bronwen,' she told him. 'And you're not

in Mumbles now.' Bronwen looked under the sofa and all the tables and behind piles of papers and eventually came across it in the cloakroom, wedged in the toilet.

'Oh, Daddy,' she sighed. She leaned against the wall and bit her lip. Mrs Cornish really wasn't enough now.

FIFTEEN

'Nice house, Donna,' said Zoe.

'Oh, ta. How do you like your coffee?'

'Just black, please. Don't suppose you've got a biscuit, have you? I drove from Matthew's place and didn't get round to breakfast.'

'Who's Matthew?' asked Donna, taking a packet of fig rolls from the cupboard.

'He's my boy— um, fiancé.'

'Blimey, that was quick work. When are you getting married?'

'Couple of weeks. Just a register office do. You know, one or two friends and family members.'

'Oh right, well, congratulations. What's he like?'

Zoe thought about it. 'I'd say he's the opposite of Ross in every way. Just normal, and very, very nice. And it's great.' They took their drinks through. 'Talking of Ross, are you going to tell him?'

'Oh yeah, definitely. Try and get him to face up to his responsibilities.'

'You mean money?'

'Uh-huh.'

'Well, good luck. You know what they say about the Scots.'

'That they wear stupid tartan socks?'

'Oh God, those sock—'

'Hiya, Don!' yelled someone from the kitchen.

Donna pulled a face and said, 'In here, Shelley.'

Zoe watched a girl of around Donna's age, with two nose rings, acne and a cigarette come into the room and stop dead. 'The Social or the Council?' she asked Donna.

'A friend, actually. Zoe, this is Shelley from next door but two.'

'Hello,' said Zoe.

Shelley nodded and said, 'Hiya.' She drew on her cigarette. 'So how do you know Donna then?'

'Oh, we're in the same—'

'Antenatal class!'

'Um, yeah . . . antenatal.' Zoe patted her tummy. 'I'm not really showing yet.'

'You're not kidding.' Shelley plonked herself next to Donna and shouted, 'Ere, Lara! Git ere!'

Zoe watched a little blonde-haired girl with a red-raw, pus-encrusted earlobe and a bruised arm totter into the room on tiny white, wedge-heeled sandals. She had the packet of fig rolls in one hand and a half-eaten biscuit in the other.

'I knew you was up to summink, you evil little tyke. Give em ere.'

Lara tottered over to her mother, dropped the packet on the sofa and screwed up her face ready for the smack that didn't come.

'Anyway, Don,' said Shelley, popping a biscuit in her mouth and crunching noisily on it, the cigarette still burning in her other hand. 'Just thought I'd tell you I got a letter from my dad. He says Carl's right pissed off that you ain't taken Ryan to see him, not even once.' She turned to Zoe. 'My dad and Donna's Carl are in Bullingdon together, which is quite nice.'

'Carl?' asked Zoe.

Donna coloured up. 'Ryan's dad.'

'Ah.'

Shelley turned back to Donna. 'Anyway, me and Mum's getting a lift there on Sat'dee if you wanna go.'

'Maybe.'

'Go see Granddad in the nick?' said Lara, jumping up and down and clapping her tiny hands. 'Yeaaahhh!'

Shelley whacked her daughter's bottom – 'Shuddup, will you, Lara! You're doin my head in today!' – then looked up at an appalled Donna and Zoe. 'Didn't interrupt nothing, did we?'

Donna gave the room three squirts from an aerosol. 'Sorry about Shelley. I just put up with her because she's a neighbour and cos she can turn really nasty if you're not careful.'

'I can imagine. That poor little girl . . . shouldn't someone . . . ? Oh, I don't suppose it's any of my business.'

'They've got a social worker, except he's a bit useless. But they're not all like that round here, you know. Mr and Mrs Burrows next door are lovely and Naomi who baby-sits for me is really decent and won't have swearing or smoking or even shoes in her house, and ... well, anyway, it's not as bad as you're thinking.'

Zoe laughed. 'You should live where I do. I've got a heroin dealer next door and filthy noisy students opposite.'

'But anyway, I suppose you'll be moving in with, er ... ?'

'Matthew? We haven't decided what to do yet. He says he really likes east Oxford. And it's not so far for us to commute to London. I don't know. We could use his place at weekends. It's perfect for that. A lovely little hamlet. Very romantic.' Zoe looked up at a miserable-looking Donna. 'Oh God, Donna, this isn't what you want to hear. Sorry. Let's change the subject.'

'I'm gonna really give him what for when he comes to Oxford.'

'Who?'

'Ross.'

'He's coming *here*? Why?'

'Oh, I dunno. He's doing some sort of performance. Um ... what's that place Jon Bon Jovi played at ... ?'

Zoe sat staring at Donna. What could she be talking about? The Apollo Theatre? Ross said he'd been in a rock band back in the seventies, but surely ...

Donna clicked her fingers and nodded. 'I know. It's the Reunion. That's it.'

Ross's band was having a reunion and playing at the Apollo?

'Huh,' said Zoe, not totally convinced. 'Fancy that.'

*   *   *

God knows how, but I'd reached page two hundred. I applauded myself and typed on.

> At 10.15 I phoned Amanda and we talked housework. She said she was just going round the bathroom taps with an old toothbrush. 'Yes, that really shifts the gunge,' I told her, 'especially if it's a stiff one.' Amanda said mm she was particularly keen on stiff ones and what was I doing later.

I sat back and smiled, thinking, William Boyd eat your heart out, then got the fright of my life when Charlie walked in the study.

'I thought you'd gone to school!'

'The teachers are having an Inset Day. What've you written this morning? Can I read it?'

'No, go away.'

'Oh, go on, Eddie.' She pulled a chair up and sat beside me, squinting at the screen.

'You should wear your glasses,' I told her and carried on typing. *Amanda and I arranged a*

'Lost them . . . Oh, I *get* it, she's talking about willies not brushes.'

'It's a *double entendre*,' I told her, suddenly and quite horribly aware that my witty, vaguely literary pastiche was becoming *Run for your Wife* meets *Carry on Dusting*. Usually, when I suspected my standards were slipping, I read a bit of *Out for the Count* by Ross Kershaw and felt like a literary giant.

'You know . . .' Charlie was saying, showing no signs of moving, 'when I was little I thought it was when the teachers went in and got rid of all the earwigs and spiders and things.'

'Mm.' . . . *a two o'clock rendezvous in the*

'Cos I thought they were having an Insect Day.' She laughed.

'Uh-huh.' . . . *jams-spreads-and-if-you're-lucky-Marmite aisle at Tesco.*

Charlie tapped a foot and hummed and I began thinking of physically removing her. 'Look,' she said, suddenly peeling back a plaster on her thumb. 'Haven't shown you my onion-chopping injury.'

'No!' I cried, but it was too late.

'Me and Jack were making a cheese and onion sandwich last night and then the knife slipped and— You alright, Eddie?'

'Just put it away,' I pleaded – head turned to the wall, knees weak, funny feeling in my spine – and she did.

'Sorry, forgot,' she said, and returned to foot tapping while I typed. 'Couldn't help me with my George Eliot essay, could you?' she asked after a short silence.

'No, sorry.' *4 p.m. – Amanda's bedroom* . . . 'But I know a man who might.'

I got straight through to Gideon at Molefield. He sounded weary. 'Ye-es?' he sighed into the phone.

'It's Ed,' I said, and realised he'd need more than that. 'From the reading circle.'

'Ah, yes, hello.'

'Hi. Um, I wanted to ask you a favour.'

'One moment. My student's just leaving.' The phone was clonked down and I heard him say, 'So, unless you're a trendy novelist you simply have to have an active verb in a sentence. "Not like what Wordsworth did" does not constitute a sentence.'

A boy mumbled something and Gideon picked up the phone. 'Kindly shut the door!' he yelled in my ear, then said, 'Right, yes, sorry, what can I do for you?'

I explained about Charlie's coursework. 'It's *Adam Bede* and Kate only knows *Middlemarch*, unfortunately.'

'Aah, *Adam Bede*, yes. Part of the mid-century move towards realism in literature.'

'Uh-huh. Well, if you could possibly come and tell Charlie all about it that would be fantastic. In fact, how about later today?'

'Ye-es . . . it also questioned the role of spirituality and faith in ordinary life. Eliot herself was an atheist, of course.'

'Right. We'd pay you . . . or perhaps you'd like to stay to dinner? Charlie gets to choose on Mondays, so it's roast turkey, roast potatoes and all the trimmings . . . trifle.'

There was a short silence before Gideon said, 'Five thirty?'

'Yep, great. See you then.'

I put the phone down and saw Charlie's horrified expression. 'Is he the one with food down his front?'

Of course I'd completely forgotten that Kate had asked Zoe and her new bloke to come and eat with us. They were getting married, it seemed, and Kate and I were invited, but we weren't to let the others in the reading group know as they wanted to keep it small. When

I remembered, I rang Kate and told her I'd accidentally invited Gideon to dinner.

'You fuckwit!' she said, endearingly.

'Yeah, I know.'

By twenty to nine Bronwen had completely given up on Gideon. She let everything cool down, then transferred it all to Tupperware containers. He really was terribly absent-minded. The bane of a deep thinker, no doubt. She'd tried Bob and Christine's but he wasn't there and she cursed him for not having a mobile, before remembering she didn't approve of them. She then picked up her phone again.

'Malcolm?'

'No, it's Larry. Hang on.'

Bronwen was feeling strangely nervous, but as soon as Malcolm said, 'Bronwen, how lovely to hear from you,' she relaxed and chatted easily as she worked her way towards suggesting the three-flutes-and-a-zither concert at Merton.

'Perhaps Larry would like to come too?' she asked.

Malcolm laughed. 'No, no, Larry's strictly a Streisand man.'

'Ah,' said Bronwen, not fully understanding, but oddly pleased he and Larry weren't total soulmates.

She told him she was now in a relationship and Malcolm said he was very pleased for her.

'And is he a music lover?' he asked.

Gideon had one cassette: John Berjeman reciting his poetry with a background orchestra. She'd thought it quite jolly the first couple of times he played it to her, but would prefer never to hear it again. 'Not really.'

'So, it'll just be the two of us,' said Malcolm; almost seductively, Bronwen thought.

'I'll get the tickets, shall I?'

'Would you mind? I'm terribly busy with my student at the moment.'

Bronwen said she wouldn't mind at all and felt unexpectedly buoyant when she replaced the phone. Could he and Larry simply be housemates after all?

'Well,' said Kate, switching off the standard lamp and wishing she had a cat to chuck out, 'it's been a lovely evening, Gideon. All that stuff about Smollett at dinner was . . . fascinating.' Ed was fast asleep in an armchair. 'Now, did you have a jacket?'

When the final lamp went out, Gideon stood up a little nonplussed and groped his way to the hall where he found Kate holding his briefcase up. 'We must do it again some time,' she said.

'Indeed, indeed. Now remind me . . . where do I catch the bus to Marston?'

Kate sighed. It was 12.40 a.m. Zoe and Matthew had left hours ago – well, at midnight, but it felt like hours. 'You'll need a taxi,' she said. 'I'll pay. After all, you did come and help Charlie.'

'Jolly decent.'

'Half an hour!' she cried into the phone. 'Well, all right, if that's the best you can do.'

She led Gideon back into the living room, switched a lamp back on and tickled Ed under his ribs. 'Your turn,' she told him as he opened his eyes and flailed around. 'I'm off to bed. Night-night.'

Gideon smiled to himself. 'Night-night' was what Bronwen always said last thing. He thought warmly of her, but then suddenly started and looked at his watch. Ah . . .

'Donna?' called out the man from the car.

She'd just slammed the front door behind her and was walking towards the road with her boys. She didn't recognise the car and couldn't see the bloke properly. Just a pair of dark glasses.

'Yeah?' she said, frowning and shielding her eyes from the early morning sun.

The man didn't answer and before she knew it he held a camera up and took a photograph of her, then another and another. The camera was large, smooth and expensive sounding as it clicked and whirred.

'Fuck off, will you?' she shouted and turned her face away, but by then the bright blue car was roaring off down Longfellow Road, leaving her shaking on her own front path.

Little Ryan let go of her hand and ran after it calling out, 'Fuckoff car!'

'No, you mustn't say that word, darlin.'

'Jake says it.'

'Well, you shouldn't't, Jake,'

'Everyone at school does. Even Mr Tibbetts.'

Mr Tibbetts was Jake's reception class teacher. He was mid-twenties and quite fit, but was going out with Miss Kirk, the deputy head, who chewed gum even though it was banned. Sometimes Donna just wished she could get her boys into a nice little private school with a grey uniform and badges and things. 'I'm sure he doesn't.'

'It was when a bee came in the classroom. Mr Tibbett's lergic.'

'Is he? That's not very nice for him.' Donna was trying not to let her boys know how upset she was. She hadn't seen the guy's face. Who *was* he? Not a snoop from the Social, surely. It wasn't like she was secretly working or anything. She was just taking her boys to school like a normal mum. 'OK. What colour cars shall we count today?' she asked them. 'Red?'

'Blue,' said Jake.

'Like the fuckoff car.'

'Ryan! There'll be no telly for a week if I hear that again. OK . . . counting blue cars . . . ready, steady go!'

By the time they reached the school, Jake had twenty-one and Ryan had twelve. Ryan got twelve every day because that was as high as he could count. Like his dad, Donna thought, and laughed, then stopped and caught her breath. Carl! Of course! He'd sent some mate on the outside to take pictures of Ryan. It all made sense now. He probably did miss his little boy, and Jake too. If he hadn't tied up and gagged an eighty-year-old for her electric money, she'd almost feel sorry for him.

*　　*　　*

Zoe would have to get them to take it in a bit but otherwise it was perfect. A deep shade of blue that wasn't quite navy, flattering neckline. Smart but nicely understated too – she could easily walk down the street to the Lebanese restaurant after the ceremony without feeling conspicuous.

After she'd told the assistant she wanted the dress, someone came and jotted down alteration details and said it would be ready in a couple of days.

'Fantastic,' said Zoe. Everything was fantastic. She couldn't believe her luck: having Matthew and being happy. She hadn't cried in weeks!

Now for some sexy beachwear. They'd broken open their piggy banks and booked a Greek holiday and she couldn't wait. Everything in her life was going so brilliantly. Well . . . apart from work. She knew she'd been slacking, but what the hell, she was happy. She'd make up for it later.

She met Matthew for lunch in their usual restaurant and didn't mention the dress. With fingers entwined on the table, they agreed that their wedding was going to be the *best* day of their lives, that the honeymoon was going to be *fantastic, brilliant*, and that they loved each other *so* much.

But then it got to two fifteen and Zoe decided she really ought to go and show her face at work before they sacked her. Would it bother her if they did? The advertising business was full of bullshit anyway. She could sell up in Oxford and be a housewife in the Cotswolds, spending her days in a quilted jerkin and pleated skirt in a house full of dogs. She'd keep chickens and bantams and brew masses of jam and let her hair grow wild. She'd learn to ride, join a cross-stitch group, have babies . . .

Duggie was doing his Physics revision at the shop counter. 'Velocity,' he told Kate when she enquired.

'Right.'

He had books open everywhere and a pile of past papers. 'I'd do it at home only my stepdad's stripping his motorbike down in the living room and singing out of tune to Steve Wright.'

'That's OK.'

Kate carried on peeling sticky-back plastic off a table and was thinking about maybe covering the top with a mosaic, when Charlie came in and dropped her school bag.

'Wotcha, Mum,' she said, giving Kate a kiss. 'What are you doing? Can I help?'

'You could make some tea if you like?'

'OK.'

It was a bit unnerving, all this niceness, but Kate wasn't about to complain. 'How was school?' she called out.

'Really good, yeah. Got an A for my art. You know, that painting I did of Jack?'

'Hey, that's brilliant. Well done.'

Charlie stuck her head round the kitchenette door. 'Mrs Herbert wanted to know where I got my talent from.'

Kate gave her daughter a self-satisfied smile and raised her eyebrows. 'Oh yes?'

'Said I didn't know.' She disappeared to wash out the mugs and over the sound of running water shouted, 'Dad isn't artistic, is he?'

'Do us a favour, will you?' asked Kate.

Charlie handed over Kate's mug. 'What?'

'Well, I haven't read any of these short stories for tonight's meeting, so I wondered if you'd read a couple to me.'

'But I wanted to talk to Duggie!'

Kate handed over the book. 'He's busy revising, best not to distract him.'

Charlie looked disappointed, fell into an old armchair and flicked through the first few pages. 'How about "Genesis and Cat – a – stroaph"?'

This wasn't looking promising. 'Catastrophe,' said Kate.

SIXTEEN

You should have seen our jaws drop. Bronwen had a kind of bearer-of-bad-news-cum-cat-that-got-the-cream expression as she led a smallish young man with short sleeves, a dark blond quiff and a black holdall into Bob's back garden. We were having an early May bout of midsummer and Christine had covered her lawn with garden furniture for us.

'This is Andy,' announced Bronwen, 'who'd very much like to join the reading circle this evening.' She motioned him to the padded lounger everyone had avoided because Christine said you had to 'watch it'. Bronwen chuckled. 'To try us out, as it were.'

She reeled off our names and Andy gave a nervous wave and sat down, only to be immediately thrust back to sunbathing position, showing everyone he'd paid sixty-five pounds for his shoes.

Bob hurled himself forward. 'Sorry, son. Been meaning to have a look at this wretched thing since last summer when Christine's sister went arse over base.' He lifted a flap and fiddled with the arm mechanism while Andy – his head now lower than his feet – lay as still as a dental patient.

'Anyone for a cheese straw?' asked Christine. She dashed through the conservatory and reappeared with a metal tray in her oven-mitted hand. 'They're still warm but they won't scald.'

We all took one and bit in and said how delicious they were, etc., pretending not to notice the awkward situation by the lilac bush. Then, as quickly as he'd descended, Andy was shot upright and facing us again, cheeks glowing.

'Hi,' he said. 'Pleased to meet you all.'

'Cheese straw, Andy?'

'Thanks.'

'Andy's an IT account manager,' said Bronwen. 'In High Wycombe.'

'But I live in, um . . . Abingdon,' he told us.

'Aren't there any reading groups in Abingdon?' asked Kate, rather rudely, some might have thought.

'Only all-female ones.'

'How did you find out about us?'

'I . . . er . . . a friend in Oxford said she'd heard about it. You know, from a friend of a friend who . . . er . . .' He bit into his cheese straw.

I was trying to work out his age. He could have been one of those guys – like Tim Henman and Ian Beale – who will look nineteen till they die. Or, perhaps he was nineteen.

Throughout our first half he had nothing to say about *The Collected*

Short Stories of Roald Dahl, not having read them, of course, but we tried to be inclusive by each of us relating one story we'd particularly liked. He looked a tad bored and stared at Donna a lot, and I wondered if he'd expected something more highbrow.

Kate chose 'Parson's Pleasure', the story about the antique-buying con artist. 'So, the Reverend Boggis – for Boggis read bogus, by the way – tells the farmer his valuable Chippendale commode is reproduction but he'll give him twenty pounds for it because he could make use of the legs. Anyway, the farmer and his son think because he's a vicar he must have a small car, so when he goes to fetch it they helpfully saw the legs off the commode for him.'

We all laughed and someone said, 'Let that be a lesson to you, Kate,' and out of politeness I explained Kate's work to Andy. It was definitely tedious having a newcomer in the group.

'How about you, Donna?' said Bronwen, handing her one of the three library copies we'd been passing around for two weeks. It could get very expensive if you weren't careful, this reading group business. 'As the book was your choice, tell us your favourite story.'

'Oh yeah, right.' She looked at the Contents page then flicked through. 'Page four five four. "Lamb to the Slaughter". Brilliant.'

'Mm, I liked that one too,' said Zoe.

'What happens is this husband comes home from work and tells his wife, who's just a housewife, I think . . . not that there's anything wrong with being just a housewife . . .' Donna looked directly at me, and Kate laughed.

'Carry on,' I said.

'Anyway, he tells her he's been seeing someone else and is gonna leave her, the total bastard.'

'Bastard,' echoed Zoe.

'When he's finished, the wife doesn't say anything, just, "I'll get the supper." Can you believe that? So she goes and gets this frozen solid leg of lamb, like out of the freezer, and when he says he doesn't want supper he's just gonna go, she whacks him on the head with it and kills him.'

Zoe smiled. 'Can you imagine the satisfaction that must have given her?'

'God, yeah. Then – and this is where she was dead clever – she puts the lamb in the oven to cook, goes and gets some vegetables from the corner shop like nothing's happened, chatting to the shopkeeper, then pretends she's found her husband dead when she gets back and phones the police and it ends with her and the policemen sitting down to a roast meal wondering what happened to the murder weapon. Brilliant!'

Donna's eyes glowed murderously. Come to think of it, so did Zoe's.

'Brilliant,' they both repeated.

'So what kind of things do you like reading?' I asked Andy as we dug into Christine's banquet in the conservatory: spicy chicken legs, silverskin onions, things on sticks, decorative sprigs of parsley.

'Oh, um, whassisname . . . Simon Rushdie, he's good.'

'Uh-huh.' I found I couldn't take my eyes off Andy's hair. How did he get his fringe so vertical? And why?

Pure Fiction

'And, er . . . that Amis bloke.'

'Matthew?'

'That's the one.'

'Did I hear you mention Matthew?' asked Zoe, swinging round with carrot in her hand.

'Zoe's engaged to Matthew,' Donna explained to Andy, who then looked confused. Did he think Zoe was engaged to that famous writer, Matthew Amis? But he just nodded.

'When's the baby due?' he asked Donna.

'End of July.'

'I expect Dad's excited, isn't he?'

'Er . . . yeah.'

I went outside and cornered Kate. 'Abingdon Andy's never read a book in his life.'

'No?'

'Odd, don't you think?'

'Well, you know . . . these computer types. Anyway, perhaps he just thought it was time he started.'

'And why's he carrying that bag around with him all the time?'

'God, give him a break. Maybe he's got a state-of-the-art laptop in there. Doesn't want some oaf on a sun lounger landing on it.'

'Mm, maybe.'

'I think he's quite cute.'

'You would.'

I looked over and saw Andy seated on a garden chair with his bag on his lap. On top of the bag was a heaped plate of food that he was slowly picking at. I made my way towards him.

'So how long does it take you to get here from Abingdon?' I asked.

He swallowed his mouthful. 'Oh, um, about an hour and a quarter.'

'Right.' My granny could walk there and back in that time. 'And, well excuse my ignorance,' I went on, 'but what exactly is an IT account manager?'

'Ah, um . . . nah, too boring to explain. What do you do?'

'Virgin Atlantic pilot.'

'Cool.'

'Oh no, Gideon!' we heard Bronwen cry. 'Don't sit on that! Remember . . . oh dear . . . Bob! No, no, don't worry, we can get you another plate of food.'

It had got a bit nippy outside so we were back in Bob and Christine's living room with coffee and soft drinks and biscuits and coasters and a strong smell of Glade.

'I've chosen a story from the *Switch Bitch* collection,' Gideon was telling us. 'These four stories first appeared in *Playboy*, you know.'

'I thought they were a bit porno,' said Donna.

'Indeed. The book received mixed reviews. Some saw the characters as having no sense of morality.'

Bronwen shook her head. 'Absolutely ghastly people.'

'Others felt Dahl tended to neutralise any evil or pornography in his stories by presenting the reader with a sort of cartoon version of them.'

'And such unashamed sexism,' said Bronwen.

'Anyway,' continued Gideon, 'I've chosen "The Great Switcheroo" as my particular favourite.'

'Is that the one where the blokes secretly swap beds and do it with the other one's wife?' asked Donna.

'Do you see what I mean?' asked Bronwen. Kate and Zoe nodded.

'Yes it is,' said Gideon. 'Poor Vic then has to come to terms with the fact that his wife has never enjoyed, ah . . . carnal relations with him, but finds it very enjoyable with his friend, Jerry. One . . . um . . . well, one can't help but feel enormous sympathy for Vic, can one?'

Gideon looked up sorrowfully at the group while we all thought about it.

'Perhaps he could have tried a little harder,' said Bronwen quietly.

The next day, Ross was surprised – and extremely pissed off – to hear Donna's voice on the other end of the phone. They'd all been given strict instructions not to call him at work. Who knew who might be listening in? He decided to adopt a formal tone.

'I'm very well, thank you. And how can I help you today?'

She told him she wanted to meet up when he was in Oxford next week.

How did she know about that? 'I'm afraid I have a very busy schedule that day.'

'Fuck your schedule, I want to talk to you.'

'All right, all right.' Christ, they were all tiresome or troublesome once you off-loaded them. 'If it's so urgent you can meet me from the train. I'll let you know approximately what time I'll be arriving. OK?'

'You'd better, or I'll . . . well . . . just make sure you do.'

Another empty threat. 'I'll go to the *News of the World*,' she was probably going to say. But they never did. Too embarrassed, or they were still desperately hoping he'd take up with them again. Donna most likely wanted to get things off her chest. A pretty little chest, he seemed to recall.

Bob was on the riverbank. He hadn't caught anything yet but he'd got to the bit in *Crime and Punishment* where Raskolnikov commits his horrible murder.

'Damned fool,' he said out loud, then hid his book again, not wanting to be seen reading. Fishing was a time for contemplation. Either that or staring at a tree on the other bank, making out you were thinking deeply. The book had disturbed Bob's peace of mind and he felt an overwhelming need to speak to Christine. He got his new mobile out and surreptitiously called her. Mobiles were another no-no; could frighten the fish off, and what's more you were supposed to be getting away from the world, not text messaging it.

'How are you, love?' he whispered.

'Fine. Just serving Gideon his dessert.'

'Oh, aye?' Gideon got a whacking great lunch as well as dinner at weekends. What with that and the weekday sandwiches Christine packed up for him, Bob often wondered if they were making any profit at all out of their lodger. 'What's he having?'

'Treacle sponge and custard. I'd keep some for you only I'd imagine Gideon will want seconds.'

'And thirds, no doubt. Listen, while I'm on the phone could you ask him something for me?'

'What's that?'

'Ask him if Raskolnikov pays for his crime. I'm guessing he does, what with the title, only I'm not sure I'll get through ten thousand pages or whatever it is. You know me.'

Christine chuckled good-humouredly. 'Just a tick,' she said.

Bob stared at a tree on the opposite bank while he waited, contemplating his diminishing pay-as-you-go units, until Christine eventually came back, calling out, 'Let me heat that custard up for you, Gideon. No, no. No trouble. Hello?'

'Yep,' said Bob. 'I'm still here.'

'He says to tell you there are many forms of punishment. The total deconstruction of one's identity, for example.'

'Right. Clear as mud, as usual. Well, I'll see you later then, love.' He lifted the lid of his Tupperware box and looked at the last, now curling, sardine sandwich. 'I could be back a bit earlier today.'

Bronwen wasn't sure why she was feeling so on edge. It wasn't as if Gideon hung out in the city centre in the evenings, along with all the foreign students and concert-goers and youths who'd bussed in from outlying towns.

She was in a popular Thai restaurant off the High Street having dinner with Malcolm; the concert having finished at the early hour of 9.20.

'Shall we order a bottle of wine?' she asked.

'Why not?' He picked up the menu again. 'Red or white?'

'Oh, you decide.'

'Well, you're having beef and I'm having duck, so red I think.'

'Lovely.' He could be manly and decisive after all. She watched him call the waiter over and order.

'Tell me about Larry,' she said. They'd exhausted the concert on the walk from Merton College Chapel to the restaurant, both agreeing that the little group needed to lengthen their repertoire if they were going to charge people twelve pounds a ticket.

'Larry? What can I say . . . he's my best friend. The perfect person to share a house with. Extremely easy-going.'

'Really.' So far so good, thought Bronwen, straightening her back and lifting her breasts.

'Loves to cook.'

'Mm, I gathered that.'

'Doesn't hog the remote control. Lets me watch the football, even though he hates it.'

She laughed. Football! Of course Malcolm wasn't gay.

'And . . .' he grinned and wobbled his head, 'we've just celebrated our tenth anniversary.'

'Oh.' She breathed out and let her chest sag and wondered if she actually felt relieved. 'Congratulations.'

'Thanks. Now,' he said, just as the wine arrived. He filled her glass and then his. 'Tell me about *your* man.'

'Well, Gideon lectures—'

'Ah, so sorry,' Bronwen heard someone sounding awfully like Gideon say.

She spun round to see him attached – apparently by a jacket button – to a seated woman's hair. The woman looked in some pain, her head back at forty-five degrees while Gideon fiddled.

'Almost there,' he was saying before finally disengaging himself. 'There. Dreadfully sorry. I, ah . . .'

'Gideon?' cried Bronwen.

'Bronwen!' He ambled over. 'Bit of a coincidence.'

'Yes,' she said, feeling the colour rise in her cheeks. How must this look? She turned to Malcolm. 'This is Gideon, my, um, partner.'

'Hi.' He extended a hand and Gideon took it.

'This is Malcolm,' continued Bronwen. 'Who's gay, by the way.'

Malcolm looked shocked, while Gideon quickly pulled his hand away. 'Yes, um . . . don't suppose you know where the gents are? The waiter directed me down here.'

Malcolm pointed. 'Round that corner.'

Gideon thanked him and started heading for them.

'But what are you doing here?' called out Bronwen.

'Oh, departmental dinner. Bit of a chore, really. Seven English lecturers all talking about their pet authors.'

Bronwen could imagine. She turned back to Malcolm, who said, 'Actually I'm bisexual.'

'I'm sorry, I didn't mean to blurt—'

'And . . . well, Larry and I have something of an open relationship.' He smiled rather attractively at her.

'Oh, I see,' she said. Well, she thought she did.

She poured them both more wine and flashed back to life with Mother Teresa. So rewarding and uncomplicated. Should she simply give up on men and do something useful? Go and save Venice from sinking? Malcolm certainly wasn't one to become entangled with; Lord knows where he, or Larry, had been. And Gideon . . . so in his own head and not exactly the kindred spirit she'd been hoping for. She waved at him, now making his way back to the stairs, one trouser bottom caught in a sock. Dear Gideon.

SEVENTEEN

On the rare occasions I'd needed one I'd always borrowed Will's suits, but as he was being a total prick about my writing I decided to buy my own to wear to Zoe's wedding. And besides, who knows when I might have to look smart for a literary function? I'd hardly want to go and collect my Whitbread Prize in rags. I never liked his suits anyway, or the way he hung the jackets on a hook behind his passenger seat.

'I'm looking for hip but smart,' I told the young man who'd come to my assistance. 'The kind of suit Ian McEwan might wear.'

He frowned and scratched his head. 'Do you mean Ewan McGregor?'

'Oh, OK. Something Ewan McGregor might wear. But not in *Star Wars*, ha, ha.'

He led me through the shop in his pale lemon shirt. 'We're after more of a *Trainspotting* look, are we, sir?'

I laughed but he didn't, and I stopped and pulled a face. Perhaps Burtons would be safer?

'Kidding,' said the assistant, and I wondered if young humour was becoming too dry and subtle for me.

'My God,' cried Kate. 'You look so shaggable!'

'You mean I don't normally?' I gave her another sexy-young-guy-on-the-catwalk twirl, hand on hip.

'You can't go to the Register Office like that. Zoe's bound to take one look at you and dump Matthew. Any sane woman would.'

This was almost too many compliments. Almost.

'So I look all right then?'

'Mm. Like Hugh Grant, Brad Pitt and Boris Becker all rolled into one.'

'Boris Becker? Is he attractive?'

'God, yeah.' She rolled her eyes like a teenager, then bounced off the bed. 'Shall I show you what I'm wearing to the wedding?'

'It's not unlucky or anything?'

'Not unless we make it a double wedding.'

We both gave an embarrassed laugh, then she slipped behind the wardrobe door and made swishing and wriggling sounds, before appearing in a tight little dress in a shade of blue that was perfect for her.

'Now we both look shaggable,' I told her, adding, 'Although of course you always do.'

Charlie was at the cinema and Georgia slept.

'How about it?' I asked.

'As long as you don't crease me.'

'OK, no ripping my shirt buttons off then.'

256

'Spoilsport.'

We did both get very crumpled. What's more, my new shirt would have to be washed and would never look so crisp. Kate had put thick red lipstick on, making the whole thing wild, abandoned and, well, messy. I made a note to slip the episode in my novel, and to perhaps add one or two laundering and ironing tips.

Maybe she wouldn't kill Ross Kershaw with a leg of lamb after all, thought Donna, putting *Crime and Punishment* to one side with a shudder. She switched off her bedside lamp and lay for a while imagining how their meeting might go. She thought she'd suggest going to the Chicago Rock Café, just up from the station. He wouldn't bump into anyone he knew there, that was for sure. She'd ask nicely for child support, and he'd say, 'But of course. How much do you think you might need?' Anything to keep her quiet. You never know, perhaps he'd set her up in a little house. Somewhere nice. North Oxford, maybe. No more Shelley! She turned on her side and pulled the duvet up. Her digital alarm clock said 21.38. God, she was knackered.

'So you're alright for Thursday, are you?' Kate asked Duggie on Monday afternoon. 'No exams or revision classes or anything?'

'Nah. Anyway, I get more done in the shop.'

'Really?'

'Mm. It's not like I'm rushed off my feet with customers.' He laughed. 'Especially on a Thursday.'

'No. The wedding's at two, so I should be back here in time to lock up.'

'Cool.'

Kate said goodbye and put the phone down. Where would she be without Duggie? So dependable, and affable with it. He probably wouldn't be able to do as many hours when he was in the sixth form, though. She'd have to drag Ed away from his writing, unless he was producing bestseller number two by then, of course.

'Kate?' said Ed. He was staring at her from his armchair, *Crime and Punishment* open on his lap.

'Mm?'

'Do you feel like playing wedding guests again?' He grinned, bobbed his eyebrows and closed the book.

'But you've only just got the lipstick off that shirt.'

'You could be a bit more careful this time.'

'And anyway, Charlie's in her room.'

'She won't hear your cries of ecstasy over her bass.' He pointed at the vase of white lilies on the coffee table. 'I'll wear a buttonhole if you like.'

'Hmm . . . and maybe I could wear my wide-brimmed hat with the ribbon round it?'

'Now you're talking.'

The next day I let the shirt soak in Vanish while I dropped Georgia off at Christine and Bob's. As usual, Georgia seemed thrilled to be arriving there, falling happily into Christine's arms, as she always did, with wide eyes and a big smile. There was something almost womblike about their place. Lots of pinks and creams and deep-pile carpets. And a pinkish-beige Draylon three-piece suite you'd scoff at, but so soft and heavenly to sit on after over-stuffed canvas. Christine wore a pinny dusted with flour. Radio Oxford was playing Petula Clark in the background. I wanted to hang out there all day myself.

'See you at four,' I said reluctantly, kissing Georgia's cheek and handing over her teddy. As usual, she ignored me and laid her head affectionately on Christine's shoulder.

'We've got lots of things planned for you today,' Christine told her. 'Oh, yes, we have.'

I smiled and waved as I made my way down the path, wishing Georgia would sometimes look mildly bothered about my departure. It was kind of embarrassing that she didn't.

I got back to a message from Bernice saying they might not be able to have Georgia for the coming weekend after all as the TV was in for repair. It took me a while to work out what she meant, then I had a depressing image of my daughter, inches from some Stallone movie, lager in one hand and a kebab in the other. This was to be her third stay with her mum. Last time I'd had to fetch her early Sunday morning due to Clive's golf. That one had puzzled me too.

I rinsed the shirt and gave it a quick spin. Good wedding weather, I thought, as I hung it out on the line, then began wondering how Kate would react if I proposed. Perhaps I should do it tomorrow at the Register Office. Rejection would be awful, though, particularly as we were living together. It would be like her saying, well, I've tried you out, Ed, and have found you wanting. I knocked the idea on the head and went to my work. Page 284. Time for a climax, perhaps.

'Ah, ha, ha, yes, very droll,' said Gideon, sitting up in bed with Smollett. It was almost midnight. He laughed again and Bronwen stuck a finger in her ear under the duvet. Had Gideon even noticed *The Best Ever Guide to Great Great Sex* on the bedside table? There was a section on food she thought he might be interested in. The authors suggested a variety of things you could do with strawberries and yoghurt and honey and root vegetables. Surely that would be up Gideon's street? She opened one eye and watched him chomping on his late-night snack – warm milk and an Eccles cake – and wondered if Malcolm and Larry ever smothered each other in chocolate spread.

At the library the next day, she worked on automatic pilot. Scanning, stamping, filling shelves and making quiet small talk with the borrowers, but all the while considering her relationship with Gideon and what exactly it was bringing her. She'd always seen herself with a sort of David Attenborough type: sexy, witty, attentive and engaged with the world. Someone who'd enthuse about her almond-shaped eyes and delight her with rainforest anecdotes. Whisk her off on an adventure at a moment's notice. But where was such a man to be found so late in the day? She sighed and scanned four overdue books. If her David Attenborough wasn't going to show up then perhaps she should find a good home for Daddy and take off. There was always a project somewhere in the world that needed an extra pair of hands.

'That's two pounds forty, please,' she whispered.

The woman across the counter paid up resentfully, saying it was most unfair and wasn't the library service supposed to be free.

'What's unfair,' said Bronwen, far louder than she'd intended, 'is keeping the books five weeks when others might like to read them.'

The woman stormed off with a 'Well!', leaving Bronwen suddenly aware of how tired she was and how she no longer wanted to be kept awake at night by an enthusiastic snorer.

Ross hopped on the train in the nick of time, as did the guy with a black holdall immediately behind him. They sat opposite each other, and for the first part of the journey listened to a woman directly behind Ross talking into her phone, complaining endlessly about her unfaithful partner.

'It was when I came across the spare pair of underpants in his briefcase . . . Some little tart at the office . . . Four months, can you believe it?' and so on, drifted Ross's way and distracted him from his Union speech notes. 'Anyway, when he said he had to go to a weekend conference in Bournemouth, and I checked at his office and there was no conference, that was the last straw. So do you know what I did to the stinking little love rat?' The woman laughed. 'I don't know if I can tell you.'

Ross noticed that newspapers and books had been put to one side, and that most of his neighbours, including the guy opposite him with the Tintin quiff and the holdall on his lap, had an ear stretched towards the woman on the phone.

'Well, I sprinkled a mixture of mustard powder and chilli powder inside his underpants ... No, honestly. He phoned me from Accident and Emergency in Bournemouth ...'

Ross grimaced and stuck a finger in each ear, then thought back to Donna's teeth digging into him, and the tenderness he'd experienced for weeks, and how she'd completely ruined oral sex for him for ever. Women could be so vindictive. If only he could live without them.

When the train eased itself into Oxford station he spotted a rather attractive-from-the-back young blonde waiting on the platform. Turn around, he willed her as he crept closer, and, to his utter horror, she did. Oh Jesus, he thought, not *again*. God, they were bloody hopeless. Was it so hard to remember one little pill a day? He was about to hide behind a hand, but Donna had spotted him in his window seat and was giving him a half-hearted wave over her voluminous middle. 'Fuck,' he mouthed.

When the train finally stopped and Ross took a deep breath, closed his briefcase and stood up, he could have sworn the young guy opposite was smirking at him.

'I am *so* sorry,' Kate told Zoe as they waited for the 1.45 wedding to finish, side by side in almost identical deep blue, just-above-the-knee dresses.

'Oh, don't worry. It's not as though *Hello!* magazine's doing a six-page spread. Only this lot will see us.'

Kate looked around at the little group. There were Zoe's mother and grandfather, Matthew's parents and his younger sister, and half a dozen others she hadn't been introduced to. Ed was talking in whispers to a couple of them, hands in his trouser pockets and a slight patch on his tie where they'd worked at a lipstick mark. She fancied the pants off him, and, due in part to the setting no doubt, had the urge to take him into a corner and propose. But she wouldn't be that brave. If he said no, she'd always wonder why: her age, perhaps, or the fact that she didn't appreciate his jazz collection. Charlie, even. When they were all called through to the next room, he came over and slipped his arm round her waist.

'The dress looks much better on you,' he whispered.

'Yeah?'

'Mm, you fill it out more.'

'Well, thanks.'

After the ceremony, Ed was pronounced official photographer and found camera after camera being thrust at him before the owners dashed back to take their places in the line-up. Luckily, it was another sunny day, so he didn't have to worry about light as he stood perilously close to the traffic roaring along Park End Street.

'Can I have some big smiles?' he called out. 'Say Brie!'

'Brie,' they all said.

'Perfect.' He clicked someone's camera, then took the one tucked under his arm and clicked again. 'Now can I have just the happy couple?' he asked, wondering if he'd missed his vocation.

The little crowd dispersed, leaving a radiant Zoe and a proud-looking Matthew, arm-in-arm, heads tilted together.

'Another lovely smile, if you please,' said Ed, just as Zoe let out a pained wail. And then another.

Her lily-of-the-valley fell to the ground and she ran headlong into the traffic on her high heels. A bus was forced to slam on its brakes and everyone held their breath as Zoe headed towards Donna, walking along the opposite pavement with a man wearing a flat cap and turned-up collar, despite the twenty-two degrees.

'Bastard!' said Zoe when she reached them. She pulled the man's cap off and slapped his face. 'You've ruined my wedding day. Bastard, bastard. God, I hate you.'

'Yeah, me too!' said Donna, slapping his other cheek.

Ross looked unsurprisingly stunned, and with a hand to his face bent down to pick up his hat. 'Jesus Christ,' he said. 'What's the matter with you fucking women? Can't take a little rejection, eh, Zoe?' He stood upright and ran a hand through his hair. 'And if you think I'm admitting paternity, Donna, you can think again.'

'Ross Kershaw?' someone called out from behind them.

All three turned to find a man with a camcorder and a holdall just feet away. 'Terrific,' he said, before spinning a hundred and eighty degrees – camera still held to his face – and running in the direction of the railway station.

'What the hell's Abingdon Andy doing here?' Ed asked Kate, as if she would know.

'Go and run after him and find out.'

'Get lost.'

Ross flagged down a taxi and dived in, and Zoe and Donna slowly made their way through the passing cars, arms linked for mutual support, towards the wedding party.

'Where's Matthew?' asked Zoe. 'Matthew?' She turned a full circle, hands on hips. 'Fuck, he's probably getting an annulment.' She pushed her way through the next wedding party, now gathering for photos on the steps. 'Matthew!'

'Do you think he's gone off for his Lebanese meal?' said Ed.

'God, I hope that's still on. I'm starving.'

'I suppose we could start making our way—'

'Kate!' someone shouted, and they both looked in the direction of the voice. It was Duggie, running and panting and very red in the face. 'Good, you're still here.'

'What?' she cried The shop had burnt down, she knew it. 'What's happened!'

Duggie was waving things at her, and before she knew it there was a tabloid in front of her nose. 'Last night's winning numbers,' he gasped, pointing at the paper. He then plonked a lottery ticket on top. 'My numbers.'

Kate and Ed's eyes darted back and forth between the two. Five of the six numbers were the same *and* he'd got the bonus ball.

'Duggie!' said Kate.

'Bloody hell!' said Ed.

'I know!' said Duggie.

*　　*　　*

'Anyway, he gets off the train in this hat like what my granddad used to wear . . .'

Zoe tutted. 'Great disguise, isn't it? Why don't you try the aubergine dip thing, Donna? It's really good.'

'Yeah, OK. Pass it, can you? Then he says, "Look, I don't have much time. Where are we going?" Can you believe it? No hello, how are you, when's the baby due. Nothing.'

'I expect he was in shock.'

'Maybe. I said, "The Chicago Rock Café," and he said, "Typical," and then he didn't say another word till we saw you. Oh God, what crap timing! Now, not only have I spoilt your wedding, which I'm really, really sorry about, but Ross has disappeared and I'll never get another chance to talk to him.'

'Oh, I think you will,' said Zoe, dolloping aubergine on to Donna's plate. 'We're not going to let him get away with this.'

'Mm, yeah well . . .'

'How come that Andy guy was with you?'

'He wasn't.'

'No?'

'Weird, eh?'

Next to Zoe was Matthew, who was trying to get Duggie to phone the National Lottery people before he lost his ticket.

'Yeah, but what if they say five numbers only pays out like a hundred and eighty quid or something? I'd be seriously gutted, I tell you.' He examined the item on the end of his fork. 'What's this?'

'A kibbeh. It's made out of lamb.'

'Looks like a turd,' said Duggie, chuckling briefly then popping the whole thing in his mouth and talking through it. 'Think I'll buy a brand-new bike. Something big, like 750 cc or something. Then I'll polish it in the middle of our living room and watch my stepdad's face.' He stabbed at another kibbeh – 'They're alright, these!' – and Matthew, with one hand on Zoe's thigh, wondered why there was a strange sixteen-year-old with a windfall at his wedding feast.

When Zoe's mother and I had exhausted the best route from Leicester to Oxford as a subject, I turned to Kate, who may as well have been holding a trumpet to her ear, so obviously was she listening in to Donna and Zoe.

'What?' she said, jumping.

'I said I want to take you home and ravage you on the hearth rug.'

'No you didn't,' she whispered back. 'You said, did I think this was as good as your Lebanese food.'

'And what are Zoe and Donna talking about?'

'They're comparing different forms of torture.'

I laughed. 'And how's Matthew doing?'

'Think he's OK. He's caressing Zoe's leg.'

'How about his friend with the red face?'

'Isn't keen on the baba ghanoush but fancies Matthew's sister. He's just told her he trains horses.'

'And Duggie?'

'Planning to buy a motorbike and looking round for ketchup.'

Zoe's mobile rang. You'd have thought she'd switch it off for her wedding. She pulled something the size of an after-dinner mint from her bag and said, 'Hello? . . . Oh, hi, Bronwen. How . . . Oh, thank you. Yes, it went really well.' She cupped a hand over her phone and pulled a face at us. 'How come Bronwen knows about the wedding?' I immediately looked at Kate, who blushed, while the rest of us shrugged. 'What? Oh dear, poor you,' Zoe was saying to Bronwen before covering the phone again. 'Her father collapsed. He's in hospital. She seems upset.'

'Tell her to get a taxi and come and join us,' said Matthew, half his arm, I could see now, so obviously in her lap.

When Zoe hung up I turned back to Kate. 'How do you do that?' I asked.

'What?'

'You know – know what's going on all round the table?'

'Not sure. Female multi-tasking, I suppose.' She bit into a falafel and practically swooned. Which answered my original question, I guessed.

'Oh, the cad!' exclaimed Bronwen half an hour later. She felt exhausted, but the delicious food was helping. She knew her eyes were red and swollen and her skirt crumpled, and on arriving at the restaurant had explained that she'd not slept a wink. She stretched her arm across the table and squeezed Donna's hand. 'Men can be so callous.' She shook her head in despair and watched Donna's bottom lip quiver. 'And are you going to have anyone with you at the birth, dear?'

Donna shrugged. 'Dunno. My mum was there the first two times, but I think she's getting a bit fed up with it.'

'Well, if I can be of any assistance . . . I've helped deliver many a child in my work around the world.'

'Yeah? Any white ones?'

Bronwen was startled, but thinking about it, no, she'd never delivered a white child. She smiled to herself. Just when she thought there were no more new experiences to be had!

Over in Marston, Christine was quite worried about Gideon. Never in all his time there had he turned down a wedge of her Madeira when it was offered – usually when, as now, they'd all settled down for *Fifteen to One* during his free afternoon. Not only that, but he had a dreadfully sad expression and hadn't shouted out a single answer. Christine's eyes darted between her television and her lodger, and occasionally over to Bob to see if he'd registered something was up.

'William Shakespeare!' cried Bob, who didn't normally get a look-in.

Gideon shook his head and quietly said, 'G. K. Chesterton.'

He was right, as usual. He rarely got the pop and soap questions, but he seemed to know an awful lot about other things. He became silent again and let Bob get eleven questions in a row wrong, then when the programme finished he announced that he was going to his room for a bit of a lie down. 'Should Bronwen phone,' he added flatly, 'would you kindly tell her I'm indisposed for the indefinite future?'

'Yes, of course,' said Christine, with a barely discernible leap of the heart.

SUMMER

EIGHTEEN

'Dear Dr Adams,' wrote Rupert,

> Thank you for sending us your manuscript LOVE IN THE TIME OF COLIC. Although well written, and packed with useful household tips, we feel unable to make you an offer due to the recent flooding of the market with Daddy-lit novels. Should, however, you have anything of a more thriller/crime/adventure nature we would be pleased to consider it . . .

Unbelievable! I ripped the letter in two, swore, dropped it in the waste-paper basket and instructed my computer to print me out another copy of my three-hundred page novel. Did I have enough ink? Probably not. Jesus, what a drag. Fucking Rupert was making a big mistake, that was for sure. I opened my *Writers' and Artists' Yearbook* and circled the names of one or two promising-sounding agents and publishers I hadn't tried before, my eyes occasionally wandering to the letter in the basket.

After a while I leaned over, took it out and read it again.

'. . . thriller/crime/adventure . . .' Surely that would sum up *Climb and Punishment*? From a desk drawer I took the three chapters and synopsis Rupert had so off-handedly rejected six months ago, and reread them. The boy was obviously a fool, put on this earth to play around with the lives and emotions of sensitive, creative souls like myself . . . not even shaving yet, I bet. How reassuring it must have been when businesses were run by adults. I looked up the publishers' number and phoned them.

'Could I speak to Rupert Jones-Bellingham, please?'

'Just one moment.'

'Rupert Jones-Bellingham,' said a deep, mature-sounding voice.

'Oh,' I said, surprised. 'I'm sorry, but how old are you?'

'Excuse me, who is this?'

I quickly apologised and introduced myself. 'I've just received a rejection letter from you,' I told him, 'and it's left me somewhat confused as to what exactly it is you're looking for.'

Actually, he was very pleasant. I explained about the original story I'd sent him, which he claimed to have no memory of. 'It's possible my assistant read it. We do get a lot of manuscripts.'

'I'm sure,' I said sympathetically.

'So it's a Himalayan mountain adventure, is it?'

'Uh-huh. With a strong spiritual element and a lot of humour.'

'Sort of . . . *Seven Years in Tibet* meets Bill Bryson?'

'Absolutely.'

Bronwen was beside her father's grave watching the casket being lowered, Gideon to the left of her, Malcolm to the right; each holding one of her elbows in the palm of his hand, as though about to push her into the hole after Thomas.

Bronwen was damp-eyed, as were many in the gathering: people who'd ignored and almost forgotten her father for the past twenty years – former colleagues, students, old neighbours and once-dear friends – but who had in some way been touched by his work or his warmth.

All alone now, thought Bronwen. She looked at Gideon and then at Malcolm. Well, almost. Malcolm had been most supportive, providing a shoulder and helping her with the arrangements. It was rather nice having a gay friend, even one who occasionally flirted and made suggestions and left her feeling a little confused. And Gideon . . . well, he'd managed to find his way to the funeral, and on the right day. Poor Gideon. It had been a bit of a blow, she knew, her suggestion that they redefine their relationship. But he'd taken it well and thrown himself into his life's work on Haworth. They were obviously going to remain friends, so all had ended well. And how wonderful it was to be getting a good night's sleep again. Perhaps there comes a time in a woman's life, thought Bronwen, when all she wants in her bed is a lavender sachet.

'Amen,' she said quietly to the vicar's prayer. She'd sell the house, of course. Far too big and rambling and in need of repair. Not a place she'd cared to stay in for some years now, but still, her childhood home, full of wonderful memories. She gave an audible sob and both Gideon and Malcolm tightened their grip.

*   *   *

'Thank you for coming, Donna,' said Bronwen. 'That was very sweet.'

Donna waddled down Bronwen's hall towards the door. 'No, I wanted to. You are going to be my birthing partner, after all.' She stepped out into the hot August sun and giggled. 'I thought I might have to get you out of bed last night.'

'Really?' said Bronwen excitedly.

She patted her enormous bulge. 'Just a bit of wind in the end.'

'Well, as I said, any time of day or night. Listen, are you sure you don't want a lift? I'm sure Malcolm would—'

'No, it's all right. There are loads of buses.'

Bronwen waved Donna goodbye and went back to stop Gideon and Malcolm talking about her.

'Of course, Thomas struggled with alcoholism,' Gideon was saying.

Bronwen gasped. 'My father hardly touched alcohol!'

Gideon looked perplexed while Malcolm laughed. 'Dylan Thomas, not your father.'

'Oh, sorry.' Bronwen hooked her arm through Gideon's and said, 'Let me introduce you to Charles. He chose Dylan Thomas as his specialist subject on *Mastermind*. There isn't a thing he doesn't know.' She winked at Malcolm, who gave her a grateful look and turned his attention to a youngish man in a velvet suit.

'It's worth how much?' cried Bronwen. She was talking to Michael Watts, of Watts, Watts and Higson, her father's solicitors.

'Around one and a quarter,' he repeated.

'Million?'

'I know,' he said, 'shocking, isn't it? North Oxford prices have absolutely skyrocketed. Done up it would be more like one and a half. All that land, the croquet lawn . . .'

Michael Watts knew the property well, having played there with Bronwen as a child – a little carelessly at times – his father being a close friend of Thomas's and the one then taking care of all his legal affairs.

Bronwen was flabbergasted. It seemed almost immoral. 'What could I possibly do with all that money?' she asked. But as the words came out of her mouth, plans started formulating themselves and her eyes did a joyful little jig. 'Golly,' she said, after a sharp intake of breath.

Poor old Bronwen, thought Kate. She was reading Thomas Thomas's obituary in the paper, when she should really have been taking paint off a chest of drawers. It was too hot for stripping, but she eventually put the newspaper to one side and pulled on her thick rubber gloves, deciding she'd better take advantage of Duggie being there.

He continued to come to the shop, even though he didn't need the money. Kate had talked him out of buying second-hand furniture with his winnings, and to put it away in case he decided to go to university. He wasn't a millionaire but there was more than enough to keep him in clubs, beers and takeaways for three years.

'Yeah, you're right as usual,' he'd said. 'My mum and stepdad are hardly going to be paying my rent and setting up a monthly allowance for me. Still, if I hate, like music technology or whatever I'm doing, I can always leave and start my own little business.'

'True.'

'Or go and be a sex tourist in Thailand.'

'The world's your oyster, Duggie.'

Since his win, Kate had started secretly buying lottery tickets. A tax on the poor, Ed called it, but, she thought, sometimes it could help the poor out. Which was more than Ed was doing with his rejected novels. As usual, business had been quiet during the summer months; people spent their money on holidays, and the tourists rarely ventured as far as Kate's shop. How would they get a sideboard back to Japan anyway? She kept circling job ads and leaving them for Ed to trip over, but he'd set his heart on saving their bacon with a six-figure advance.

She stopped her stripping, pulled her rubber gloves off and gave him a call.

'Hello,' he said.

No, not quite right. 'Ed or Will?' she asked.

'Will. Thought I'd pay Ed a quick call and as usual I'm left holding the baby.' He laughed annoyingly. 'How are you, Kate?'

'Fine. And you?'

'Terrific. Business is booming.'

'Mm, mine too.'

'That's not what Ed tells me.'

Jesus. 'Oh, he knows nothing. Head stuck in his writing all the time.'

'My sad deluded brother.' He laughed again. 'What was the purpose of all that study? Eh? All that taxpayers' money?'

Will had a point but Kate wasn't going to let him know it. 'He's had some encouraging comments from an editor.' Kind of. 'And anyway, he's going to be tutoring this coming academic year. Oh! Customer's just come in. Better go. Maybe see you later, if you're still there.'

'Oh, I doubt it. Busy, busy.'

She put the phone down and stuck her tongue out at it. There was no potential customer. Hadn't been for a couple of hours. She popped her head into the shop. Duggie was at the counter, teaching himself chords on his acoustic guitar for the six pounds an hour she was paying him. She leant against the doorframe, folded her arms and sighed. Nothing was quite how it should be.

Donna's waters broke at the bottom of Headington Hill and by the top she was having her first contraction. 'Ouch,' she said, stroking her bump. She told the guy beside her she thought she might be in labour and could he go and ask the bus driver to stop, and like quick.

The young man shrugged and pulled a face and said, 'I sorry. I here learn Inglis. I no understand.'

She turned to the people behind her who looked equally young, foreign and blank, then tapped the shoulder of the Japanese girl in front. 'I don't suppose you speak English, do you?'

She smiled and nodded, Japanesely. 'I am student of ranguages at school in High Street. But Engrish not so good.'

Donna thought she'd try shouting, slowly. 'Can . . you . . . tell . . . the . . . driver . . . I'm . . . having . . . a . . . *baby*?' She pointed at her tummy and then did a cradling motion with her arms.

'Aaahh,' said the girl reverentially. 'I tell driver? Yes?'

'Yes!'

'Sorry folks,' shouted the bus driver, taking an unscheduled left at the traffic lights and heading for the conveniently nearby John Radcliffe Hospital. 'Slight detour!'

There was some grumbling and moaning amongst the passengers, but Donna thought, Sod them, and got out the mobile Bronwen had insisted on buying her, 'just in case'.

First she phoned her mum to ask her to take care of the boys and to bring her already-packed case to the hospital, then she called Bronwen and told her what was happening.

'Oh, Donna, are you sure?'

'Well, I've been through it twice before so I reckon I know what to expect.'

'OK. I'll be there as soon as I can.'

'But what about your party?'

'Well, I'd hardly call it that. Anyway, Malcolm can hold the fort.'

*　　*　　*

Bronwen finished handing out the coffees, then got her little stool from the kitchen and stood on it in the living room.

'I'm terribly sorry, everybody,' she shouted out to a suddenly quiet crowd. 'I'm afraid I'm going to have to leave you and go off and be a birthing partner.'

Most of the elderly people there seemed not to know what she was talking about, so Bronwen explained about Donna, being single and so on.

'Awfully bad timing, I know, but I did rather commit myself.'

'From the grave to the cradle, eh!' a retired and slightly deaf lecturer thought he was whispering to his wife.

'Oh yes, very good,' said Bronwen, and everyone chuckled, turning it into a much less sombre do.

Gideon shared a taxi, which, after dropping Bronwen off, took him on to the railway station with a suitcase that bulged with books and clothes. He was off to spend a week on the Yorkshire Moors, researching the Brontës and Haworth, as well as doing some preparatory reading for next term: reading he was not looking forward to.

'Considering the ethnic mix at Molefield,' the departmental head had said at the meeting back in May, 'it seems appropriate to run a course that encompasses African, African-American, Afro-Caribbean and Asian writers. Wouldn't you agree?'

They had all agreed, whilst Gideon had remained quiet. Not an area he'd ever dipped into himself, unless one counted *Midnight's*

Children, which he'd failed to finish. Would the characters speak in strange lingoes, he wondered. Might be tricky to teach.

'I thought I'd give this module to you, Gideon, and let Fiona take over The Nineteenth-Century Novel.'

Gideon had frozen, swallowed hard and said, 'Ah, yes. An interesting challenge. Thank you.'

When the train pulled in he got on and heaved Toni Morrison, Arundhati Roy and a dozen others up on to the rack above his seat, then settled down with Christine's lunchbox and a dog-eared copy of *The Tenant of Wildfell Hall*. He'd turn to Vikram Seth, he decided, after changing trains at Birmingham.

Kate hung up and bounced into the kitchen. 'She's had a little girl!' she told me. 'Isn't that fantastic!'

'Yeah, great.' I was sitting considering an advert for A level tutors that she'd cut out and stuck to a can of Fosters in the fridge. 'But why do people always say that?'

'What?'

'Little. She's had a *little* girl, or she's had a *little* boy. I mean it's hardly going to be a fully grown human, is it? And even if it's an eleven-pound monster they still call it little.'

'God, you're a grump this evening.'

I couldn't disagree. The thought of teaching nice-but-dim rich kids, no doubt. The 'small and friendly college' needed tutors in Maths, English, Physics, Computer Studies and History; none of them exactly my thing. I knew this 'small college' – i.e. bottom end of the tutorial market – scene well from friends. The college does bugger all and charges the parents a fortune for each hour of tuition, out of which they'll give the tutor – who's using his/her own house, gas, electricity and teaching materials – around thirteen pounds. Still, I thought, thirteen pounds an hour . . .

'Why don't you phone them?' asked Kate.

'I can't teach those subjects!'

'Wimp.'

'Nagger.'

'Emily Jane.'

'Pardon?'

'Donna's little . . . sorry, Donna's *baby*.'

'That's nice. I thought about Emily, but there were too many vowels. Emily Adams.'

'Sounds fine, but Georgia suits her. Didn't Bernice mind her being given your surname?'

I looked at her, incredulous.

'No,' she said, 'I suppose not.'

I got up from the table, tucked the ad in my shirt pocket and drained the lager. 'Thought I'd do a bit of writing,' I told her, chucking the can in the recycling box. 'Finish off Chapter Ten.'

Her silence spoke volumes.

NINETEEN

Donna sat up in bed trying to find Ross resemblances in Emily's sweet little face. More like she, Donna, had been as a baby really. Fair hair, though not much of it, and blue eyes. But did all babies have blue eyes to begin with? She bent and kissed the top of her head. A daughter . . . she couldn't believe it.

'Donna?' said a familiar voice. She looked up just as a camera's flash went off.

'What . . . ?'

The camera was lowered to reveal Andy. He smiled at her and said, 'You look lovely, you know.'

'But why do you keep taking photos of me? Has Carl got you to do it?'

'Who?'

'Carl. My ex.'

'No. No one's got me to do it.'

Andy put his camera away, zipped up his bag and wandered towards the bed. 'She's just like you.'

'Yeah?'

He pointed at the chair. 'Do you mind if I . . . ?'

'No. Go ahead.'

'I suppose I should explain,' he said, as he sat down and inched the chair nearer to Donna, who nodded, said, 'Yeah, you'd better,' and kissed her daughter's head again. A girl! She still couldn't believe it. Jake and Ryan would adore their little sister and be dead protective, she just knew it.

'You see . . . I was going out with someone who got caught up with Ross Kershaw.'

Donna started. 'Oh?'

'Mm. Annie, her name was. Is. We both worked for the same bank. Anyway, to cut a long story short, she met him on a train, fell for him, got knocked up then jilted by him, had an abortion and has been a shadow of her former self ever since.'

'Yeah well, that sounds familiar!'

'We tried to get back together, but it wasn't the same. I couldn't totally forgive her, she couldn't forgive herself and neither of us could forgive him. He has no idea what he's done, that's the trouble. That's why I detest him.'

'So why all the photos?'

'I had a feeling Annie wasn't the only one, so I started following him. Wanted to get something on him. Annie had some wild tales, I'll tell you. And . . . I dunno . . . go to the press with the story, I suppose.'

'Shit, you won't, will you? Look, I really don't want this little one—'

'No, don't worry. Well, not without your say-so, anyway. It's just become a bit of a mission, really. Or maybe an obsession. I'm using up all my annual holiday on it.' He touched Emily's little hand with a forefinger. 'You know, I wanted Annie to have the baby, even though it wasn't mine. I would have helped her bring it up.'

'Wow, you must be quite a nice person?'

He laughed. 'Yeah, I am. And I'm really sorry about taking your picture outside your house. I was just trying to get loads of evidence together for the story. You know, "Council House Single Mum to have MP's Child". Well, I guessed it was his. I couldn't see any signs of another man in your life.'

'God, you mean like you've been my whatsit . . . stalker? I should be really pissed off with you, but I'm not. Must be this one.' She kissed Emily again. 'How did I look in those photos? Crap, I bet.'

'Well, a bit surprised and cross. But beautiful.'

'Oh yeah, *I'm* sure.'

His hand moved from Emily's to Donna's. 'No, really.'

It was something of a shock when Kate and I walked into Donna's small ward to find her holding hands with Abingdon Andy.

'Andy?' I exclaimed, flowers in my hand. Kate went over and hugged Donna.

'Actually, it's Dave.'

'And you're not from Abingdon, are you?'

'Ealing.'

'Ha!' I said. 'IT account manager?'

'Assistant bank manager.'

I had a feeling that sounded grander than it was. 'Do you mean counter clerk?'

'Hey, Ed,' I heard. 'Come and look at Emily. She's gorgeous.'

Dave stood up and offered me his chair. 'Well, we can't all be airline pilots.'

'You what?' said Kate.

Later, at the reading group, we all said how it didn't feel quite right without Donna.

'Or Gideon,' added Bronwen.

'Or Gideon,' we agreed.

However, it was good that Donna wasn't there because after a brief chat about *The Unbearable Lightness of Being* we began plotting on her behalf.

'I thought we could call ourselves The North Oxford Literary Society,' said Zoe.

'Perfect!' cried Kate.

Bob said, 'Bloomin scoundrel,' not for the first time. 'You wait till I get my hands on him.'

'I think we should all agree to a non-violent approach to this,' Bronwen told him.

'Bah,' said Bob, folding his arms. 'He wants shooting.'

'Shall we compose a letter now?'

'Ooo, yes,' said Kate, rubbing her hands together and possibly salivating.

I took out some paper and a pen and asked the group how they thought we should address him. 'Dear Mr Kershaw or Dear Ross Kershaw – what do you think?'

'Don't tempt me,' said Bob.

'Or me,' said Zoe.

I started writing. 'Dear Ross Kershaw . . . yes, that looks fine. Not too formal, not too informal. Right. How about . . . I am writing on behalf of the North Oxford Literary Society in the hope that you might be interested in giving a talk about your magnificent novel, *Out for the Count*.'

Kate clapped and said, 'Brilliant! Tell him we'll be selling his book, and perhaps he wouldn't mind signing copies.'

I nodded. 'OK. But first, how about . . . The NOLS is made up of, um . . . artists . . . that's you, Kate; authors, that's me; media executives . . . Zoe; people from the book world . . . Bronwen; academics, Gideon . . . and . . .' I stopped and pondered on Bob and Donna. 'Many avid book readers.'

Zoe smiled and fiddled with her wedding ring. 'What writer would turn that down?'

'And let's face it, he's not even a writer,' I said, studiously ignoring Kate. I knew exactly what kind of look I'd get.

'Ah, no television, I see.'

The Yorkshire landlady bristled. 'Well, if it's not good enough for you, there's plenty more B & Bs around.' She held the door open and gestured him out of the room.

'No, no, it's fine. Rather nice view of the moors. I'll take it.'

Gideon was, in fact, desperate. He'd hired a car in York, gingerly driven south-west at thirty-five miles an hour and stopped for a large and lengthy dinner before realising the time. 'NO VACANCIES' he kept seeing as he negotiated narrow winding roads in the dimming light, until he happened upon the appropriately named Moorview Bed and Breakfast, a pink bungalow with a rose-filled garden and a 'VACANCIES' sign in the window.

'There'll be hot water first thing, but leave enough for my other guest should you use the bathroom first. Breakfast will be served between seven and eight thirty. How would you like your egg?'

'Oh . . . ah . . .'

'Fried, poached or scrambled?'

'Oh, fried, please.'

'You'll be wanting two, I expect. You look like a man who eats a good breakfast.'

'Splendid.'

When she'd gone, Gideon unzipped his case. The jumble of books had rather messed up Christine's neat packing. Everything was a bit creased, but still, he was in the English countryside, not Paris. He picked up two books and held one in each hand, weighing them up. Vikram Seth or Anne Brontë? Hm, perhaps Brontë tonight and Seth tomorrow. Now, where did Christine tuck the alarm clock, he wondered and began rummaging. And rummaging . . . Oh dear.

Gideon jumped and opened his eyes wide at the sound of the thumping.

'Breakfast'll be finished in ten minutes,' he heard, words which immediately filled him with dread.

'Please wait for me!' he called out.

'You'll have to get your skates on then.'

Within four minutes, Gideon was entering a room of pink-checked tables.

'Good morning,' a woman in khaki shorts and hiking boots said. She was standing and dabbing at her mouth with a napkin. 'Lovely day.'

'Yes,' Gideon managed, still shell-shocked and suffering slightly from the sunshine beaming through a wall-length window.

'Are you on a walking holiday too?' she asked with a friendly smile.

'More of a literary one really.' He rubbed a bleary eye and took a better look at her. Something rather Penelope-like, he noticed. A little younger, perhaps. Slimmer legs.

'That sounds interesting. I'm an English teacher, you see. Anyway, you must tell me all about it. Well, if you're staying that is. I'm here for another six days.'

'Actually, I wasn't . . . well, yes, I probably . . .'

'Tea or coffee?' barked the landlady through a hatch.

'Oh, tea, please.'

'Well, have a good day,' said the departing woman.

'Yes, you too.'

'Cereals are on the side!' he heard.

'Right oh.'

Gideon poured himself a large bowl of cornflakes and wondered if the other guest had a TV in her room. Being not so far from *Emmerdale* country he thought he'd quite like to catch it later.

Duggie arrived to find Kate looking forlornly at a stack of bills on the counter.

'You alright?' he asked.

She picked up the top one. 'College complaining because I'm behind with the shop rent.'

'Oh dear.'

She put the letter to one side and went on to the next. 'Council wondering what's happened to my Council Tax direct debit. I cancelled it, you see.'

'Right.'

'Huge phone bill Charlie's run up.' She waved it at him. '*That* I'm really cross about. We bought her a mobile so this wouldn't happen, but she never tops it up.'

As Duggie approached Kate he could see she was really quite upset. 'My mum cries over bills too,' he told her. 'Only then a few days later my stepdad'll turn up with a wad of notes and it all gets sorted.' He shuffled from foot to foot and stuck his hands in his trouser pockets. 'Look . . . I dunno, maybe I can help? You know, a bit of a lend?'

Kate wiped an eye with the back of a hand and laughed. 'How do you know I'd ever be able to pay you back?'

'Tell you what,' he said brightly, swinging his school bag off his back and missing Kate by millimetres. 'You know how much I like that leopard-skin Chesterfield?'

'Yes?'

'Well, I'll buy it off you. It'll look good in my new room, as long as I keep all the other slobs in the house off it.'

'Sorry?' said Kate. She piled up the bills again. 'What slobs? What room?'

'Oh right, yeah, haven't told you. I'm moving out. Getting a shared house with some geezers. Well, maybe. They're like students and things.'

'When?'

'Not for a month and a bit. It's not that definite, cos some of them are still trying to get the deposit together. But I'll give you the money for the sofa now. Collect it later. I want to paint my room first anyway. Already found the paint. Gunmetal grey. Should look bad.' He did a kind of shoulder-shrugging-hand-flicking-rapper-like thing, which reminded Kate of his age.

'Doesn't your mum mind? With your A levels and everything?'

'Doesn't seem to.'

Kate looked at the bills, then over at the reupholstered Chesterfield. Just under a thousand pounds. That should clear everything for the time being. Probably didn't have any choice, she thought, and wondered how many other businesses had been saved from insolvency by their work experience kids.

'OK, Duggie, it's yours. Couldn't get the money to me today or tomorrow, could you?'

'I dunno. I'll try.' He took a SOLD sticker from the counter drawer and stuck it to the back of the Chesterfield, then settled himself on it with a smirk, arms behind his head, feet up on the arm. 'If this doesn't impress birds, nothing will.'

Kate smiled and kept her mouth shut. Ed had taken one look at it and said given the choice he'd rather house Mike Tyson.

'Hello, is that Dr Edward Adams?'

'Yep.'

'This is Ross Kershaw. You wrote to me about giving a talk? The letter was forwarded to me here in Scotland.'

Ha! We'd decided a 'Dr' might sway him, as might the mention of a generous fee. Better sound a little plummy, I decided, if he could hear me, that was, over Georgia trundling back and forth in her baby walker. Had sanded floorboards been such a great idea?

'Good of you to call,' I said. 'Are you able to accept our invitation? I'd imagine it's rather a long way to come during the summer break.'

'No problem. I'm going to be in London on and off throughout the summer.'

Of course he would be. Not much young totty in the Scottish wilderness.

'Super,' I said, perhaps for the first time in my life. 'The society will be delighted.'

We agreed that I would contact him nearer the time to confirm the arrangements.

'If I'm going to be answering questions,' he said with a little Scottish laugh, 'I guess I should read my book again. Can't remember what was in it now.'

Stilted and clichéd dialogue, improbable women, every 'said' followed by an adverb, I felt tempted to remind him, when Kate burst through the living-room door with a gleeful look.

'Nine hundred and fifty!' she shouted.

I shushed her and waved her out the room and she looked rather pissed off.

'Personally,' I said, 'I can't read it enough times.'

'Sorry, Kate.' I went over and wrapped my arms around her waist. 'But guess who that was?'

'Rupert, wanting your book?'

'No, better. Ross Kershaw saying yes to the talk.'

'Hey, what a great day!'

'How did you make nine hundred and fifty?' I asked.

She looked smug and casually said, 'Someone bought the leopard-skin Chesterfield.'

'Bloody hell. I take it they had a white stick and a Labrador?'

'Ha, ha. Listen, how are we going to break this to Donna? I mean, she'll have to be there.'

I had a little think. 'Ealing Dave?'

We got his mobile number from Bronwen and discovered he was in Oxford visiting Donna, so we had him over to dinner and I decided he was an alright bloke, after all. Once he found out I didn't make three trips a week to New York and was in fact a failed novelist looking for bits of teaching work, he became far more open and friendly. He told us all about Ross Kershaw's relationship with his ex, Annie. Well, not *all*, I guessed, with Charlie and an almost-one-year-old at the table.

I explained about NOLS. 'You will join us, I hope? We might need all your sordid evidence.'

'Sordid evidence of what?' asked Charlie.

'Nothing,' said Kate and I.

'God, you *two*,' she said, standing up and pushing her chair back. 'You'd think I was five not fifteen!' She stormed halfway across the room, all bare midriff and low-slung jeans, then stopped and turned. 'What's for dessert?'

'Home-made strawberry mousse,' I told her.

'Oh.' She came back to the table and sat down again. 'I mean, it's not like when you were fifteen, Mum, and telly hadn't been invented and you didn't know about life and sex and were still collecting stamps and all sitting round the radio listening to Churchill—'

'I think you're getting me muddled with your *Mamie*.'

'I have watched *Sex and the City*, you know.'

'It's good, isn't it?' said Dave. 'I like the blonde nymphomaniac.'

Georgia bashed her highchair tray with her spoon and gave us one of her long babbles, consisting mostly of the 'muh' sound.

'She wants her nappy changed,' said Charlie, who tended to be right about these things.

Dave jumped up. 'I'll do it, shall I?'

Kate laughed. 'Don't be sil—'

'No, I want the practice.'

'What do you mean?'

'Oh . . . just in case,' he said enigmatically.

Actually he was a bit odd after all, I decided.

TWENTY

Zoe and Matthew were showing a youngish couple around the house.

'And this is the master bedroom,' Matthew was telling them. 'As you can see it easily takes, well, a bed.'

The man said, 'It's a bit small for two hundred and fifty thousand, isn't it?'

Zoe shrugged. 'That's Oxford for you.'

'Original fireplace,' added Matthew.

'Oh, sweet,' said the woman dreamily. 'And I love your colour scheme.'

Her partner tutted. Zoe had never got round to painting the new plaster in her bedroom. 'Let's see the garden then,' he said.

Despite the man's churlishness, they seemed keen and said yes to a cup of tea, which was always a good sign. They showed Zoe and Matthew the estate agent's details of their house up north. 'Four bedrooms, a cloakroom, a conservatory and an orchard,' said the woman. 'And all we could get was a hundred and forty.'

'Oh dear.'

'So what are the neighbours like?' asked the man.

'It's, um, quite a lively street,' said Zoe. She'd tell them later about having to get a man in a protective suit round to gather needles from the front garden. After exchange of contracts, maybe. 'Got one or two eccentrics.'

'Sounds fun.'

'Yes.'

The man dunked a biscuit in his tea. 'Two thirty-five?'

'Two forty-five.'

'Two forty?'

'OK.'

'Come on, Gideon. Almost there.'

Alison was something of a hard taskmaster. Sweat covered Gideon's entire body. His feet hurt. Wrong shoes, no doubt. 'Couldn't we stop for a little nourishment?' he called to her, shielding his eyes from the blazing sun. He had a Mars bar in his rucksack he was desperate for, but knew he was too short of breath to eat while he walked.

'Once we get to the top.'

He stopped and puffed, hands on hips, and wondered why he wasn't in the Brontë Museum. 'OK. Coming.'

It wasn't as far as he'd thought, but far enough. He heaved his bag off and dropped it with a thud. What had possessed him to bring two novels and a notebook along 'just in case'. Dear, dear, this really wasn't his idea of a good time. Alison was sweet, though; much kinder than Penelope had ever been to him, and almost as nice as Bronwen. He sat against a rock – shade at last – and watched her opening various plastic tubs, while he delved into his bag and pulled out the Mars bar.

'Oh, no you don't,' said Alison, snatching it from him and dropping it back in his bag. 'Food with slow-release energy is what you need when you're hiking. Not a quick sugar fix.' She proffered a selection of raw vegetables with one hand and assorted nuts with the other. 'You'll be good for another three hours if you eat this. Here, dig in.'

Gideon didn't want 'to be good for' another three seconds. He just wanted chocolate.

'Mm, take in that view,' Alison said. 'Glorious.'

He blinked away the sweat, chewed on a Brazil nut and held a hand above his brow as he surveyed the scene. 'Ah yes,' he sighed, slowly turning his head. 'True Brontë country.'

'Imagine Heathcliff stalking these moors,' said Alison wistfully.

'And the beautiful Cathy, hoisting her skirts and petticoats above the gorse.'

They laughed and were silent with their thoughts for a while, then Alison picked up another tub and flipped off the lid. 'Sultana?'

'Thank you.' He popped a handful in his mouth, then undid his brogues and tugged them off, together with his socks.

'Oh, poor you,' said Alison, at the sight of his blisters. 'We'll have to get you some proper footwear for next time.'

'No need, no need,' said Gideon. Next time? This was sufficient hiking for one lifetime.

'And a good thick pair of socks. I know just the shop. Celery?'

'Lovely,' he said, and munched his way through a stick. When he'd finished he slipped a hand into his bag and slowly and silently pulled out the Mars bar, then hauled himself up with the aid of the rock and began tiptoeing away on bare feet. 'Excuse me,' he said to Alison. 'Call of nature.'

Donna was feeding Emily in the shade while the boys played in the paddling pool and sprayed each other with the hose. 'Here you are, Mum,' they'd say every now and then, turning the hose on her.

'No,' she told them each time, protecting the baby with her arm. God, whoever invented school holidays should be shot. Still, Dave was being a help. Turning up most evenings and all last weekend, bathing the baby and rough and tumbling with the boys. She wasn't sure she fancied him as much as he fancied her, but maybe he'd grow on her. She'd heard it was sometimes better that way. It was love at first sight with Carl and look how that ended.

Shelley, with daughter, suddenly appeared at Donna's back door. 'Can I leave her with you while I nip down town?' she asked.

Lara had already slipped out of her dress and got into the paddling pool. 'OK,' said Donna reluctantly. It wasn't as if she could ever ask her to pay her back. Last time she'd left the boys there, Shelley's bloke, Lee, had taught Ryan how to shoot birds with his air rifle. 'Listen, you couldn't pick me up some disposals, could you, Shell?'

Shelley rolled her eyes. 'What did your last servant die of? Yeah, I suppose so.'

'My purse is on the side in the kitchen.'

'Right. See ya!'

Lara was collected at six and Dave rolled up just after seven, saying he had something he wanted to talk to her about. As she bathed Emily she hoped he wasn't wanting to move in with her. They were cramped enough as it was, what with only having the two bedrooms, and Dave was always talking about his hi-fi and his 27-inch telly and his computer. Where would all that go? She gave Emily her four-hourly feed, put her in the Moses basket beside her bed and went down to join him.

'No!' she said. Dave nodded. 'Oh my God!' she cried. 'But what if Ross turns nasty?'

'I'll have the camera rolling.'

'Ha!'

'Listen, I got us a nice bottle of wine to have with dinner.' Dave opened the fridge door and showed her. 'It's just chilling.'

'That's great but—'

'What? Don't you like white?'

'No, it's not that,' said Donna. 'The boys have had their tea but there's no dinner for us. Didn't get to the shops today.' She picked up the change Shelley had left her and dropped it in her purse. 'Tell you what, let's get a takeaway.'

'Good idea.' Dave's hand went to his back pocket.

'No, no, I'll pay. You bought the wine.' She opened her purse again and flicked through the folds. 'I've got ten . . .' she said. 'Oh . . . Hang on a minute. I know I had . . .'

Donna came over cold. Fucking Shelley. She'd kill her, she really would. God, if only Ross knew what she had to put up with. Well, maybe now she'd have the chance to tell him.

'Are you all right, Donna?'

'Yeah, yeah. Didn't get to the cash machine either. Sorry.'

Bronwen was getting to work on the study, pulling each book off her father's shelves and dusting it. She believed some to be quite rare first editions and handled those particularly carefully as she went up and down the set of wooden steps Daddy had used for as long as she could remember. Oh to have a sibling, she thought, not for the first time. She'd been packing up stuff for five evenings in a row now – items that had made her weep or laugh, or which had just puzzled her, like the overly familiar letter he'd kept from a 'Harriet' dated 1964. But the study wasn't to be cleared, just made clean and tidy to give the impression it was still in everyday use.

Soon she was surrounded by all the books, piled on the floor and the desk and every available chair. 'Right,' she said, taking the can of polish and a duster up the steps to the empty top shelf. 'Here goes.'

As she sprayed and buffed Bronwen thought about the nice letter she'd received from the children's charity, thanking her for her 'extraordinarily kind' offer. Well, what would she do with a million and a quarter, anyway? Better to put the lovely old house to some use, although still keeping it in her name, of course. No doubt there'd be all sorts of red tape to go through, but it would be worth it to provide a week or so's escape for children who have to spend most of their spare time caring for an ill or disabled parent. Poor loves. They could make it such fun! Tennis, a pool room, cosy dorms . . . The doorbell rang. 'Goodness,' she said, putting the duster down. Jehovah's Witnesses? She descended, smoothed her hair and went through to the hall. It was Ed.

'I saw your bike,' he said, locking up his own. 'Need a hand?'

Bronwen almost hugged him. Never had she been so pleased to see a man with a good pair of shoulders. Well, no, that wasn't entirely true.

She left him with the books and the polish and various instructions whilst she tackled the weeds in the front gravel and went over the front door furniture with Brasso. Just the old floor tiles in the hall to wash and the linoleum in the study to shine up and . . . well, no one would ever know it wasn't a lived-in and loved house. She'd get some flowers. Yes.

It was a very special Wednesday. 'Georgia's taken her first steps!' an elated Christine had called to tell me. 'Five in all, then Bob caught her.'

'Hey, terrific! And on her birthday, too!'

When I put the phone down I felt slightly pissed off with Georgia for doing it at their house and not at home, but then realised you'd feel a lot braver on deep-pile carpet with best underlay than on

Victorian boards with bits missing, and quickly forgave her. When I collected her later, together with the fluffy animals and other gifts Christine and Bob had lavished on her, she walked, first falteringly, then rapidly, across their living room while Bob took three or four snaps.

'Bless her,' said Christine.

'Hi, Bernice. Good of you to come.' It was 6.30 and she was in suit, heels and vamp makeup. Should I kiss her cheek? Maybe not.

Clive was heaving something out of his boot. 'Her present,' Bernice told me. 'You'll have to assemble it, I'm afraid.'

'Oh, right. Sounds interesting. Anyway, come on through. We're all in the garden. Will's here too.'

'Oh, *good*. Come along, Clive,' she said. 'Stop making a meal of it.'

At the sight of Bernice, Georgia turned and buried her face in Kate's chest. She'd started doing this with strangers.

'Happy birthday, darling,' said Bernice, oblivious. 'Mummy's brought you a fabulous present.'

It turned out to be an all-in-one desk and chair. Better than the one I use, and almost as big.

'Well, nice thought,' I said, putting the screwdrivers back in my toolbox. Georgia had pulled herself fully upright by the chair leg of her new present and her nose was just about level with the seat.

'And I got this to go with it,' said Bernice, handing me a geometry set. 'Give her a good start, as it were.'

'Oh, *I* really need one of those,' said Charlie, running over. 'My compass broke the other day.'

304

Bernice sniggered. 'You mean compasses.'

'No,' said Charlie, frowning. 'I only had one.'

Of course Georgia had no idea what was going on, but came out of her shell and threw herself into the festivities. Anything was better than going to bed.

My mother rang, wanting to speak to her. 'And what have you been doing, Georgia?' she asked. Did she seriously expect an answer? 'Having a lovely party, I bet? I expect you've got lots and lots of nice presents and that . . .' By then Georgia had crawled back to where it was all happening and I pretended I still had her on my knee with the receiver at her ear. '. . . You do like the pushalong doggie we sent you?'

I did a quiet little 'muh, muh, muh,' impersonation, then said, 'I think that means yes, Mum. Anyway, she mustn't neglect her guests for too long.'

'Is that woman there?'

'Bernice? Yes, she is.'

'Well, wonders will never cease. Your dad always says someone should give her a good hiding.'

I imagined that Clive already had. And that Will would very much like to. 'Oh, she's not all bad,' I said. Mum had once overheard Bernice describe her as a washed-out little housewife, so was never going to see any good in her. 'Better go,' I added.

'We'll be down at the weekend then.'

Christ, I'd forgotten. And had I told Kate?

'Yep. Great. We're all looking forward to it.'

*   *   *

Will was teaching Bernice some salsa steps, in a way that involved his groin being a whisker away from her rear. Clive looked on wanly, a plate of uneaten birthday cake on his business suit trousers. I thought I'd engage him in conversation, and drew up a deck chair.

'Fancy a beer?' I asked.

'No thanks, I'm driving. Bernice certainly can't.'

'Mm, she has had one or two, hasn't she?'

'Six.'

'Right.' I took a swig from my can. 'So . . . how's the textbook business? Busy time of year, I expect? Just before the new . . .' I stopped, realising he was somewhere else altogether.

Somewhere rather miserable, I guessed, as he turned his weary features my way and said, 'You don't want her back, do you?'

'No, thanks.'

'That was Gideon,' Bob told Christine. 'Says he's decided to stay up in Yorkshire a while longer.'

'Really? What on earth for?' Christine couldn't imagine Gideon roughing it in B & Bs for too long.

'Apparently, he's finished hiking over the moors and is now going walking in the dales.'

Christine stared at Bob. 'Are you sure it was Gideon?'

'Sounded like him.'

*   *   *

'Look,' said Kate, surveying all the 'SOLD' stickers. 'I really think you've bought enough things from me now, Duggie.' She was beginning to feel like his pet charity, and anyway, if he was going to buy that much stuff she needed him to shift it. 'Excuse me, but do you have *anything* for sale?' one customer had asked that morning.

Duggie said, 'Don't worry, my stepdad's got a lockup. Told me I can store some of it till I get this shared house thing sorted. But . . .'

'What?'

'Well, he said to put only the more valuable things there, so I'm a bit worried that there might be like this mysterious break-in and robbery.'

'Ah.'

Kate thought about the big house Bronwen was emptying out and gave her a call.

'No problem at all,' Bronwen insisted. 'He can store them in the master bedroom. Well, actually there are three master bedrooms. Soon to be dormitories,' she added excitedly. She went on to explain her latest plan for the house.

'Sounds great,' said Kate.

'The charity will pay me rent, so I'm not being totally altruistic! Not the market rent, of course.'

Kate thanked her profusely, put the phone down and said, 'Anything else you want to buy, Duggie?'

*　　*　　*

Alison and Gideon were the first down to the dining room, where they partook of identical breakfasts: tinned grapefruit segments, poached egg and wholemeal toast with low-fat spread.

'I thought we might attempt an eight-miler today,' said Alison. 'After you coped so well with that seven-mile walk yesterday.'

Gideon wiggled his toes in his hiking boots. Nothing felt sore. They'd obviously moulded themselves to his feet, or vice versa, since those first truly torturous days breaking them in.

Alison showed him a diagram of the circular walk through Swaledale. 'It's my favourite,' she told him.

Gideon looked out the window. 'Oh, mine too.' All the dales were his favourites. What a delightful part of the country he was in. Had the area produced any writers, he wondered, as he waited for a little more toast to arrive. He licked a finger and dabbed at the crumbs on his plate. There was James Herriot, of course, but wasn't he a Scot? And perhaps not a literary great.

'More toast?' asked the landlady, at last.

'I think we've had plenty,' said Alison. 'Thank you.'

TWENTY-ONE

'Ready, then?' Kate asked Ed. He'd been fussing with his hair and changed his shirt three times.

'Do I look OK?'

'*Yee-es.* Come on, or we'll be late.'

She went downstairs and found Georgia – pyjamas on, thumb in mouth, big blue eyes beginning to look tired – tucked between Charlie and Jack. On the screen before them, people with grotesque faces were having earnest conversations in dark rooms on faraway spaceships.

Kate bent over the back of the sofa and kissed the top of Georgia's head. 'In bed by eight, little one,' she said, for Charlie and Jack's benefit rather than Georgia's. Georgia took her thumb out of her mouth and looked up at Kate. '*Star Trek,*' she said, or so Kate was convinced.

'Don't be ridiculous,' Ed protested in the camper van. 'Nobody could say "*Star Trek*" at twelve months. All those tricky con-sonants . . . It was probably "Ta-ta". Christine says that a lot.'

Kate said, 'Mm, well, maybe,' and slowed the van to the 30 m.p.h. limit, while Ed flicked through the book on his lap and sniggered.

Gideon decided he'd go straight from the train to the reading-circle meeting. Bob had told him over the phone which book they were reading, and he'd managed to find it in Leeds. By Birmingham he'd worked his way through over half of it. Extraordinary, he kept telling himself. Why on earth was he attempting a heavy tome on the Brontës if this was what sold by the bucketful? Sex and intrigue and dastardly characters ... and a particularly light touch when it came to the prose. A good deal of sex, actually. He turned back a page and reread an exceptionally graphic section, considering, as he did so, just how much disbelief the reader was supposed to suspend. He also wondered who in the reading circle had chosen it. The idea that Bronwen might have been trying to tell him something seized him briefly, but ... well, he'd not received any complaints from Alison. Rather the opposite, in fact.

'I'm off now,' called out Bob.

'Right you are,' said Christine from the kitchen. She came into the hall wiping her hands on a tea towel. 'Got your book?' she added with a smile. Bob had twice left for the reading circle bookless, and had to turn back.

'Aye,' he said, holding up the carrier bag Christine had put his sandwich in. She guessed Bronwen hadn't had time to think about food for this evening.

'Clean hanky?'

Bob patted a pocket. 'Yep.'

'Well, ta-ta, then,' said Christine, holding the door open for him. 'Oh, and good luck!'

He kissed her cheek. 'Thanks, love.'

Zoe, Donna and Dave arrived at the same time, and a tired-looking Bronwen held open a large shiny-knockered front door for them and waved them in.

'Wow,' said Donna, taking in the panelled walls and the broad sweeping staircase, sleeping baby in the crook of her arm. 'This place is amazing.'

'It certainly is,' said Zoe. 'These floor tiles are beautiful. And so shiny.'

Bronwen brushed a strand of hair from her face with her hand. 'Lovely, aren't they? They took some cleaning, I can tell you! Decades' worth of grime in them. Still . . . do come on through. I've worked hard on the library too.'

Zoe could sympathise with Bronwen. She and Matthew had spent days packing up her things for the move to his place, then cleaning up for the new people. She ached in odd places and, looking at Bronwen rubbing at a shoulder, guessed she did too.

'Oh yes,' said Dave, placing two heavy bags on a large leather-topped desk. 'Now this is what I call a study.'

'I've got flapjacks and a pot of coffee on the go,' Bronwen told them, as her guests rotated their heads and gawped. 'But you're absolutely *not* to follow me to the kitchen. It's a shocking mess in there. There's a cloakroom off the entrance hall, freshly painted this afternoon, should anyone need to spend a penny.'

The doorbell rang and all four froze and stared at one another, 'I'll go,' said Zoe. 'It's probably just some of the others.'

Ross Kershaw was in the back of the taxi with little yellow tabs protruding from his copy of *Out for the Count*. 'A little bit about you,' Dr Adams had suggested over the phone. 'Half a dozen or so readings with explanations, plus anecdotes, then questions from the audience. That's how we find these evenings usually go.' This was Ross's first literary talk, but not the last he imagined, having read his book again. Terrific stuff.

He was halfway along Banbury Road and still hadn't decided whether to go for page 154. Too racy? Perhaps he'd take a look at his audience before deciding. Didn't want to upset any fusty old north Oxford types. On the other hand, a potential conquest might find herself going weak all over at his erotic yet sensitive prose. The taxi slowed and turned down a leafy side street and then off the road and into a wide drive, where it crunched to a halt on gravel. Ross looked up at the house through his open window. Impressive, indeed. Victorian and enormous. Virginia creeper and little turret things near the roof. Oh yes, he could get used to this set. Who needed the Front Bench?

*　　*　　*

We hadn't quite believed it was Gideon when he walked into Bronwen's father's study. Well, Bronwen's study, now. She'd inherited a veritable mansion, and in one of the most expensive areas in the UK. Gideon would be mad not to propose to her immediately, I thought, as I looked around at my handiwork. Everything shone tastefully and smelled of expensive polish. Ah, perhaps that was why he'd lost a good stone and a half and got himself a tan and a modern haircut? Ready to go in for the kill.

'Amazing what a bit of exercise can do,' he said in response to our compliments. He sat down with his copy of *Out for the Count* and said, 'Oh, no, thank you,' when Bronwen waved a plate of flapjacks at him. 'Watching the old . . .' He patted his stomach and gave her an attractive smile. He'd been quite a handsome devil under all that puffiness.

'Gosh,' said Bronwen, transfixed.

Donna looked out of the window and said, 'Ohmygodhe'shere!' before hyperventilating noisily. Dave gave her a hug with one arm and got his camcorder ready with the other. 'You'll be all right, sweetheart,' he told her. 'Get the baby out.'

'Right.'

'You OK, Zoe?' asked Kate.

'Uh-huh.'

Bob was working his way through his digits, clicking each knuckle loudly.

'*No*, Bob,' said Bronwen, wagging her finger. 'There'll be none of that.'

Gideon surveyed the shelves. 'Ah, what an honour to be in Thomas Thomas's study.'

The doorbell went. 'Ready, Ed?' asked Bronwen.

I straightened my tie. 'Yep.'

'I'm Dr Adams,' I announced, holding out a hand. 'Pleased to meet you. Do come in.'

'Hello,' he replied with a firm shake. Another handsome devil.

'Do come on through. We're all assembled in the library.'

'Thank you. Lovely evening.'

'Yes.'

I led him to the study, then once we were both through the door I shut it and stood with my back to it, quickly turning the key in the lock as I'd practised, then pulling it out and handing it to Bronwen, who handed it to Zoe, who slipped it into her bra.

'What the hell's going on?' asked our guest as he glanced around the room, his dreadful book clutched in one hand, his briefcase in the other.

Donna had Emily on one shoulder, Dave was filming, and Kate, beside me, looked as though Hugh Grant, Brad Pitt and Boris Becker all rolled into one had just walked in.

'Stop that,' I whispered, and she closed her mouth.

'Sorry.'

'Dr Adams?' pleaded Ross, but it was Bronwen who took over,

sweeping him into the middle of the room and confronting him with his child.

'We thought you might like to meet your daughter. This is Emily.'

Donna gently rolled her baby round to face him and smiled tentatively. She so obviously wanted him to fall in love with his little girl the moment he saw her, just as she had.

'This is preposterous!' he yelled, growing red in the face.

Donna flinched and bit her bottom lip while I grabbed Bob's wrists behind his back.

Zoe stood up, as did the others. 'You'll always be a heartless bastard, won't you, Ross?'

Had she got that from his book, I wondered.

Everyone was standing now, and we'd quite effortlessly and unintentionally formed a circle around him. When I felt Bronwen take my left hand, I let go of Bob's wrists and took *his* left hand. And so it went on around the group until we resembled a weird sect. It didn't help that Bronwen was in long flowing black and had a wild and hungry look to her. All we were short of was a chant.

'Donna would like you to have a DNA test,' I said bravely. 'We think that's the least you can do.'

'Jesus Christ, it is not my baby! I don't know this . . . this slut.'

Dave pointed to a large black suitcase. 'Photographs, film, cassette recordings. And she's not a slut.'

'And once paternity is established,' I continued, 'we believe it is only right and proper that you provide for your offspring.' I saw Kate shoot me the you're-a-fine-one-to-talk look she'd given me every time I'd rehearsed that line. Or maybe I was just paranoid. 'If not, I'm sure the State will see to it that you do.'

'Absolutely absurd!' was his retort. 'Now if you'll kindly let me leave . . . I mean, how *dare* you ambush me in this way? Letting me believe I was coming to a literature group to talk about my highly acclaimed novel—'

'Ah yes, talking of which . . .' chipped in New Gideon. He had both Zoe's hand and his open copy of *Out for the Count* in one palm. 'I wonder if I might refer you to . . .' he looked down, 'yes, page one five four. A little clarification, if you wouldn't mind, as to how your central character managed to satisfy *both* . . . um, let's call them peripheral characters, in the course of one elevator ride?'

'Yes, I wondered about that,' I said.

'All it would take is a little imagination,' whispered Bronwen.

Was Ross inching towards the door?

Bob had obviously noticed too. 'Stay where you are, you good-for-nothing piece of excrement!' It was the closest I'd ever heard him come to swearing. He freed himself from Kate and myself and stepped towards Ross, fists clenched in boxing pose.

'You're all completely mad,' said a suddenly terrified-looking Ross. He made a bolt for the door through the gap Bob had provided, but on the way tripped over Thomas Thomas's wooden steps and was hurled towards the floor, catching his head on the corner of Thomas Thomas's mahogany desk before landing with a clatter and a thud on Bronwen's gleaming floorboards.

That was when we all went really quiet. Particularly Ross. 'Oh dear,' said Bronwen as we moved gingerly forward to take a look. He was lying face up, eyes closed, with *Out for the Count* spread-eagled on his chest.

'Oh, great,' whispered Donna. 'Now you've killed my baby's daddy.'

Dave made us all jump with his flash, then apologised. 'Can't resist a photo op,' he explained.

'All, well . . . poetic licence, I suppose,' said Gideon to himself, flicking through pages to the rear.

'Is that blood?' someone asked, just as I noticed it too – a slow disgusting trickle behind Ross's left ear.

'Someone call an ambul—' was the last thing I heard before it all went black.

AUTUMN

TWENTY-TWO

TWENTY-TWO

It reminded Kate of one of those houses you drew as a child: four windows and a central door; chimney top right; straight front path and a fence surrounding the garden. It wasn't as old as some of its neighbours – Victorian, red brick – but pretty nevertheless. A rose, now dying, had been trained up a trellis and there were fancy bits of brickwork above each window. Nice, she thought. Shame about the location. The door was slightly open and the sound of hammer on metal could be heard.

'Hi, Kate,' said Zoe, stepping over a toolbox and greeting her with kiss. 'It's been ages, hasn't it?'

They wove their way past a young man fitting a radiator and an older one running cable down a groove in the wall. 'Sorry about this,' she said. 'Let's go in the kitchen. It's lovely and warm in there.'

'OK.'

While Zoe filled a kettle and placed it on the Aga, Kate took in the view at the back of the house. Which was nothing, basically.

321

Unless you counted a green incline up to the horizon and half a dozen sheep. She folded her arms around her middle, tightly. What was it about the country that gave her the shivers? Could it be down to that trip to a farm from her Croydon infants' school? So much mud and poo and slimy damp straw everywhere. Red-faced farm hands whacking cows with sticks. How barbaric it had all seemed.

'Lovely, isn't it?' said Zoe, sidling up to her.

'Mm. How long have you been here now?'

'Two months.'

'Crikey. Has it been that long since . . .'

Zoe nodded. 'That evening! Did you bring Dave's photos?'

Kate laughed. 'Of course.'

'And this is Donna feeding her baby in the corner of the library, looking tearful and worried. She wanted Dave to rip that one up, but then decided it was a nice one of Emily.'

'It is, isn't it?' Zoe placed the photo to one side and took the next.

'Ross coming round,' Kate said, then handed her another one. 'Ross sitting on a chair looking dazed and holding his head.'

'Oh dear, what a sight!'

'Bronwen with the tea.'

'That was a lovely tea set, wasn't it?'

'Gorgeous.'

'The ambulance arriving.'

'Uh-huh.'

'Me holding Ed's hand while they carried him out.'

'That paramedic you're looking at was cute, wasn't he?'

'Alex? Didn't notice.'

Zoe laughed and took the next photo. 'How is Ed now? Ribs healed?'

'Yes, at last. He couldn't laugh for six weeks. We couldn't even, you know . . . without it really hurting him.'

'Oh dear.'

'He's making up for it now, though. Oh, and here's a tanned Gideon trying out Bronwen's father's desk. He's even slimmer these days.'

Zoe peered at it. 'He looks a bit like that nice Australian actor. What's his name? The one in *The Piano*. Sam something . . .'

'So he does!'

'Bronwen must be kicking herself.'

'Oh, I don't know. She's got her project going now. Did I tell you Duggie moved in with her?'

'No?'

'She had all his furniture anyway, so it didn't make much difference him being there. I think she sees him as a bit of a cause as well.'

'Oh God, look at Bob's face in this one!' cried Zoe. 'Talk about furious.'

'That was when he was giving Ross a good talking to. Look. Here he is tearing up the novel.'

Zoe frowned. 'I thought that was a bit mean, actually.'

'Bob stamping on the torn-up novel . . . Oh, and this is nice.

323

Ross holding his baby daughter. Reluctantly, yes, but Emily's not to know that when she's older.'

'What's that last one?' asked Zoe, reaching for a photograph much larger than the others. 'Did you have one blown up?'

Kate went to slap a hand on it, but was too slow off the mark.

'Oh *yes*,' said Zoe, holding a headshot of Alex the paramedic at arm's length. She laughed and tilted her head first one way, then the other. 'I'd like a copy of this one.'

Bob looked over at Christine, humming away to little Emily whilst she fed her. If she took on any more nippers she'd probably have to get registered. Then she'd have him putting guard rails on the cooker and filling in the ornamental pond to comply with regulations. No, two was enough at his age. Left him time to get the fishing in, not to mention the reading. But at least Christine was making a bit of money at it now that Ed was working and young Donna had that Dave chap living with her and maintenance from the MP. Did the decent thing in the end, Mr Kershaw, though they all knew it was hush money really. It said in the paper the other day he'd be standing down at the next election to 'spend more time with his family'. Which family, Bob had wondered.

Yes, what with his pension, plus the profit they were making on Gideon now that he only seemed to want salad and Volvic for his tea, he and Christine would be upgrading the Vauxhall and holidaying in Greece before they knew it.

He took Donna's usual lunchtime call – 'She's been as good as gold,' he told her – then stretched out on the sofa with *The Color Purple* – never could spell, these Yanks – pulled out his bookmark and turned back a page to remind himself of where he'd got to. It seemed to be all about darkies and slavery and rape, not something you'd expect Gideon to have chosen, but there you go. Right, he thought, better take advantage of the temporary peace. Georgia was having an afternoon nap, and within a few minutes so too was Bob.

'Duggie?' called Bronwen through the door. 'Will you be joining us for lunch later?' She knocked twice. 'Hello?'

She tried the handle but the door was locked. Ah well, probably asleep. All that effort he'd put into the games room mural, no doubt. So many nudes! Perhaps she'd get one of the workmen to 'accidentally' paint over it. Though she wouldn't want to hurt Duggie's feelings after his generous donation to the charity. If he was still keen to be involved, they'd find him something else to do.

Ah . . . no, not asleep. She could hear him singing, suddenly quite loudly. Probably had his headphones on. He had rather a nice voice, actually. Perhaps she'd get him to entertain the children with his favourite songs some time. Once they'd arrived, of course. Another couple of months should see the place ready. How exhilarating it was to be busy on something worthwhile again! Not getting herself all knotted up and careworn over men. In fact, they were barely entering her thoughts these days in any kind of romantic or sexual capacity. Although, having said that, it was hard not to let one's eyes drift down to Damian the carpenter's taut, down-covered, lower abdomen when he was shirtless and stretching to work on a shelf bracket.

She let the image fade, slowly.

Right! Now, what was next? Oh yes. She'd fetch the spade and fork from the garage ready for Gideon. He'd never find them himself, tucked away behind Duggie's new 'bike', as he called it. Bronwen had always thought of a bike as something that came with a bell and a wicker basket. And gears, if you paid a little more. Not something noisy and blindingly red, whose wing mirrors made it roughly the size of Poland. Still, he seemed thrilled with his new machine, despite not quite managing to get beyond the drive with it yet.

She pulled up her sleeves, blew a strand of hair from her face and set off for the garage, making a slight detour to see how Damian was getting on.

Gideon was at the gym. He was on the cross-trainer, trying to maintain the right heart rate, but this was proving difficult as he had to keep releasing one of the machine's sensored handles in order to hoist his shorts back up to his waist. The one negative aspect of the fat-burning programme was constantly having to downsize one's gymwear. Perhaps he'd get Alison to pick out something flattering for him in the Peaks at the weekend.

Now would he have time for the weights? He had promised Bronwen he'd turn over her father's old vegetable patch. Ah, or was that tomorrow? He stopped and hitched his shorts up again. Of course a couple of hours with a shovel would probably do the same amount of toning, and he really didn't mind helping Bronwen out. After all, with all her Indian experience, she was proving a valuable source of lecture material for *The God of Small Things*.

He looked longingly over at the leg press. Another ten minutes, then he'd go.

'Come in, er . . .' I said. Shit, what was his name?

'Jamie.'

'Jamie, yes, of course.' Did teaching adolescents affect your memory, I wondered. Could explain Gideon.

'How are you getting on with . . . um . . .'

'Equilibrium?'

'That was it. Cup of tea?'

'Got coffee?'

'Yep. Chocolate digestive?'

'Yeah, ta.'

Jamie got his books out and plonked them on the dining table, while I killed time in the kitchen. Organising refreshments and talking football could take up a good quarter of an hour-long tutorial.

'Good result on Saturday, eh?' I said on my return.

'Brilliant. Did you see that last goal?'

'Superb.' I pretended I'd got Sky Sports; it was easier that way.

Towards the end of Jamie's hour I was pinching my arm under the table to keep myself awake. I'd had five students in a row that day and had found it hard to stay articulate, informative and animated for that long. Nice kids, though, ranging from fifteen to nineteen. Some a little less keen than others. And one or two of them had that teenage-boy aroma that can get a bit much when you're sitting next to them explaining Rank Coefficient Correlation at length.

Four and a half minutes left. Should I pack him off early? Some of the kids report you for that, I'd heard. Four and a quarter. Please hurry up, clock. Once Jamie went I'd have exactly an hour to spend at the computer, writing. Chapter Twenty-six. Almost ready to send to Rupert. I was winding it down now after the denouement on the beaches of Goa. My protagonist was back north in the mountains again, and had, amazingly, met up with beautiful Rosa, the woman he'd lost track of in Chapter One. Giving the book a satisfyingly circular form, I felt. Should they have sex, though? This I couldn't decide. Better to leave the ending romantic and open-ended, perhaps. All the better for a sequel . . .

I felt my arm being tapped. 'Can I go now?' asked Jamie.

'What?' I said, springing my eyes back open.

'Only it's five past.'

'No need to put your hand up, Donna,' said Caroline.

'Oh, OK.'

Donna was in a small classroom with a group of people from all different backgrounds. Three or four women like herself who had children. Only they were a bit older – the women *and* the children. Then there was Kieran in his forties, who'd told them all he used to be a heroin addict. Some were kids who'd messed up at school and done crap jobs for a couple of years. She quite fancied Ben, but he was a bit immature, doing stupid things when Caroline wasn't looking. Actually, he was very immature. But then she'd probably got used to being with older men. Try as she might, she couldn't see Ross flicking things around the House of Commons with a rubber band.

'What did you want to say, Donna?'

'Right. Sorry.' She held *Middlemarch* in one hand and twirled her hair with the other. 'Well, the reason this is such a brilliant book is that George Eliot knows everything that's going on in everyone's lives, as well as what's going on in their heads. You know, like people who believe in God think He does.'

'Well observed, Donna,' said Caroline. 'Now, does anybody know the term for this?'

Donna smiled and shot her hand up. 'Omniscient narrator?'